Praise for the Orchard Mysteries

"Meg is a smart, savvy woman who's working hard to fit into her new community—just the kind of protagonist I look for in today's traditional mystery. I look forward to more trips to Granford, Massachusetts!"

—*Meritorious Mysteries*

"An enjoyable and well-written book with some excellent apple recipes at the end." —*The Cozy Library*

"A wonderful slice of life in a small town . . . The mystery is intelligent and has an interesting twist . . . *Rotten to the Core* is a fun, quick read with an enjoyable heroine, an interesting hook, and some yummy recipes at the end."

—*The Mystery Reader* (4 stars)

"Full of rich description, historical context, and mystery."

—*The Romance Readers Connection*

"There is a delightful charm to this small-town regional cozy. . . . Sheila Connolly provides a fascinating whodunit filled with surprises." —*The Mystery Gazette*

"A true cozy mystery [with] a strong and feisty heroine, a perplexing murder, a personal dilemma, and a picturesque New England setting . . . Meg Corey is a very likeable protagonist and her future in Granford hopefully guarantees some further titles in this delightful new series."

—*Gumshoe Review*

continued . . .

"[An] example of everything that is right with the cozy mystery . . . [A] likable heroine, an attractive small-town setting, a slimy victim, and fascinating side elements . . . There's depth to the characters in this book that isn't always found in crime fiction . . . Sheila Connolly has written a winner for cozy mystery fans."

—*Lesa's Book Critiques*

"A warm, very satisfying read." —*Romantic Times* (4 stars)

"The premise and plot are solid, and Meg seems a perfect fit for her role." —*Publishers Weekly*

"Meg Corey is a fresh and appealing sleuth with a bushelful of entertaining problems . . . One crisp, delicious read."

—Claudia Bishop, bestselling author of the Inn at Hemlock Falls Mysteries

"[A] delightful look at small-town New England, with an intriguing puzzle thrown in."

—JoAnna Carl, author of the Chocoholic Mysteries

"Thoroughly enjoyable . . . I can't wait for the next book and a chance to spend more time with Meg and the good people of Granford."

—Sammi Carter, author of the Candy Shop Mysteries

Berkley Prime Crime titles by Sheila Connolly

Orchard Mysteries

ONE BAD APPLE
ROTTEN TO THE CORE
RED DELICIOUS DEATH
A KILLER CROP
BITTER HARVEST

Museum Mysteries

FUNDRAISING THE DEAD
LET'S PLAY DEAD

Bitter Harvest

Sheila Connolly

BERKLEY PRIME CRIME, NEW YORK

THE BERKLEY PUBLISHING GROUP
Published by the Penguin Group
Penguin Group (USA) Inc.
375 Hudson Street, New York, New York 10014, USA
Penguin Group (Canada), 90 Eglinton Avenue East, Suite 700, Toronto, Ontario M4P 2Y3, Canada
(a division of Pearson Penguin Canada Inc.)
Penguin Books Ltd., 80 Strand, London WC2R 0RL, England
Penguin Group Ireland, 25 St. Stephen's Green, Dublin 2, Ireland (a division of Penguin Books Ltd.)
Penguin Group (Australia), 250 Camberwell Road, Camberwell, Victoria 3124, Australia
(a division of Pearson Australia Group Pty. Ltd.)
Penguin Books India Pvt. Ltd., 11 Community Centre, Panchsheel Park, New Delhi—110 017, India
Penguin Group (NZ), 67 Apollo Drive, Rosedale, Auckland 0632, New Zealand
(a division of Pearson New Zealand Ltd.)
Penguin Books (South Africa) (Pty.) Ltd., 24 Sturdee Avenue, Rosebank, Johannesburg 2196,
South Africa

Penguin Books Ltd., Registered Offices: 80 Strand, London WC2R 0RL, England

BITTER HARVEST

A Berkley Prime Crime Book / published by arrangement with the author

PRINTING HISTORY
Berkley Prime Crime mass-market edition / August 2011

Cover illustration by Mary Ann Lasher.
Cover design by Annette Fiore Defex.
Interior text design by Laura K. Corless.

For information, address: The Berkley Publishing Group,
a division of Penguin Group (USA) Inc.,
375 Hudson Street, New York, New York 10014.

ISBN: 978-0-425-24276-6

BERKLEY® PRIME CRIME
Berkley Prime Crime Books are published by The Berkley Publishing Group,
a division of Penguin Group (USA) Inc.,
375 Hudson Street, New York, New York 10014.
BERKLEY® PRIME CRIME and the PRIME CRIME logo are trademarks of Penguin Group (USA) Inc.

PRINTED IN THE UNITED STATES OF AMERICA

10 9 8 7 6 5 4 3 2 1

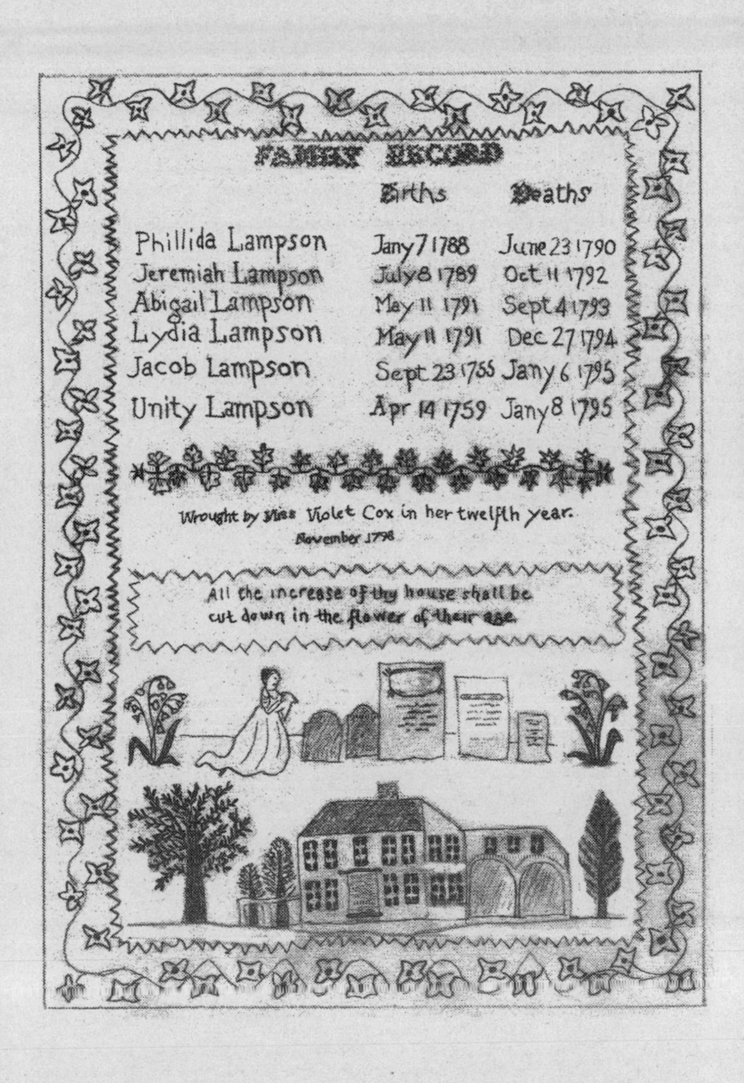
FAMILY RECORD
Births Deaths
Phillida Lampson Jany 7 1788 June 23 1790
Jeremiah Lampson July 8 1789 Oct 11 1792
Abigail Lampson May 11 1791 Sept 4 1793
Lydia Lampson May 11 1791 Dec 27 1794
Jacob Lampson Sept 23 1755 Jany 6 1795
Unity Lampson Apr 14 1759 Jany 8 1795
Wrought by Miss Violet Cox in her twelfth year.
November 1798
All the increase of thy house shall be
cut down in the flower of their age.

1

Meg Corey surveyed the drifts of paper that covered her dining room table, and all but growled with frustration. The harvest was over—her first apple harvest, her first try at farming. Would it be her last? The apples were picked, sorted, and delivered. She'd started in January, and now in December she'd survived storms and accidents, and had learned more than she'd ever realized there was to know about apples and their cultivation. Now the question was, had she made any money, or was this just one extremely expensive hobby? One she couldn't afford?

In an earlier life she had been a financial analyst. She should be able to sort out the mess of receipts and invoices scattered in front of her. The problem was, she had delegated the task of analyzing the results to Briona Stewart, her orchard manager and housemate—young, untried, and eager Bree. It was Bree's responsibility, and part of her job description, to manage the financial side of the orchard operations. Unfortunately, Bree might be brilliant when it came to judging when to prune and when to pick, but she was lousy at keeping records, and there were far too many bits of paper with pieces of essential information scribbled on them that Meg couldn't begin to decipher. She was conscious of year-end looming. Sure, she could wait to file her taxes, but she wanted to keep on the good side of the IRS and the state. More important, she wanted to know whether it was worth going forward with the orchard, or whether she should cut her losses now and find some other way to make a living. If that was even possible in the current economy.

Meg abandoned contemplating the mess of papers when she was interrupted by a knocking at her back door. She went through the kitchen to open it and was greeted by a rush of cold air and Seth Chapin: next-door neighbor, renter of part of her ramshackle outbuildings, and good friend—or more. They were still negotiating the "more" part. But he wasn't alone; not only had he brought Max, his still-young golden retriever, but Seth also was accompanied by two goats, around whose necks he'd tied a rope so he could control them. Meg recognized the goats because they were hers.

"Missing something?" Seth asked.

"I hadn't noticed. Where'd you find them?"

"Over at my place. They just showed up and wanted to play with Max. Good thing I was home, or who knows where they might have ended up."

Meg shuddered as she considered the less pleasant possibilities. "Thank heaven they didn't head across the road. Or into the woods—some idiot hunter might have decided they were small deer. Well, we'd better get these two back where they belong, and see how much damage they did on the way out. Let me grab a coat."

Meg reached behind the kitchen door for one of her grubby but warm down-filled jackets, pulling a hat and gloves from various pockets. "Okay, ready." She closed the door behind her. "Dorcas, Isabel, what were you thinking?" she said, as she took one rope from Seth and led the way to the goat paddock. "I give you nice food and a shelter, and I even talk to you now and then. What more could you want?" The goats gave her sidelong glances but otherwise ignored her.

When they reached the near side of the paddock, fenced in with sturdy posts and wire mesh around the perimeter, Meg examined the fence. "This side looks okay," Meg said. "It's cold out here! I thought maybe it would stay above freezing for a little while longer."

"This is New England—get used to it," Seth said. "Besides, your apples are safely harvested, so you don't need to worry about weather for a couple of months, right?"

"If I don't freeze to death first. That furnace is definitely not up to the job." Meg followed Seth around the left side of the paddock, past the corner where the goat's shed blocked her view from the house.

"Have you had it tuned up recently?" Seth asked.

"Uh, no. I took one look at it when I first got here in January and prayed it would survive until the spring, which it did. But this year it's really limping along. Of course, I keep the heat cranked down, to save money. My sweater collection is growing by leaps and bounds."

"I'll take a look at it once we get your goats sorted out. Ah, here's the problem," Seth said, pointing. Meg could see where one post was splintered at the base, near the ground, and the wire fencing was trampled down.

"That wood doesn't look rotten to me. To snap it off like that, the two of them had to have worked together, didn't they?" Meg asked.

"Maybe. Goats are smart, and determined. Here, you hang on to them and I'll get something to shore it up. Maybe we'd better inspect the rest of the posts while we're at it." Seth headed off toward his workshop at the end of the long driveway.

Meg stood with the goats' ropes in hand and turned toward her house. She'd managed to get most of the trim painted over the past summer, but that only made the rest of the paint look shabby. The roof should be replaced sooner rather than later, but that was one expensive project she was going to put off as long as possible. Storm windows would be nice, but that was a pipe dream. Well, if her many generations of ancestors had managed to survive New England winters in this house, she could, too. She'd just have to toughen up.

Seth emerged from his workshop carrying several lengths of lumber and a toolbox, Max frisking around his feet. When he neared Meg he said, "I should train Max to carry my toolbox or something—he's got far too much energy and not enough to do."

"That would be cute. Maybe you could put him on your business cards. Do you need me to hold anything?"

"Just the goats, for now."

That was enough to keep her busy, as Dorcas and Isabel kept tugging her in different directions, wrapping the rope around her legs, and fending off Max, who really, really wanted to play. She was relieved when Seth said, "That should do it. You can stick them back in the pen now."

"Good." Meg walked back to the front to let them in through the gate, and followed them in to check on their food and bedding. Everything looked okay. She scratched their heads one last time and let herself out of the gate again. "You want some coffee? Or are you busy?" she asked.

"Coffee sounds good. And I can take a look at your furnace."

"Seth, you don't have to do that."

"Why wouldn't I? I'm your tenant, sort of, so it's in my best interest that you don't freeze to death. Should I leave Max outside?"

"Won't he be cold?"

"With his coat? No way."

"Fine, then. Come on in."

Meg led the way back into her kitchen, and while Seth stopped to secure Max to a handy hook outside her back door with a long piece of rope, she hung up her coat and put the kettle on to boil. Seth came in and started prowling around, and Meg suppressed a smile: he and Max shared the same kind of restless energy. They were a good match.

"What are you working on?" he called out from the dining room.

"Trying to sort out the financials for the orchard business," she shouted back. When he returned to the kitchen she went on. "I didn't have time during the season to keep any kind of running tally, although I probably should have. And Bree wasn't much help—she still owes me a lot of information. I know we paid the workers what we paid them last year, but I have the feeling that's not competitive. And I had no idea how to price my apples."

"Are you worried?" Seth asked, finally sitting down.

"I really don't know. At least I've still got a few dollars in the bank, but I don't know what late invoices are lurking, and I know we haven't been paid for some of the last deliveries." Meg busied herself making coffee, then set a mug in front of Seth and sat down with her own. "Don't laugh, but I really thought I'd have some more time to work on my family history, and to do some of the cataloging I promised the Historical Society. Silly me."

"They'll wait—they've waited this long. Any word from your folks lately?"

"We talked over Thanksgiving weekend. They send their regards."

"I hope they'll be back up this way sometime soon."

"Wasn't that one visit enough of a disruption for you? But I'm sure we'll see them again soon. And it was lovely of Rachel to have me and Bree over for Thanksgiving dinner." Seth's sister and her family ran a bed-and-breakfast in a ramshackle Victorian house in Amherst, and Meg, Bree, and even Bree's boyfriend Michael had all joined Seth and his mother at Rachel's feast. "She's such a great cook—I'm jealous."

"She'd be happy to give you some tips."

Meg laughed. "I'm sure she would, but I just don't have the time. Maybe once I get these numbers lined up I'll feel better. Right now it's nagging at me."

Meg's cat Lolly strolled in and sniffed at her half-full dish, then looked plaintively up at her. "No, silly," Meg said. "Finish what you've got." She turned back to Seth. "You have any big projects planned?"

"Not at the moment. Most people don't want to work on their houses during the holiday season—it's either before, so they can show off to the relatives, or after, when the relatives have said nasty things about how shabby their place looks. Speaking of which, let me check out that furnace." He stood up and plunged down the rickety wooden stairs to the cellar before Meg had time to protest.

She shivered. Even in the kitchen it was cold. Lolly seemed to agree, because she jumped into Meg's lap and curled up in a tight ball, her tail over her nose. "So it's not just me, huh?" She could hear Seth clanking and banging around beneath her feet. That furnace had to be at least thirty years old, maybe more. The last owners of the house had been a pair of maiden sisters who'd been born in the house and lived in it their entire lives—and hadn't changed anything, as far as Meg could tell. She had a vision of them weathering each winter, adding layers one at a time to keep warm—and probably going to bed as soon as the sun set, in order to conserve heat. When Meg's mother had inherited the place, she'd continued the long tradition of neglect, renting the house out to a series of tenants. Had they ever complained about the cold? Meg wondered.

Seth came clomping back up the stairs and dropped into

a chair. When Meg cocked an eyebrow at him, he said, "It's not good. Your firebox is cracked."

"What the heck does that mean?"

"It means you're losing heat, and possibly leaking fumes."

Meg sighed: one more problem, and an expensive one, no doubt. "Do I have to do something right this minute? It won't explode or anything, will it?"

"It's not life-threatening, but I won't promise it will last the winter."

"There's no patch job you can do?"

He shook his head. "Nope. It's a cast metal heating chamber, and once it goes, it's gone. From the look of it, it's had a good long run, but it's reached the end of its time. Sorry, Meg."

"I guess I knew it was coming. Tell me, is the furnace more or less important than the roof? If I have to prioritize?"

"Can't say without taking a look at your attic and seeing if it's leaking, or maybe I should say, how badly it's leaking. Have you been up there lately?"

"No. I don't like it up there—it's dirty, and kind of creepy. I took one look at it when I moved in and I haven't been back since."

"I can check it out for you."

"Seth, I appreciate the offer, but you can't do everything. You aren't a roofer!"

"But I know some guys—"

Meg interrupted him, "Yes, and I'm sure they'll give me a good deal." When Seth looked hurt at her comment, she went on, "Sorry, I'm being ungrateful. It's just that all these things that absolutely, positively must be done keep landing on my head, and I have no idea how I'm going to pay for them. That's why I need to know if I've made any kind of profit this past year."

Seth smiled. "I know. Houses—and businesses—will do that to you. You can plan all you want, but there's always something that sneaks up on you. At least you don't have to worry about floods. Or earthquakes—we don't get a lot of those in New England."

"Granford will probably be the epicenter for the first one in two hundred years, with my luck."

Seth drained his coffee and stood up. "I've got some inventory to check, and I'll let you get back to your paperwork. Let me look into options for a new furnace for you."

There was no stopping him, the ever-helpful Seth. "Fine. Thank you. And thanks for catching the goats."

"My pleasure. See you later."

He headed out the door, leaving Meg at the table with her coffee and a warm and purring cat on her lap. On reflection, she realized she wasn't devastated by the news of her ailing—no, *dying*—furnace; at least, not as much as she would have been a few months earlier. She'd proven to herself that she could cope with all sorts of crises, and at least this one had an easy solution, even if it was an expensive one. Funny, she'd left a job managing six- and seven-figure amounts of money for municipalities, and now she was worrying about a couple of thousand here and there.

She looked down at a very content Lolly. "Hey, cat, I've got work to do. Want to come along? The lap goes with me."

2

Meg was enjoying breakfast the next morning when Bree stumbled down the back stairs that led from her room. Her slight frame was buried under layers; she had on a turtleneck under a heavy wool sweater, corduroy pants, thick socks, and even a hat jammed down over her long dark hair. "Morning," Meg said. "Are you cold?"

"Freezing. Is the coffee hot?"

"It is. I'm sorry, apparently the furnace is on its last legs. Seth diagnosed it as terminal yesterday. Besides, I think your room"—Meg nodded her head toward the room over the kitchen—"was intended for the hired hands, and they didn't need heat, right?"

"Well, *I* do." Bree sat down with a mug of coffee and wrapped both hands around it.

"Then let's hope it keeps going a little longer, because I can't afford to do anything about it right now. Speaking of affording, how're you coming with those figures?"

"I'm working on it," Bree said, avoiding Meg's eyes.

This was the part of being "management" that Meg really didn't like. "Bree, it's important. We've talked about this before. Working out our profit and loss statements may not be much fun, but it is necessary."

"I hear you!" Bree snapped. "Look, cut me some slack, will you? I've worked hard, and I need a little downtime. I want to spend time with Michael, 'cause he's just as busy as I am during harvest season. You have a problem with that?"

"No, not at all. Look, this is still all new to me, and it's the first set of numbers I've run through, with nothing to go on from prior years. I'm anxious about getting all the details right, and I need to know how we came out. We've both worked hard this season, and I really want to believe it's paid off. But I won't know until I see all the numbers together, you know?"

"Yeah, yeah," Bree muttered. "What about that little surprise you and your mother found? You sell that, you've got a nice piece of change in the bank."

Meg sighed: she'd thought of that, too, more than once. "I don't feel right, doing that. I'm still thinking about it. But we can't run a business here if we depend on windfalls to drop on our heads. We need to make this work. How about you get all the pieces together for me by midmonth? And by that, I mean *all* the invoices and statements and whatever other pieces of paper you've got, in some sort of order. Deal?"

"Whatever," Bree said, sounding like a sulky teenager, and Meg had to remind herself that Bree at twenty-two wasn't far past that age. "Listen, you need me for anything else? I thought I'd go over to Amherst to see Michael, maybe spend a night or two."

"You tell me. We don't have to think about pruning or anything until January or February, right?"

"You were paying attention!" Bree smiled. "Yes, you're right. Right now, as you keep reminding me over and over, is the time to catch up on record keeping and make some assessments about how we did. We also need to review the trees we've got, and what you might want to put in, thinking ahead. Assuming there will be an 'ahead'?"

Meg smiled. "Depends on those numbers you give me. Go play with Michael, and have fun. I can keep busy here."

"Yes, ma'am." Good humor restored, Bree bounced out of her chair and snagged a banana from the counter. "I'm going to leave before you change your mind."

Ten minutes later she came down the stairs with a bag slung over her shoulder. "Hey, before I forget—they're talking about a big storm coming. Keep an eye on the news, will you?"

"Is there something I need to do with the trees?" Meg asked.

"No, they either make it or they don't. But a bad storm can really mess things up—like power, and driving anywhere."

"Okay, I hear you. But I really think you're just looking for an excuse to stay over in Amherst a bit longer."

Bree gave her a grin. "Maybe. Bye now!" And she slammed out the back door. Meg heard her car start up, and watched from the kitchen window as Bree pulled away. So did Dorcas and Isabel, from their now reinforced pen.

Meg turned away from the window, feeling lost. She'd been working her tail off since she'd arrived almost a year earlier, first trying to make the house livable—sealing up the worst of the cracks, and even refinishing the kitchen floor. And then she'd been caught up in the demands of the orchard, and her parents' unexpected visit, and by the time she caught her breath it was December. She still had numbers to crunch, but she'd just given Bree a reprieve. She refilled her coffee mug and sat down, trying to decide what she should do.

She attempted to picture herself out shopping for some decent furniture, at least for the most visible front rooms, since what she had at the moment had been handed down—and should have been thrown out—by decades of transient tenants. But buying furniture would take money, so scratch that. The home improvement wish list included the roof, storm windows, and somewhere in the mix, a second bathroom. Again, none of those was going to happen until she had figured out her financial situation. And she had to factor in the dying furnace, which was pretty close to the top of the list. More money. Funny—up until last year, when she'd lost her banking job, she had always had more than enough money. She hadn't been rich, but her salary had exceeded her needs and even her wants, and she'd been content. Now she had to look at every penny she spent. She wasn't used to it, and she wasn't happy about it.

At least working online doing genealogy, her latest interest, was free. When her mother had visited recently she had begun to piece together the family tree, with some surprising results. In the thick of the harvest Meg hadn't had time to digest what her mother had found; maybe this was a good opportunity to do that. And she could make a list of questions to ask Gail Selden at the Historical Society in town. Of course, she'd have to smooth the way with Gail by showing her some progress in the Historical Society records that she had agreed to catalogue—very slowly. The material was often fascinating, especially when she stumbled upon a document that shed light on farm life in the nineteenth century, and even her own house—the Warren house. She had a skeletal outline of her Warren ancestors, thanks to her mother, and maybe this was the opportunity to flesh them out a bit, so to speak.

But she'd blanketed her workspace, otherwise known as the dining room table, with business records, and she didn't want to disturb them. So, where to go? It would have to be another room altogether. The kitchen was too busy, and she needed the table space to eat there. The two rooms across the central hall were freezing: she wasn't using them and kept their doors shut most of the time to conserve heat. But the front parlor was the only place she and Bree had to sit or do anything, so she would have to brave the cold and set up across the hall. With a sense of purpose Meg crossed the hall and pushed open the door.

The front room was absolutely freezing, its windows partially frosted over, and she hurried to open the heating vents. There was little furniture, but Meg had found a folding card table and a couple of matching chairs, and they would do. She needed a light, and a plug for her laptop and printer, and she'd be set. And maybe if she left the doors open to the rest of the house, the temperature in the room would rise above what she estimated was about fifty degrees. Could she keyboard wearing gloves?

At least moving furniture around and setting up her new workspace kept her warm for a while. She had placed the table so she had a view out the window (although not too near it, because she could feel cold eddies of air sneaking in around the sash), from which she could see the barest edge of the orchard up the hill. Funny—for the first few weeks she'd lived in the house, she hadn't even known she had an orchard. How much things had changed!

Meg booted up her laptop and pulled out a folder of notes her mother had left for her. It seemed like a lifetime ago now, even though it had been only a month, but the harvest had taken all her energy and attention. She used to think that genealogy was for retired grandmothers with too much time on their hands, but that was before she'd found herself living in a house that her ancestors had built—by hand—over two hundred years earlier; ancestors who had farmed the land, raised families in the house. Who had, in some obscure way, made her who she was today—or who at the very least had contributed a fragment of DNA, without which she would have been someone else. So she felt she owed them something. Besides, once she had gotten into it, she had discovered that the process was kind of fun. She opened the folder and started reading.

Four hours later Meg sat back and realized she had forgotten to eat lunch. Her pile of papers had increased twofold, and she'd managed to work her way back to the mid-1700s, when the paper trail, or at least what was available online, became sparse. She knew that Stephen Warren had built her house, probably in the 1760s, although there was no handy document saying "built house today," so she'd had to make some inferences from land records. He'd been too old to fight in the Revolution, although both of his sons had fought. One of whose direct descendants had stayed in this house until some twenty years ago—that record might be hard to beat, in the modern world. What's more, one of Stephen Warren's grandsons had ended up living in the house next door, and handing it down to his descendants as well, although that house had passed out of the family much earlier in the twentieth century. So much history, and here she was living in the middle of it.

She was about to shut down her computer when she remembered Bree's warning about the weather. She clicked onto a weather site and read with a mixture of anxiety and skepticism about a burgeoning storm that seemed to be headed right in her direction. Of course, it was still at least a day away, but already comparisons were being made to prior memorable storms: the blizzards of 1996, 1978, and even, for heaven's sake, 1888. None of them meant anything to Meg. Still, she thought, it couldn't hurt to stock up on the usual supplies—basics like bread and milk and batteries. And cat food. No doubt everyone in the Connecticut Valley would have the same idea, but she wasn't in a hurry and wouldn't mind waiting in line. And she should make sure the goats were battened down, or whatever one was supposed to do with goats, before the storm hit.

She turned off her computer and headed for the back door. Outside, wrapped in her warm coat, she looked up at the sky:

pale, wispy clouds moved slowly across it. Apparently they didn't know about the storm. There was a slight wind, but all in all, everything looked very ordinary. As she walked to her car she noticed a glint at the end of the driveway, and she headed toward it to explore. Someone had thrown a glass bottle, which had shattered, scattering shards across the drive. *Kids?* She couldn't recall hearing anything breaking, but from the back of the house she might not have noticed. It was a good thing she had seen the glass, though, because if she had driven over one of the larger pieces she could have lost a tire, and that was another expense she didn't need right how. Meg carefully gathered up the pieces and deposited them on her back step to be disposed of later. Not thrown out, she reminded herself, recycled, as Seth kept telling her.

Meg got into her car and headed for the nearest supermarket, the next town over. Granford had no market of its own, unless you counted the one-room general store in the middle of town, which doubled as the local pharmacy and sold souvenirs and T-shirts as well. As she had predicted, the parking lot was jammed, even at this time in the afternoon, and she ended up parking at the far end of the lot, snagging a cart from someone who had just finished loading her own car. "Looks like a bad one," the woman said as she slammed the trunk shut.

"Could be," Meg agreed amiably, although she wasn't at all sure about it. Inside the store people milled around looking mildly frantic. The bread was long gone, but Meg collected eggs, cheese, pasta, flour, and an assortment of other staples, not forgetting the cat food. She added some fresh vegetables—imported from some other hemisphere, which annoyed her—and declared herself finished, then joined the long line at the cash register. At least all the cash registers were staffed today, which was unusual.

Twenty minutes later she reached the head of the line. "Think it'll be a bad one?" she asked the teenaged girl in front of the cash register.

The girl looked blankly at her and shrugged. "Paper or plastic?"

Apparently the panic hadn't trickled down to the high school yet. And students would probably be thrilled at the prospect of a snow day. "I brought my own," Meg said.

Back outside, Meg checked the sky again: no change. Maybe this monster storm was all media hype, or a vast conspiracy designed to sell bread and milk, or just to ramp up the anxiety level among the general population. At least she'd be ready—just in case.

She spent a quiet evening at home, watching television—a rare treat. She even managed to stay awake long enough to check the eleven o'clock news, where the approaching storm was the lead headline. The talking heads looked serious and concerned. When she flipped through the channels, she found the same thing on every station, although their time estimates varied a bit. Okay, she'd done her duty: she'd stocked up. There was nowhere she had to be the next day, and nothing she could do to prepare her trees for whatever was coming. She was willing to bet they had survived earlier storms, and losing limbs was a fact of tree life. Meg figured she was as ready as she was going to be.

3

Meg allowed herself the luxury of sleeping in the next morning, which currently meant staying in bed until the dark sky shaded into gray. She lay nestled in her blankets and quilts, and listened for a moment. She could hear snow spitting against her windows—that wasn't good. No howling winds yet, but when a lone vehicle passed along the road in front of the house, the sound was curiously muffled. The snow had clearly begun.

She checked her clock: almost seven, later than she had expected. The clouds must have darkened the day. And then she realized what she wasn't hearing: the furnace, which her aged thermostat was supposed to goad into action at six thirty. She listened harder. No, no ticking of the heating ducts, expanding and contracting as warm air and cold did battle within her mostly uninsulated walls. Maybe, she thought optimistically, the house was already at her normal daytime temperature of sixty-eight degrees? She stuck an arm out from under the covers, and could tell immediately that the temperature in the room was nowhere near sixty-eight. She wasn't even sure it was near sixty.

What next? Well, obviously, get out of bed, put on lots of warm clothing, and go down to the cellar to see if she could prod the slumbering beast to life. Although, she admitted to herself, her expertise amounted to fiddling with the thermostat and cursing a lot. At least if she went down and looked at the furnace—and spoke kindly to it?—she would know whether it was sulking or just plain dead. For a moment she thought nostalgically about her former apartment in Boston, where there had always been ample heat and hot water, and someone to complain to when things didn't work. Well, she had Seth. Who would most likely tell her that the furnace's time had come and she needed a new one, which would definitely cost more money than she had.

When Meg gathered herself to climb out of bed, she realized that Lolly had crawled under the quilt and was glued to her legs. It must be really cold. Meg extricated herself from the sleeping cat and dashed for her closet, pulling out heavy jeans, a flannel shirt she didn't remember she owned, and a fisherman's knit sweater someone had brought back for her from Ireland. And socks. She thought wistfully about long underwear, but she'd never had any reason to buy any—until now. She made a mental note to order some online. Meg managed to dress in record time, then brushed her hair. Hairbrush in hand, she drifted over to the window on the west side, from which she could usually see the orchard. Not today: the orchard had disappeared behind a wall of white flakes, swirling erratically. Small, dry flakes that looked serious and determined. By her best guess there was already several inches of snow on the ground.

She went down the hall to the lone bathroom, where she brushed and washed. Emerging from the bathroom, she checked Bree's room at the back: as she had suspected,

Bree hadn't come home last night, and with this weather she probably wouldn't be back for a while.

Downstairs it was, if anything, colder. Meg put the kettle on to boil and went to check the thermostat. It read fifty-two degrees. She rotated it back and forth, but there was no reassuring click indicating that the furnace had started. Maybe the thermostat had gone bad, spontaneously? She heard the kettle whistle in the kitchen, and went back and made coffee, strong. She scrabbled through the provisions she'd bought yesterday—yes, she had milk, so she could make oatmeal. That sounded warm and comforting, and she wanted both at the moment.

As she was putting her oatmeal into the microwave to heat, Lolly finally stalked in, looking unhappy. Hunger had apparently won out over warmth. Meg opened a can of cat food and dished it up, then laid the food at Lolly's feet. "There you go." Lolly sniffed at it, then wolfed down half. Then she retreated to her favorite place in the kitchen, the top of the refrigerator, which, Meg realized, was warm. Smart cat.

Fortified with coffee and oatmeal, Meg felt ready to brave the cellar. She was growing increasingly fond of the house the longer she lived in it, but she still disliked the cellar. It was old: half the joists holding up the first floor were actually logs, some with bark still on them. Part of the floor was still dirt, although someone had added a thin and now-crumbling layer of concrete to the area around the furnace. And it boasted a vigorous spider population. Meg didn't even want to think about mice. She wondered briefly whether any mouse with the gall to venture upstairs would inspire Lolly's primitive hunting instincts. Not likely. Meg wasn't even sure Lolly knew what a mouse looked like—although, she had to admit, Lolly had survived on her own for a few weeks when her former owners had abandoned her and moved to another state. Still, she'd rather not find out how Lolly handled mice.

Quit stalling! Meg squared her shoulders and marched

to the door in the dining room that led to the cellar, and pulled it open. Turning the light on, she made her way carefully down the rickety wooden stairs and crossed the floor to confront the furnace. It was still and silent, and Meg felt helpless. Wasn't there a button to push, a switch to flip, a prayer to say? All she could tell was that it wasn't doing anything at the moment.

Was the oil tank full? She checked the massive tank a few feet away. The gauge looked ancient, but it did show a line at the halfway mark. She tapped the gauge, but it didn't shift. She knocked on the metal side of the tank, and it didn't sound hollow.

She had exhausted her options. Time to call Seth.

Upstairs, she poured herself another cup of coffee and retrieved the phone. She hated depending on Seth to fix anything and everything. Not that he wasn't willing to do it. If anything, he was too willing. He was Mr. Fix-it, not only for her but for the whole town, as a selectman, and even beyond if she counted his sister Rachel in Amherst. And the price was right: nothing. He honestly liked to help people. Still, even he couldn't fabricate a furnace out of thin air, and she had no idea how long it would take to obtain and install a new one. Or how much it would cost. With a sigh, she hit Seth's speed dial button.

He answered on the second ring. "Hey, Meg, you're up early. What's up?"

"I think my furnace is dead."

"Sorry to hear that, but I did warn you. I'll come by and take a look at it again, but I don't think I have any magic fixes up my sleeve. Lousy timing, with this storm."

Meg hadn't even thought about that. If it kept snowing for long, suppliers probably wouldn't be delivering large equipment anytime soon. "I know. Have the forecasters changed their minds?"

"Nope. They're having a wonderful time making dire pronouncements, and the snowfall estimates keep going up."

"Where are you? Home? Were you planning to come over to the office today?"

"Yeah, I'm at home, but I can be there in half an hour or so."

"Seth, you don't have to do that. I can keep warm for a bit."

"Look, why don't you come over here and stay until this is over? Where's Bree?"

"With Michael in Amherst. What about your mother?"

"She went over to Rachel's yesterday. You could join them there, if you don't want to stay at my place."

"I'll think about it."

"Well, we'd better check that the rest of the house and barn are ready anyway. And maybe get the goats into the barn—they'd be better off there than in the shed."

"Thanks, Seth." *Again.* "See you soon." She hung up the phone.

Seth arrived twenty-five minutes later, coming overland with Max frisking through the snow. "No change in our patient?"

"None," Meg said. "You didn't drive?"

"I took a look at the roads and decided it wasn't worth it. Even if I made it, there are always idiots who decide they have to go out, and they usually end up in a ditch or stuck in the middle of the road. You'd think anybody who'd lived around here for a while would figure out how to drive in snow—or to stay home. Anyway, I pulled out my trusty snowshoes."

"You have snowshoes?"

"I do, and I know how to use them. I hate to say it, but it's bad out there, and it's going to get worse before it gets better. Let's go down and take a look at the furnace. Hi, Lolly." Seth rubbed the cat's head in passing. Meg followed him down the stairs.

In the cellar, Seth poked and prodded the furnace, removing cover plates, testing wires, pushing a few buttons, all with no results. He straightened up and turned to her. "It's hopeless. Sorry, but you're going to have to replace it."

"Well, you did warn me," Meg said glumly. They turned their backs on the moribund furnace, and Meg led the way upstairs. In the kitchen she said, "Maybe that'll be my Christmas present to myself—a new furnace. How much?"

"Depends. You want to switch to gas?"

"That'll cost more, right?"

"You'd have to run a gas line. The unit would be about the same in cost, and it's anybody's guess what the long-term operating costs would be, compared to oil. Your call."

"How much?" she asked again.

"Six, seven thou, maybe. But it's not like you have a choice—you need a furnace, and there's no used furnace store. Wish I could give you better news."

She sighed again. "So what do we do now?"

"I make some calls, see who's got what in stock. That is, if I can find anybody at work. If they're smart, they stayed home today. This isn't going to happen today, or probably even tomorrow. From what I'm hearing, nobody's going to be going anywhere for the next couple of days."

"So you're saying I'm going to freeze my buns off here?"

"Hey, I said you could stay at my place. Lolly, too. I'm not sure we'd make it over the mountain to Rachel's in Amherst, even with four-wheel drive."

Meg thought about that for a moment. She'd never been past the first floor in Seth's house just over the hill, maybe a mile away, although he'd spent plenty of time in her house, both downstairs and upstairs. But somehow it felt wrong; it felt like she was abandoning her house. "Is this storm really going to be that bad?"

"Maybe. Probably. They're saying this could be one for the record books."

"I feel I should be here in case something happens. Look, this house has been here since the seventeen hundreds, and they didn't have furnaces then, right? So how did they manage?"

"Fireplaces. Yes, you've got a couple, but the chimneys aren't in the best of shape."

"But would they work, at least for a little while?"

"I'd have to check to see if either one is clear. You don't want to find out the hard way that birds or raccoons have been nesting there for decades—you don't want to risk a chimney fire. Are you serious about this, Meg?"

She realized belatedly that she had probably hurt his feelings. "I'm just exploring my options. It's not that I don't want to bunk with you, but I feel kind of proprietary about this house. Can you at least take a look, please?"

He gave her a quizzical look. "I guess so. Got a flash-light?"

She pulled one from a drawer and handed it to him, then followed him out of the kitchen into the front parlor. Seth knelt on the hearth and jiggled a handle she hadn't noticed. It resisted for a time, then with a screech it shifted, and a shower of black soot fell onto the bottom of the fireplace. He backed away quickly and stumbled into Max, who had been watching with great interest. Seth looked disgusted. "Good thing I wore work clothes," he said, sticking his head into the opening and peering up. "I can see daylight, so no nests. But the mortar's pretty much gone, and there are some bricks missing."

"But will it work, for now?"

"I think so." He backed out of the fireplace and slapped his hands on his now-blackened jeans. "You have any wood?"

"If I have any firewood, it's been there for a while," Meg said. "I do know there's some construction rubble out in the shed."

"You don't want to burn that—you don't know what the stuff has been treated with. Let me go check."

He went out through the back door. Meg followed as far

as the kitchen, wondering at her own reluctance to take the easy route and stay with Seth. At least his house had heat. It wasn't like they hadn't spent the night together before. But the idea of "roughing it" the way her ancestors had—not that they had had a choice—was kind of appealing. It could be an adventure.

Seth came back, stomping his boots on the back steps. "It's really coming down—I think there must be a couple more inches since I got here. The short answer is, yes, you've got some firewood out there, although it looks ancient, and some of the scrap wood would be okay. That covers your heating. Look, Meg, if you're set on this idea, why don't I stay here?"

She smiled at him. "I like that idea. It's not that I don't want to spend time with you, it's just that I don't feel right leaving the house."

"Meg, the house has survived quite a few years without you in it."

"I know. But I haven't spent a full winter here yet, and I want to keep an eye on things. Is that strange?"

"Kind of, but the worst that can happen is that you'll spend a very cold and miserable couple of days."

"With you."

"There is that." Seth laughed. "Well, one good reason to stay, I guess, is that if it gets really cold, we should keep an eye on the water pipes. Some of them aren't insulated, and you don't want them to freeze and burst."

"Okay," she said slowly. "How cold? How fast?"

"Twenties, maybe? As I say, you don't have much insulation, so the pipes aren't protected. We could rig up some lightbulbs on extension cords—that's usually enough to keep them from freezing."

"I knew there was a reason I kept you around. So, what first?"

"Let's get the goats into the barn, and maybe we can

find some more wood out there while we're at it. You'd better bundle up."

Meg pulled on most of the outerwear she owned, as well as her boots, then followed Seth out the back door, shutting it in the face of a disappointed Max, who Seth had decided should stay inside. It was like entering another universe. She could no longer see the steps outside the door because they had disappeared under snow. Gusts blew snow in every direction, including into her face. If she hadn't known where the barn was, she would have been lost: it wasn't until they were within a couple of feet of it that its dark bulk emerged from the swirling whiteness. Seth reached it first and pulled open a door. They stepped inside to relative silence. As her eyes adjusted Meg could see where snow drifted in through some of the many cracks between the old boards.

"We should clear out a stall for the goats," Seth said. "You'll have to put out some hay, and some food. And if you find anything that looks burnable and isn't holding something up, leave it in the center here."

"Gotcha. Which stall looks best?"

Seth looked around him. "They all look pathetic. But how about the one that backs against the apple storage chambers? At least there's one solid wall to block the drafts, and the rest looks okay."

Together they hauled random pieces of ancient farm equipment and a roll of wire fencing out of the stall. Luckily Meg had been keeping the goats' hay inside the barn already, since there wasn't room in their shed outside, so they spread some on the wooden floor of the stall and stacked the remaining bales around the perimeter. Meg added feed to a trough that had been part of the stall for as long as it had been there, and filled a bucket with water from the rusty tap inside the barn. Now all they needed were the goats.

"You want me to get the girls?" Seth asked.

"Will they come to you?"

"Sure. They love me. They came over to my place yesterday, didn't they?"

"I thought it was Max they had a thing for."

"Love my dog, love me. I'll go round them up."

How did Seth stay so cheerful? Meg wondered. Throw a major storm at him, and he just goes down his checklist of things to do: make sure mother is secured. Check in on poor Meg, who is clueless. Herd goats. Build a fire. What couldn't he do?

He was back a minute or so later with Dorcas and Isabel trotting behind him, on the same rope leashes he had used before. "Listen, didn't you replace the locks on the doors, after that pesticide incident?"

"Uh, yes. Plus to protect the equipment I keep in here. Why?"

"Looks like someone tried to jimmy the back one again—there's a bunch of new gouges."

"Do you think they got in?"

"Hard to say. Is anything missing?"

"Honestly, I never come out here, or at least, not past the holding chambers. The tractor is still here, obviously, but I don't think anyone would be tempted to steal it. As for the rest, I have no idea what I've got. You think someone was looking for something, or just wanted a place to hang out? Like teenagers?"

"Maybe. No harm done, apparently. Let's get these two settled." He led the goats into their new temporary home, and they explored it thoroughly before trying out the feed. Seth latched the gate behind them.

"Will they be warm enough?" Meg asked.

"Sure. They've got shelter, and they've got each other. How do you think animals survived in the wild all these years?"

"I didn't think about it. Are we done here? My fingers are getting numb."

"And they aren't going to get a lot warmer in the house. Remember, I offered you a nice warm place."

"And I thank you, but I'm staying."

"Then so am I."

When they emerged into the blinding snow, Meg realized there was someone else in the driveway, or at least another truck.

"Seth?" someone called out.

"John?" Seth replied. Meg giggled: this was like a game of Marco Polo, with the three of them trying to find each other in the snow.

A shadowy figure came into focus, bundled to the eyeballs. "Hey, Seth, I wanted to check if you'd need me for plowing? Oh, sorry, I didn't see you, ma'am."

Seth looked back and forth at Meg and John. "You haven't met? Meg, this is John Taylor—he lives down the street from you, toward Ludlow. John, meet Meg Corey."

John stuck out a gloved hand. "Nice to meet you. Sorry I haven't been by to introduce myself before now."

"Hey, I've been so busy with the orchard that I haven't been around much, so I probably would have missed you anyway."

"Looks like you had a good harvest this year."

"I did."

"Just came over to talk to Seth. So, Seth, can you use me for plowing?"

"Sure. I'll call you as soon as I have the details. Once the snow stops."

"Right. Thanks. Good to meet you, Meg." He climbed into an ageing pickup truck and pulled out onto the road.

"I haven't seen him around before," Meg said as the truck disappeared. "Which is surprising, since it's not like there are a lot of people living on this road."

"John doesn't socialize much. He's having a rough time—he's got a sick kid, and he just lost his job a few months ago and had to move back in with his mother. I plan to hire him when I need another pair of hands, so you'll be seeing him here, on and off. And I've been throwing what municipal work I can his way, like snowplowing. His wife can't work because someone's got to stay home with their child full-time."

"Sad," Meg said.

"It is. Come on, let's get out of the weather!"

"Right behind you."

4

Meg followed Seth into the house, and they stripped off their outer clothing, shaking the snow from each piece; it melted quickly on the floor, making puddles. Max was eager to help, and excited about being inside with some of his favorite people. He kept bouncing around their legs, and Meg had to remind herself that Max wasn't even a year old yet—still a puppy, albeit a large and boisterous one. Lolly watched the scene from atop the refrigerator, keeping out of the fray.

"So, now what?" Meg asked. "Are you hungry?" She was surprised to see that it was lunchtime already. "I did stock up on staples, so we won't starve. Oh, except I didn't think of dog food. Will Max eat cat food?"

"I can go back and get a bag of kibble."

"Seth! You want to go back out in that?" Meg waved out the kitchen window, which showed nothing but white.

"Why not? It's daylight, I've got the snowshoes, and I know the way. Give me lunch and I'll be ready to brave the storm."

"If you say so," Meg said dubiously. If it had been up to her, Max would have eaten whatever she could find. "Ham and cheese work for you?"

"Sounds good."

Once lunch was over, Seth donned all the pieces of clothing he had taken off.

"Are you going to take Max with you?" Meg asked.

"I don't think so—he doesn't have snowshoes, and it's getting pretty deep out there. Besides, if we got separated, I'm not sure I'd find him again. He's never seen snow, and I'm sure you've noticed he's easily distracted."

Meg conjured up an image of doggie snowshoes and laughed. "He'll be okay here. Won't you, Max?" Max responded by drooling on her hand. "How long will you be? Just so I can send out the Mounties when you don't show up."

"This isn't the Arctic, Meg. I'm walking home and back again. I've done it a thousand times, even in the snow. An hour, maybe? I've got to make sure my place is secure, too. Don't worry—I'll be fine. You'll be fine. Maybe you should start cooking dinner—that at least will keep the kitchen warm. We'll wait to build a fire until I get back. Anything else you can think of that we need?"

"Just you." As he headed for the door, she grabbed his coat and pulled him back and kissed him.

When she let him go, he smiled and asked, "What was that for?"

"I'm sending you off into a howling blizzard in search of dog food, a truly noble calling. Thank you for humoring me about staying here."

"Hey, I get it. Although you may find one experiment as Meg Corey, Pioneer Woman, is enough for you."

"Take care." He gave her a salute then strapped on his snowshoes. She watched him as he disappeared into the driving snow—it took him only a couple of seconds to vanish. She turned to the dog. "Well, Max, what shall we make for dinner? How does minestrone sound to you?" Max wagged his tail enthusiastically. "Minestrone it is."

Seth had been right about a warm kitchen. She kept all the doors closed, and put a large pot of water on the back of the stove before she began chopping vegetables and opening cans. She had it easy—at least she had fresh vegetables, not to mention store-bought cans of beans and tomatoes. A century or two ago, people would have eaten what they raised—period. Probably December wouldn't have been too skimpy, but she could imagine that February might be grim, after the fall harvest crops had run out. The apples would have survived that long—dried, maybe, and she thought she'd seen some mention of putting them in barrels, well packed in straw, and submerging them in a pond over the winter. It sounded a bit extreme, but what did she know? She had modern refrigeration.

The soup started to smell good. It was hard to go wrong with the basics: onions, carrots, beans. The nice thing about minestrone was that you could toss in whatever you had on hand, and no one could argue with you about messing with the recipe. And it was kind of cozy to be working in the warm kitchen while the snow swirled around the house. The windows were steaming up. Lolly slept on, and even Max was quiet at the moment, which was a blessing. Should she make something to go with the soup? Corn bread? Did she have cornmeal? She couldn't remember. Actually, she couldn't remember the last time she'd really cooked. She'd been so busy with the harvest, and so exhausted at the end of each day, that she and Bree had relied mostly on takeout and microwave foods, even though she shuddered at the salt and sugar content. Rachel had taken care of Thanksgiving. So this was really the first chance she'd had to indulge in cooking for pleasure. She could make the corn bread, and then leave the oven on and try for an apple pie. At least she knew she still had apples.

After an hour and a half Meg began to wonder if she

should worry about Seth. Sure, he knew his way around, but she'd read stories of Arctic explorers who got disoriented in the snow and lost all sense of direction—and sometimes their frozen corpses weren't found for decades. That was not a comforting thought. Still, up until now, if Seth said he was going to do something, he did it, with a minimum of muss and fuss. And usually three other things at the same time. Besides, she had no idea what she would do if he didn't reappear soon. Call the police? Then there would be multiple people wandering around in a blizzard, which only increased the chances of someone getting lost, with possibly fatal consequences.

Stop it, Meg! Why was she getting so morbid? A minute ago she had been cheerfully chopping vegetables; now she was envisioning frozen corpses in the snow. Seth knew what he was doing—didn't he? She trusted his judgment. If he said he could walk home and back in a howling blizzard, she was going to believe him. Until when? Two hours? Three?

Her increasingly frantic thoughts were interrupted by a stamping at the back door. Seth looked like an abominable snowman, his winter jacket and hood covered with an inch or so of the white stuff. The image was exaggerated by the large pack he was wearing on his back. How much dog food had he brought? Was he preparing for a long siege?

She pulled open the door as he was brushing the last of the snow off his legs. He took off the snowshoes and left them leaning against the house outside the door before stepping in. "Something smells good."

"You took long enough."

Something in her tone made Seth look at her more closely. "Sorry. Were you worried? I was making sure my place was closed up tight, and I checked Mom's, too. Oh, and when I was coming back I noticed one of your cellar windows had come loose. I didn't notice that when I looked at the furnace earlier. But it was probably held in by one of those old hook-and-eye rigs, and since the wood is old, a good gust of wind could have knocked it loose. I wedged it closed, but I'll take a look at it from downstairs. Hi, Max—you being good?"

"He's been asleep, mostly—you woke him up. Have you seen or heard any updates on the storm?"

"The weather forecasters are having a great time outlining disaster scenarios, but they're paid to make news," Seth said. "Why don't we turn on the TV and check on the latest?"

Meg flipped on the small television she kept in the kitchen. Not surprisingly all channels were running continuous coverage, and she watched in fascination, flipping among channels, as each outlined details of a storm that exceeded anything she—and they—had ever heard of.

"Wow. They're saying it could go on for another day, with record snowfalls. So, what now?"

Seth smiled. "You want me to show you how to build a fire in your fireplace?"

"Oh, goodie. Yes, please. You're sure it's safe?"

"The biggest risk for chimney fires is when you have a buildup of creosote inside. Since nobody seems to have used this for years, and since I've already made sure there are no obstructions, I'd say we're good. You *do* have a fire extinguisher, don't you?"

"Of course I do." She noticed he was smiling. "Oh, you're joking. Okay, big man, make the little woman a fire."

"Piece of cake," he said. Coatless, he went out the back to the adjoining shed and returned with an armload of split logs and smaller pieces of wood for kindling. "Get the door, will you?"

Meg obliged—and was shocked at how much colder the dining room was than the kitchen. She led the way through to the front parlor and stood and watched as Seth laid a fire.

"You have any newspapers?"

"I thought that was cheating."

"It's not my favorite method, but they'll do in a pinch. Yes or no? Otherwise I'll have to start using those historic records you've been sitting on. I bet they'd catch fast."

"Don't even think it. Yes, I have some newspapers. They're even stacked up for recycling." Meg went back through the kitchen and collected a stack of papers, marveling again at the differences in temperature. She returned to the parlor and thrust them at Seth. "Here. Will these do?"

"Just fine, thank you," he said, turning his attention back to the fire. In a couple of minutes he had a nice small fire going, and he watched it carefully to make sure the smoke was going up the chimney. Finally he said, "It's drawing nicely. The old builders knew what they were doing. Of course, if this was your only heat, you kind of had to get it right. Now, close off the doors to the hall and the dining room to keep the heat in. We don't have a whole lot of wood, and we don't know how long this storm might last."

"Surely not more than a day?" Meg said.

He shrugged. "I wouldn't count on anything."

"This is kind of scary," she said, shivering.

"Why?" he asked. "We have food, heat, electricity, and companionship. What more do you want? Do you happen to have any oil lamps handy?" When she stared blankly at him, he went on. "I'll take that as a no."

"You're thinking we'll lose power?" she said.

"It's possible. I think there are some old lamps out in the barn. The question is, is there any kerosene for them? Only one way to find out."

"What, you're going out in that again?"

"It's going to get dark soon. It's better to be prepared now than to fumble around later."

"By any chance were you a Boy Scout?"

"How'd you guess? Look, you stay here and I'll go check in the barn. I'll take Max along—he probably needs to go, and he can burn off some energy." Seth went back toward the kitchen, whistling.

He *was* actually enjoying this! Meg stood in front of the fire as it began to cast some heat into the room, her arms wrapped around herself. She was pretty sure that the house would survive; at least she knew it was structurally sound. The barn? The roof was pretty iffy, but the skeleton was good—Seth had checked when he installed the apple holding chambers. So she might be cold, but she wasn't in any danger, and there was plenty of food. And companionship. She was going to have a sleepover with Seth. Sure, they'd spent nights together, but not prolonged periods of time with little to distract them. They'd actually have time to talk, unless Seth went into his manic fix-it mode. Was this good or bad?

Good, Meg decided. There were issues they'd both been tap dancing around for months, and maybe now they would have time to explore some of them.

Seth was back in minutes, and after stamping off the snow—again—he came from the kitchen bearing two remarkably rusty but intact oil lamps that Meg dimly remembered hanging in the barn. "We're good. You might collect any candles you have. Dorcas and Isabel said hi."

"Are they all right?"

"They're fine. Probably bored. Listen, you should also bring down blankets and pillows—I don't think you'll want to sleep upstairs."

"Even with a bed warmer?"

"Even with." He smiled.

She went upstairs and started collecting quilts and pillows. He was right: it was freezing upstairs, and it wasn't even dark yet. She wondered briefly if she had a chamber pot lurking in a dark corner. Making a trip to the bathroom later wouldn't be pleasant. Maybe a bucket?

Downstairs she dumped her trove of bedding on a chair. "So now what? What did people do in the old days?"

Seth prodded the fire carefully. "When they weren't working, you mean? Read. Sewed, since clothes were scarce and probably needed a lot of mending. Knit. Sat around the pianoforte singing. You don't happen to have one of those, do you?"

"Sorry, no. I'm not particularly musical anyway. And I'm not very good at knitting."

"Well, there are games—cards, backgammon, cribbage. Poker, if you want to be more modern. You have any games or cards?"

"Maybe, although I'd have to hunt for them. I never had time for that sort of thing in Boston. Everyone I knew was always working, and even when we had time off, we'd usually just go to a bar or restaurant or watch a DVD."

"There are plenty of games at Mom's house."

"Seth Chapin, don't you dare go out in this weather just to get a cribbage board or whatever! Worst case, we can make our own playing cards."

"Now there's the pioneer spirit!"

"Can we leave the fire unattended? Because I was thinking of baking something."

"As long as there's nothing flammable nearby, I think we'll be okay—you've got a good, broad slate hearth here. Can I help?"

"You can lick the bowl, if I can figure out what dessert is."

"Sounds good. Let me go downstairs and check that window, and you go start whipping up something in the kitchen."

"Yes, master."

5

While Seth poked around in the cellar—again—Meg inventoried her supplies. What was she in the mood for? The idea of peeling all those apples, and then trying to make a piecrust, had lost its charm. She wanted something solid and sugary. Not cookies: cake. Or gingerbread. Did she have molasses? She rummaged in her cupboards and triumphantly pulled out a sticky bottle. *Yes!*

Seth came in, looking perplexed, as she was melting butter in a pan.

"What?" she asked.

"I don't know why that window came open. The wood was pretty sound, all things considered, so it would have taken some real force to pull the eyebolt out, which is what happened. A freak gust, I guess. What're you making?"

"Gingerbread. I thought it fit the scene. You know, real Currier and Ives stuff. You know anyone with a one-horse sleigh?"

"Sure, but he's over in Hadley, remember? I don't think he'll be stopping by tonight."

They spent a companionable hour cooking, or rather, Meg cooked and Seth watched and commented.

"You know, this is pretty sexist," Meg said, as she slid the gingerbread into the oven and set the timer. "Me doing all the housework and you sitting there and kibitzing."

"How about I wash the dishes?"

"Deal. I hate washing dishes. Was yours a traditional household? I mean, your mother cooking, your father doing the heavy stuff?"

"Kind of, even though Mom usually had a job. Well, early on she was working for Dad, doing the billing and accounting. She trained us kids to do a lot of the housework, although we bickered about it."

"Forward-thinking woman," Meg said approvingly. "I don't think I ever saw my father with a sponge in his hand. We did have a cleaner who came in once a week. I know it sounds kind of pampered, and I guess it was. It was a rude shock when I started living on my own and realized that things got dirty and stayed that way until I did something about it."

"You poor thing! So did you hire Merry Maids cleaners?"

"I did not! I learned. Good thing, or I'd be totally lost with this place. And now I've acquired even more skills. You ready for minestrone?"

"Starving."

"Good."

She fed Max and Lolly—putting Lolly's dish on the countertop, since she didn't trust Max not to scarf up any food he could reach—then dished up the minestrone. "I think there's a bottle of wine in the fridge. Should I open it?"

"Why not? I promise you I'm not driving anywhere tonight."

Meg realized she hadn't heard a vehicle pass for quite a while—not even a snowplow. "I don't think anyone else is either. Who orders the plows out? The selectmen?"

"You're looking at one, remember. The answer's yes, but the snow-removal budget has been cut each year for a while now. And right now, if we sent out the plows—all two of them—the snow would blow right back over the roads in minutes. It's a judgment call, but the plan is to wait until morning and see what's what. Of course, the state is responsible for the highways, so they'll do Route 202—when they feel like it. Don't hold your breath." Seth dipped into his soup. "Hey, this is great."

After dinner Seth cleaned up the dishes as promised. Back to the front parlor, Meg found that the fire had burned down to coals. It might have been sixty degrees in the room, but after passing through the unheated dining room it felt almost balmy. She'd managed to find a deck of cards in a drawer, and when Seth arrived they quibbled for a while, trying to find a card game in which they were evenly matched.

"Look, I played hearts in college, and then bridge, but we just weren't into poker," Meg grumbled. "Are we going to be reduced to Go Fish? War?"

"Kind of mindless, aren't they? You ever tried Russian Bank? Spite and Malice?"

She shook her head. "I've never even heard of them. Did you play a lot of cards with your family?"

"On and off. Dad was always very competitive, and not particularly patient. But Mom and the three of us kids used to play, back in the Dark Ages before video games. I guess we kind of outgrew it. I know we stopped before I went to college."

"My folks played with some regular bridge groups, but I didn't have sibs, so that was kind of limiting—just three people. We did jigsaw puzzles for a while—I think Mother still has all of those, in the attic." She hesitated a moment. "You know, we could just talk."

Was it her imagination or did he stiffen slightly? "About what?"

"Don't go all funny on me—that's talk with a small 'T,' not a capital one. It's just that you and I have been through a lot, some of it pretty intense, and we've been physically intimate, but there's a lot I don't know about you, or you about me. That's all. I didn't mean to make you uncomfortable." When Seth didn't answer immediately, she wondered if she'd done something wrong.

Finally he said, "Let me take Max out, and you can figure out whether you want to leave Lolly in the kitchen. Oh, and check the weather forecast one last time. Is there any of that wine left?"

"I think so. I've probably got another bottle." Was that an agreement to talk, or an evasion?

"Good," he said. He stood up abruptly and Max followed, and Meg could hear him putting his boots back on and slamming the door. She followed more slowly. If Lolly was going to stay in the parlor with them, she needed to bring the litter box along. The cat's dish was empty, so she wasn't hungry. Meg decided they might need all the warmth they could get, so she carried the box into the front room. It was definitely warmest in front of the fire, so Meg arranged the quilts and blankets in what looked like a large, messy nest on the floor, then went back to the kitchen. She found another bottle of wine and collected a corkscrew and two glasses and made another trip to the front of the house, setting them on a low table. Then back again to the kitchen. Seth and Max came in, and Meg shivered at the cold wind they brought with them.

"Still coming down hard," Seth said, pulling off his boots. Max shook himself, scattering snow and water in all directions. "Did you check the news?"

"No, I forgot." She turned on the television again, and they stood silently, watching. Every time Meg had tuned in today, the snowfall estimates had increased, and now they were saying at least thirty-six inches were expected, with a lot of drifting. And it wasn't going to stop anytime soon. She turned to Seth. "Seen enough?"

"I think so. Come on, Max." He went to the door to the dining room and opened it, holding it while Meg scooped up a protesting Lolly and turned off lights, then he opened the door to the front parlor and let them all pass before him.

"Do we have enough wood?" Meg asked.

"It'll do. We may need to conserve it for tomorrow."

"What, you're not going to go out and chop a tree down?" When Meg put Lolly down, she prowled briefly around the room, locating her litter box, then returned and curled up on a blanket near the fire. Max settled himself on the other side of the fireplace, keeping a watchful eye on Lolly.

Meg looked at Seth and quailed inwardly. She was the one who had suggested "talking," but now that they were here, alone, she felt nervous. Was she unhappy with the status quo? Did she want to change anything? Not really. But as she'd said to Seth, she felt that while they were very close in some ways, they were still near strangers in others. And time was a rare luxury in both their lives. Meg grabbed a blanket, wrapped it around herself, and pulled one of the battered armchairs closer to the fire.

Seth watched her for a moment, then followed suit. "What is it you want to know?"

"I don't have an agenda. This isn't an inquisition. It's just that I know bits and pieces about you, but there are some large gaps. Can't I be curious?"

"Is this one of those 'where are we going' talks?" he asked, neutrally.

"No, that's not what I want. Or maybe it is, indirectly. I mean, if you're hiding something important, I'd rather know sooner than later, before we get too involved."

"What makes you think there's anything to know?" His gaze returned to the fire.

Meg considered how to answer that question. "Look, I know Rachel, and I've met your mother, and I think they're both great people."

"And Stephen?" he asked, his voice tight. Meg knew he avoided mentioning his black-sheep younger brother.

"I know *about* Stephen, and a little about what made him the way he is. And now you've met both my parents and seen them, us, together. I'll be the first to admit that I haven't always judged them fairly, but I'm working on it. But, I guess—Seth, you hardly ever say anything about your father. Why is that?"

Seth got up to poke at the fire, threw on another log. "He's dead. You know that. What's to say?"

From his tone it was clear that Seth was trying to shut down the conversation, but Meg wasn't willing to accept that. "As far as I can see, you have great relationships with both your mother and Rachel. You look out for them. In fact, you look out for just about everybody." *Except yourself*, Meg wanted to add, but held back.

He finally looked at her. "What do you mean? I like to help people."

Meg struggled to find the right words. "You know, when we first met, I had trouble figuring out whether you were helpful to me because you liked *me*, or because that's the way you were with everybody. I'm not sure I've decided what the mix is, even now. And, I suppose more to the point, I know you were married once—heck, I've met your ex, remember?—but I don't know why that didn't work out. I mean, you're great husband material. And of all the people I know, you should have kids. If we're going to have any kind of long-term relationship, whatever it is, I'd like to know what went wrong."

In the near-dark Seth sighed and sat back in his lumpy chair. "I told you, Nancy wanted bigger things than I did. She thought I was more ambitious than I turned out to be, and she wanted a different life, one beyond Granford. Is that a problem for you? That I like my life here? That I like the people here, and I'm happy to be able to be useful in some way?"

"No, Seth, that's not what I'm saying," Meg protested. "I admire you for it. But I guess the question is, where are *you* in the equation? Do you have what you want? Or are you so busy being big brother to the community that you lose sight of your own wants and needs?"

"Jesus, Meg, you sound like a therapist. And before you ask, yes, I have experience with therapy—Nancy and I tried it, back when things started falling apart. It didn't really change either one of us. It just prolonged the breakup. Do we really need to talk about this?"

After a long moment Meg laughed. "You know what? I don't think we do. Look, if there's anything you ever want to tell me, I'll listen, but I suppose I have no right to pry into your personal life."

"I wouldn't say that, Meg. But I just don't think this is the time to get into it. All right?"

When will the right time be? she wondered. At least he'd left the door open a crack.

The fire was mesmerizing, and they sat for a time in silence. Meg was almost startled when Seth began to speak again.

"You asked about my father," he began tentatively, talking more to the dark than to her.

"Yes," she said, fearful of discouraging him. She waited.

"He died when I was in college. I was putting myself through Amherst with a combination of scholarships, loans, and whatever work I could scrounge, and Mom wanted me to finish. But I knew there wasn't going to be enough money for Stephen and Rachel to go. So when Dad died, I finished my last year, then I came back to Granford and picked up where he had left off with the business. It wasn't that I'd always hoped to be a plumber, but the family needed the money, and it's steady work. I'd worked with him on and off, in high school and summers, so I knew what I was doing, although I had to get licensed. A couple of friends helped with the hands-on stuff in the beginning, and Mom kept the financial side going until I could come back."

"How did he die?"

"Heart attack. He was just past fifty, but he'd been a smoker and a drinker most of his life, and he'd ignored his high blood pressure for years, no matter how much Mom pushed him about it. Which wasn't much—she knew he wouldn't listen, and she wanted to keep the peace."

He stopped, and the seconds spun out until Meg wondered if that was all he was going to say. Then he began again. "Nancy and I got married right after graduation. She really wanted to believe that running the plumbing side of things was only temporary—that when Stephen and Rachel were set, I'd close the business down and go back to graduate school."

"But you didn't."

"I didn't. She couldn't see that I wasn't cut out to be an academic, and I couldn't convince myself to try, just to please her. Maybe I wasn't any better at plumbing, but it paid the bills. It was honest work, and I like working with my hands. With people."

"I think your father would be proud of you."

"No, he wouldn't."

Meg was surprised at the unexpected bitterness in Seth's voice. "Why do you say that?"

"Because he was a bully, and he figured the world owed him something. He thought he wanted kids, because that's what men were supposed to do, and then when he had them he said we were always in the way. He hated me when I stood up to him, but I was only trying to protect the younger kids."

"Was he abusive?"

"No—at least, not physically. I think Mom would have called the cops on him if he'd ever hit her—and he knew it—even though that's hard to do in a small town. But it was easier for her to just go along than to try to argue. That was another way she looked out for his blood pressure. When he worked up a real head of steam, didn't matter over what, he'd turn red and start yelling, and she'd calm him down."

Meg thought about her own family and her upbringing, so restrained and proper—and emotionally distant. She could count on the fingers of one hand the times either of her parents had actually raised a voice in anger. "But you did turn out well."

"Did I? I spend a lot of time and energy trying to fix other people's problems. Did you know that's true of a lot of eldest children? We're the fixers. We're always trying to smooth things over. But you're right—I don't have a whole lot to show for it, personally. Sorry, Meg, but you did ask."

It wasn't far off what Meg had thought: Seth's outgoing, cheerful exterior hid a lot of inner doubt. "You've got friends. You've got the respect of the community. You've got a profession you enjoy." *And you've got a sister who's made a good life for herself, and a brother who hasn't.*

"I guess. What you said, about not being able to tell whether I was helping you just because I help everybody? That works both ways. I couldn't tell if you cared about me, or whether you were clinging to me because I was there and you desperately needed a lifeline at the time."

"I wasn't sure myself, in the beginning. Honestly, probably some of each. I'm grateful that you were there. But I'm not clinging now. It's been a tough year, but I've survived. I'm proud of myself for sticking it out. I'm proud of myself for taking on new things and making them work. I couldn't have done it without you, Seth, but now that I've proven to myself that I can make it on my own, I get to choose whether I *want* to do it alone."

"Do you?"

"No."

He didn't respond, but in the wavering light of the fire Meg saw him smile. He stood up and held out a hand, then pulled her out of her chair. "We should try to get some sleep," he said. "Can you get comfortable in front of the fire?"

"Sure, I guess. I'll sort out the blankets and stuff."

While Seth stoked the fire one last time, Meg rearranged the blankets and pillows, building almost a wall to block the cold air behind them. She nestled under a quilt, and Seth slipped in behind her and pulled the quilt over them both.

"Conserving body heat, are we?" she joked.

He kissed the back of her neck. "More than that, Meg."

"I'm glad you're here, Seth."

"So am I."

6

The night passed slowly for Meg, although she was glad for Seth's warm presence. Despite all the padding, the floor was uncomfortable and unfamiliar. The coals popped and snapped periodically, startling her, and the wind howled around the corners of the house. When gray light slowly filled the room, Meg took stock. Seth was still asleep, his body curved around hers. Lolly had joined them sometime during the night and was curled against her belly, on the side closest to the fire, and Max lay on the other side of Seth. When Meg slid her arm cautiously out from under her layers of blankets to look at her watch, she was surprised to find that it was after eight o'clock. If her cold nose was any indication, it was freezing in the room, and the fire was out. She lay still, enjoying the lingering warmth under the blankets, and listened. No sound of vehicles on the street. No sound of anything, actually, except the wind and the scratch of snow against the windowpanes. So the forecasters had been right: it was still snowing. How long would it continue?

She could feel the shift in his body as Seth woke up. "Hey," he said, into her neck. "You get any sleep?"

"Enough, I guess. It sounds like it's still snowing. Do we have to move?"

"Not on my account." But at the sound of his master's voice, Max had gotten up and was now circling them. Seth sighed. "I guess he needs to go out."

He disentangled himself from the covers and stood up, pulling his clothes into place. Meg shivered in the cold draft his departure had generated, and decided she might as well get up, too. As she did, she realized why the room was so dark: there was snow piled up against the windows along one side. She crossed the room and said, "Seth, look at this!"

He joined her by the window. "Wow. I can't remember that I've seen this much snow more than once or twice in my life. And it's still coming down. We should check the news and see what they're saying now. Come on, Max."

He headed for the kitchen, Max at his heels. Meg followed, and Lolly, not wanting to be abandoned, scampered in front of her.

In the kitchen Seth pushed the switch on the small television. Nothing happened. He turned it off and on again, with no results. Then he turned toward Meg, looking troubled. "The power's out."

"Oh? Oh." Meg's slow brain kicked into gear. No power meant . . . no light. No stove. No hot water. "What are we supposed to do?"

Seth's mouth twitched in a half grin. "I guess what people used to do when the house was new. We've still got firewood. You have any cast iron cookware?"

"A couple of skillets, and I think some former tenant left a Dutch oven thing—I put it on a shelf out in the shed because I don't use it."

"Then we can cook. In case you're worried, you can still flush—that doesn't take electricity. The cell phones may work, but the batteries won't last long. Let me take care of Max, and I'll bring in some more wood so I can get the fire going again. And you can whip up a nice, hearty one-skillet breakfast for us—I don't want to waste any more wood than necessary."

"Yes, sir! I'm on it, sir!"

Seth pulled open the back door, with Max bouncing at his feet, but then had to wrestle the outer storm door against the piled snow. In the time it took to clear enough space for him to get out, a lot of cold air rushed in, and Meg shivered. Seth was right: they had the essentials, but she had better organize some cooking implements. She wasn't too sure how to handle cooking in a fireplace. She wondered if coffee was out of the question, and then realized that she had only whole beans, and the grinder wasn't going to be much use. Too bad she had never acquired one of those kitschy hand-cranked grinders that were usually sold as decoration. Could she just whack the beans with a hammer? It looked as though she was going to have to settle for tea, if she could find something to boil water in. Which she couldn't do until Seth brought in more wood and started a fire. How the heck had people managed in the old days?

Meg started pulling open more cabinets—and thinking. Last night had been . . . unexpected. Put two rather conflicted people in forced seclusion in a dark room with a fire, and look what happened. What Seth had said had confirmed some things she had thought or sensed—mainly that he was trying to be everything to everybody because of his own family's history. Was that a bad thing? He was a good person, and he did make a difference in a lot of people's lives. Could he dial that back and pay a bit more attention to his own wants? Could she, should she ask that of him? Trying to change people never worked, and anyway, she was still working on keeping her head on straight. As she had told him, she'd had a difficult year, with a lot of changes, and she hadn't processed them all yet. And she couldn't draw any conclusions until she knew if her business was turning a profit.

What if it wasn't? Would she cut her losses and quit? Leave Granford? Leave Seth? She'd pretty much exhausted her capital, between the barn improvements, buying a tractor, upgrading some other much-needed equipment, and getting necessary supplies, so if it turned out that the orchard couldn't support her, she'd have to find some other income. Which wouldn't be easy, given the local economy. That was one problem she didn't think Seth could fix. She wondered briefly if he was helping to support his mother. He certainly didn't live like he had a lot of money. Not that money or possessions seemed to matter to him.

Once she'd located her skillets, and a pot that would withstand a fire, Meg had little left to do. She pulled out her cell phone and turned it on, and was surprised to get a signal. She hit the speed dial number for Bree's cell.

Bree answered after the fourth ring. "Wha?"

"Sorry, did I wake you?"

"Meg? Sort of. You okay there?"

"Well, the furnace quit and the power's out, but other than that, I think so. How about you?"

"'Bout the same—no power, and the furnace here has an electronic ignition so it's not working either. This is a bad one."

"You heard anything about when it's going to stop?"

"Not since last night. Don't expect to see me anytime soon."

"That's fine. I'll manage. Seth's here."

"Oho!" Bree chortled.

"Whatever. Enjoy your time with Michael, and I'll see you when I see you. Bye."

Seth still wasn't back, so Meg decided to check the rest of the house and make sure there were no problems. She put Lolly's food on the counter, then headed for the hallway. When she pulled open the front door, she found the outer storm door blocked by drifted snow as well. Peering out, she realized she couldn't even tell where the road began: the snow rolled on unbroken as far as she could see. She slammed the door shut quickly, and poked her head into the room across the hall. More or less the same: snow piled at least up to the windowsills outside. Upstairs she used the bathroom, briefly splashing very cold water on her face, then checked out the other rooms. All were equally cold, colder now than the ground floor rooms. She shut the doors behind her again, and went back downstairs in time to meet Seth coming into the kitchen with an armload of wood.

"Bacon and eggs work for you? We can toast bread or bagels or whatever on forks, right?" she asked. "Oh, and I talked to Bree. It sounds like it's as bad in Amherst as it is here."

"I'm not surprised. I'll get the fire going."

An hour later they were swabbing their empty plates with toast that was only slightly burnt. "What now?" Meg asked. "Do we have to do the dishes? I mean, there's no hot water."

"You could boil some. But I'd wait until you have a whole batch of dishes. We do need to ration the wood."

"So how are we supposed to keep warm?" When she saw Seth's expression, she giggled. "I mean, apart from that?"

"We keep moving. Is there any cleaning or sorting you need to do?"

"Well, we can't run a vacuum. But I'll admit there are parts of the house I haven't even touched—no time and no need. Maybe this is a good opportunity. Can we skip the attic?"

"Why?" Seth asked.

"I don't like it. There may be bats. And other things I'd rather not think about. Giant spiders. Rats. Besides, it'll be freezing cold up there, won't it?"

"If I recall, it's not insulated, so, yes. There should be enough to keep us busy in the rest of the house, anyway. We can do some triage while we're at it—you know, figure out what repairs need to be done, make a priority list, that kind of thing."

Meg grimaced. "I'm not sure I want to know. I probably won't catch up in my lifetime."

"One step at a time. You ready?"

Meg braced herself and headed out into the freezing hallway and up the stairs. "We might as well look at the two rooms on the east side first—since I'm not using them, I haven't done much in there."

"Makes sense. Uh, if we're supposed to be cleaning, shouldn't you take something along to do it with?"

"Oh. I guess I'm trying to avoid that. Dust cloths?"

"It's a start."

"Your mother trained you well."

It was, in fact, an interesting process, cleaning out a long-neglected room, and Meg found it did keep her warm. She kept a pad of paper in her pocket, making notes of which furniture she wanted to get rid of—heck, some of it was little better than firewood—and what she thought she should acquire, if she ever found the time and money. She resolutely ignored the growing length of that list. Since the house had been built in the later eighteenth century, there were few closets, and those that existed were sadly inadequate for modern storage. Nineteenth-century renovations hadn't improved things much. The basic problem was, there were no places to even think of putting closets.

"You could build out a false wall," Seth suggested, "and fit closets in that way."

"Maybe," Meg said dubiously. "But that would make the rooms too small, and we're limited by the placement of the windows. Maybe in this room?" They were standing in the back bedroom, which was depressingly gloomy because of the storm, not to mention cold and none too clean. "At least all those tenants didn't feel compelled to change things. I would hate to have to peel off a lot of cheap wallpaper and vinyl floor tiles."

"Amen!" Seth said. "I see plenty of that, and it's a lot of work just to get rid of it so you can start fresh. Getting old glue and paste off is not fun. You're lucky."

"I deserve a little luck here somewhere, don't you think?" She surveyed the rather bare room. "Are we done in here?"

"I think so. How about the front bedroom?"

"Mother used that when she stayed here, so I spiffed it up a bit, at least on the surface. She didn't complain about the bed, so I guess it's all right. I wonder what happened to the rest of the sisters' furniture? You'd think they would have held on to something from the family."

"Who knows? Maybe the family divided everything up—you know, if the sisters got the house, the rest of them shared the contents? Or something like that." They moved into the front bedroom.

"The two front rooms have closets, if you can call them that—they weren't intended for modern clothes," Meg said.

Seth pulled open the closet door and contemplated the empty space. A few wire hangers dangled from a modern plastic rod stretched across the closet. "Hey, at least there's something. It looks original to the house."

"I'm guessing this was the master bedroom, or whatever they called it back in 1760. Although you once said you thought the nursery was next to the room I'm using. Maybe they reserved this for important guests. Do you think George Washington ever slept here?"

"Unlikely, but imagine all you want. Did your mother use the closet?"

"Probably. She's tidy that way, likes to hang up her clothes." Meg joined him at the closet. "Although I'll bet she brought her own hangers."

"There's something on the shelf. Maybe she left something behind?"

"She didn't mention that she was missing anything. Where?" Meg stood on tiptoe but still couldn't see anything on the lone shelf.

"Shoved in the back there." He pointed.

"I don't see it. Can you boost me up?"

Seth offered her his joined hands, and she stepped up, hanging on to his shoulder. He was right: there was something wadded up in the back of the closet. It looked like an old rag, and even from where she perched she could see it was covered with dust. "I think it's been there quite a while. Can you get any closer?"

Seth wobbled a foot or so nearer, and Meg stretched out to grab the rag from the back of the closet. Dusty was an understatement: it was covered with a layer of powdery dust that had to be half an inch thick. Meg was obscurely pleased that there had been lousy housekeepers in the house before her.

"Got it. You can put me down now." Meg stepped back to the floor with her prize. She shook it, sending a cloud of dust into the room, and they both sneezed. She teased out a couple of corners and stretched it out gingerly. "What the . . . It's a sampler! Look."

"I thought a sampler was one of those things where girls tried out different stitches and made alphabets and the like," Seth said, trying to decipher the details through the dust.

"What? No, I think there are different kinds. Oh, look at the flowers, and—is that a house? And tombstones? This is so interesting. And maybe sampler isn't the right word, but I don't have a better one."

"It looks old. Is it intact?"

"I think so. Linen, do you think?"

Seth took it carefully. "Looks like it. And I think the thread is silk. If it had been wool, I'd bet the moths would have gotten to it years ago. Nice. Wonder if it comes from the Warren family?"

Meg took it back from him, then walked to the window to get more light. "I don't know. What a lovely thing it is, though. I wonder if there's anybody who does conservation of this kind of thing around here?" she said, distracted, her eyes on the shabby piece of cloth in her hand. "I think it's dated—it looked like seventeen-something. Wow."

"Do you want to finish our cleanup, or are you itching to get a better look at your discovery?"

Meg looked up at him and smiled. "What do you think? The dirt will still be here tomorrow, but this is a piece of history I'm holding. Besides, if we don't look at it now we'll lose the light. Unless you think we'll get power back anytime soon?"

"I won't put any bets on it. Maybe fifteen minutes from now, maybe tomorrow. But I doubt repair crews are going anywhere fast today."

"Then let's go take a look at this."

Downstairs, Meg looked around. "I can't clear off the dining room table, because I'll mess up Bree's system, whatever that is. So I guess that leaves a card table—I was using one for my computer in the room across the hall, but I'm sure it's too cold in there. I don't suppose I should wash the sampler?" At the look of horror on Seth's face, she said quickly, "I didn't think so. I'll leave that for a professional. But at least we can take a look at it and figure out what it's about. You want lunch first? It'd better be cold sandwiches. We can do something hot for dinner."

"Good thinking. Can you contain yourself that long?"

"I think so. But let's eat fast."

7

As they ate their sandwiches, standing in the now-cold kitchen, Seth said, "You know, you're easily distracted."

"I am not!" Meg mumbled through a mouthful of bread. "I'll admit I don't like cleaning, but I can be focused when I need to be. This is not an ordinary situation. Aren't you even curious about what we've found?"

"Of course I am. I'm just pointing out that we left that other project half finished."

"And that bothers you? Okay, we can go back to it later. Heck, for all we know this blizzard will go on for days, and we'll have plenty of time for housecleaning. You finished eating?"

"Yes." Seth dusted the crumbs off his hands. "Lead on."

Meg pulled the card table into the front parlor, where the coals from the dying fire were sending out little eddies of warmth. Seth added one log to it as Meg unfurled a clean sheet on the table. "Gail will be so proud of me! At least I'm keeping it clean." She carefully laid the fragile piece of cloth flat on the sheet, smoothing it out gently. "Maybe I should take some pictures, in case it decides to crumble to dust immediately."

"You must be thinking of Egyptian tombs. This is quite a bit younger."

"I know, but it can't hurt." She retrieved her camera from the sideboard in the dining room, came back, and snapped a series of photos, including close-ups of the details. "You know, sometimes you can use software to edit pictures and increase the contrast, make them easier to decipher. I've done it for tombstones."

"I can see that makes sense," Seth said, apparently warming to the process.

"Maybe I should have gotten a shot of it in situ," Meg said dubiously.

"Meg, this isn't a crime scene. You found it in your closet. Why would anyone worry about provenance, anyway?"

Meg shrugged. "You never know. What if it turns out this was made by Abigail Adams or Emily Dickinson or someone like that? It could be valuable."

"Let's just take it one step at a time. As you pointed out, it won't be light out much longer."

"Okay, okay. So, here we have a piece of hand-embroidery, and we're guessing it's silk thread on a piece of linen. It measures maybe two feet high, and eighteen inches across, I'm guessing. It's in pretty good condition, all things considered—no holes or tears. The colors are a bit faded, but that's not unusual, is it?"

"It hasn't been exposed to light in a while, so it's better than it might be. Go on," Seth replied.

"You know, this is really kind of interesting. There are five panels, it looks like. The big one at the top—that's a family record! How wonderful! All the births and deaths, neatly lined up. Then there's a line for who made it—I'll have to wait to decipher that when I can clean it up a little more. Then a row of tombstones."

Seth was warming to the subject. "You notice there's only one person mourning, a girl or woman on the left. Maybe the girl who made it? And clusters of flowers, probably to fill in the spaces on the side. A nice flower border, too—I wonder if it's purely decorative, or if they represent a real plant?"

"Interesting thought," Meg said absently, still studying the embroidery. "Then a quotation of some sort, and then at the bottom, a white house. You think it could be this one?" When Seth looked skeptical, Meg protested, "Yes, I know, it's a pretty generic Colonial, two stories, roof, and chimneys. But look at the addition at the back—doesn't that look just like my shed? And then there are trees—oh, look, Seth, at that little group with a fence around it. Do you think they're apple trees? They've got these little red dots—it looks like each one is a single knot."

"Could be," Seth agreed. "Besides, I'd hate to rain on your parade."

"I'm bowled over by your enthusiasm, sir. I think it's a wonderful piece. Can you make out the surname?"

"It looks like Violet Cox to me for the maker, and, Lamb-something for the rest of them."

"How odd—I don't recognize either name from around here. I suppose things could have changed a lot since this was made. Are there any Coxes around here?"

"Not that I know of at the moment, but there could have been during the eighteenth century."

"I'll have to check on that. So we have the parents at the bottom of the list, and then a lot of children. Oh, dear—most of the children seem to have died very young. How sad. How awful that would be, to watch your family die. But I don't see the name Violet Cox on the family record. I wonder where she fit? Maybe a cousin? I don't think it would have been her married name, because it says she was, what, twelve when she stitched this?"

"Most of these were done by young girls or women,"

Seth said amiably. "Needlework was considered an important skill among young ladies."

Meg looked away from the sampler to stare at him. "Now why on earth do you know that?"

"I once wrote a college paper on early New England attitudes toward death, and mourning samplers came into it. Death was a lot harder to ignore in those days. People were vulnerable to a lot of diseases, and there were always accidents, fires. There's a reason why all those cemeteries were close to town—they saw a lot of traffic."

Meg shivered, and not from the cold. "I wonder why this is here in this house, and why it was forgotten? And, look, the parents died close together, not long after the last of those children."

"Could have been an epidemic. There was a lot of diphtheria around in those days. Typhoid. Even measles could be deadly."

So much death, Meg thought. Did she really want to know what happened? Not exactly, but she did want to know what had brought this piece of cloth and the history attached to it to her house. She knew who had been living in it in 1800. Was the girl a relative? Had the family in the sampler lived—and died—around here? Or was the sampler something that someone had once picked up at a yard sale, and then tossed into the closet and forgotten?

"You've gone quiet," Seth said.

Meg smiled ruefully. "I'm just wondering how much I want to know about a family that had such rotten luck—all the kids dying like that, and then the parents. Mostly I'm curious about what the piece is doing here. Well, there's not much I can do about it right now. If we had power I could go online and at least find out if there was anyone with that surname in Granford at the right time. But we're stuck back in the nineteenth century, and it's a little too snowy to walk over to the town hall and ask to see the records. So maybe we should just get back to work? It'll be dark soon, and it may take us a while to put dinner together, what with having to cook it over an open fire."

"You might want to talk to Gail Selden, once you can get to town, and I'll see if any of the thanatologists I consulted when I was in college can shed any light."

"The what?"

"Thanatologists. People who study death, and how culture copes with it."

"Seth Chapin, you are a font of information, even if it is a little creepy. Okay, back upstairs for now. Oh, first let me take care of this before Lolly decides it would be nice to sharpen her claws on it." Meg found a clean towel and rolled the sampler into it, setting the bundle on the sideboard, where she hoped it would be safe. It would be a pity for it to be destroyed after it had waited so long.

They finished exploring the front bedroom, which since it was on a corner and had two windows, still had enough light to see by. There were no more surprises, happy or otherwise.

"The other front room?" Seth asked when they were done.

"My room? I went over that pretty closely when my parents were here, remember? I don't suppose anything else will turn up, and it's in pretty good shape. So now what?"

"I say we call it a day. It'll be dark soon."

"Sounds good to me."

Downstairs the light was fading fast. Max followed them around, but Lolly opted to stay as close as possible to the dwindling fire. The snow was still piling up against the windows. "Is this ever going to end? What's the longest Massachusetts storm on record?"

"That I can't tell you, but it should blow itself out soon."

"How long will it take to clear the roads?"

"What, you're in a hurry to get rid of me?"

"No, nothing like that. It just feels so odd, to have no options. You think the goats are all right?"

"I'll check on them when I take Max out, which should be sooner rather than later, from the way he's acting. How about I stoke up the fire, and then take Max out while you rustle up some grub?"

"That's sexist—careful or I'll give you nothing but beans."

"You'd regret it later."

"I could make you sleep in another room."

Seth just shook his head and laid a few more logs on the fire. "And retrieve my cold corpse in the morning."

"Oh. I hadn't considered that. But with these temperatures you'd keep until I figured out what to do with your body."

Seth snorted. "Come on, Max."

Meg followed them as far as the kitchen. What could she make? Or maybe she should make Seth cook—she knew he knew how. Of course, to be fair she'd have to go out and get the wood and stoke the fire, and she wasn't about to assume she could handle that. Better to cook. And fast: it was cold in the kitchen.

The result was sort of a goulashy concoction of beef, tomatoes, and onions, with a bunch of herbs and paprika thrown in. She mixed the ingredients together in the cast iron Dutch oven, which conveniently had little feet on it to hold it over the coals while it cooked. She waited until Seth deemed the coals ready and spread them around so she could settle the pot on top. How long the mess would take to cook was anybody's guess—she'd just have to keep poking at it. She checked her watch: five o'clock, and already night-dark.

"Now what?" she asked.

"You sound like a bored kid. Relax. Is there another bottle of wine somewhere? We can pull up the chairs and huddle in front of the fire and have a drink."

"But we did that *last* night," she said with a mock whine.

"Yup, we did. Nobody ever said colonial life was exciting, except for the occasional Indian attack or war. Mostly you worked hard to stay alive, fell into bed, made a few babies, then got up and started all over again. On Sunday you might take some time off for church."

"Oh, come on. There had to be some socializing."

"Weddings and funerals. Quilting bees. Sharing the harvest chores and celebrating when it was done. I don't think anyone should romanticize the lifestyle, but it worked, because here we are."

"Yes, we are. Just like all those forebears, sitting in front of the fire, grumbling. Soon to be followed by snoring." She stood up quickly. "I'll go look for that wine."

In the kitchen she found a bottle of red, and collected two glasses—and Lolly's food, to save herself yet another chilly trip. Back in the front parlor she handed the bottle with a corkscrew to Seth, then refilled Lolly's dish while he opened the wine. When she was done, Seth handed her a glass.

"What should we drink to?"

"Survival." Meg raised her glass, and Seth echoed her motion.

Dinner proved better than she had expected, especially after Meg had had the brainstorm to make up a corn bread crust and bake it on top of the stew for the last half hour or so. Or maybe the wine made everything taste better. Either way, she wasn't going to complain. Stomach full, head swimming slightly, she sat cocooned with blankets in her chair staring at the embers of the dying fire, until she nodded off.

She half woke when Seth nudged her gently. "Bedtime. I stoked the fire, and Max has done his stuff."

She was too sleepy to think of a comeback, so she followed him meekly to their now-familiar nest in front of the fire, where they snuggled in for the night.

Maybe pioneer life wasn't for her, but this she could grow used to.

8

The first thing Meg noticed was the brightness. She didn't even need to open her eyes to tell that something had changed that morning: the sun had come out. She could hear Seth in the kitchen, talking on what had to be his cell phone. No doubt organizing the Granford digging-out process. She wondered if he had enough clout to get her driveway plowed quickly, and then felt ashamed of herself. She didn't need to go anywhere, and Seth's car was back at his place anyway. He'd have to hike back overland to get it, if that was even possible.

She pulled off the blankets and stood up, once again dislodging Lolly. The sun rose on the other side of the meadow, but all she could see was blazing blue sky and an endless expanse of white. She couldn't even tell where the fence around the goat pen was, the snow was so high. It was beautiful—and it was going to be a pain to get rid of. Couldn't they all just wait until it melted? Not likely: Meg remembered mounds of snow in the middle of Northampton early in the year that had lasted weeks.

"Hey, you're awake." Seth came into the room, looking ridiculously energetic.

"Brilliant deduction, since I'm standing up. What time is it?"

"Just past eight. I had to check in with the snowplow guys. They've got to dig themselves out before they can tackle the roads. It may be a while."

"Do you need to be somewhere?"

"Not yet. Don't you wish you'd gotten a plow blade for that tractor of yours?"

"No! Then someone like you would expect me to use it. You want breakfast?"

"Sure. I'll build up the fire again—let's hope this is the last time."

"Still no power?"

"Not yet, but the guys I talked to said the electric company's working on it. Maybe by the end of the day."

"Have you checked in with Rachel and your mother?"

"Yup. All's good there, and the kids are thrilled to get to stay home another day. Look, I've got to take Max out, and I'd better dig a path out to the barn and make sure the goats have enough food."

"Shall we do the traditional thing again? You make the fire, I'll make breakfast. Unless you see a handy varmint out there and want to shoot it for breakfast instead."

"If I brought back a rabbit, would you be prepared to skin it?" he asked.

"In your dreams. Go!"

In the kitchen Meg assembled eggs, bacon, bread. She swabbed out the skillet they had used the day before, still unwashed since there was no hot water. Cold water and grease were not a pleasant combination. She could hear the rhythmic sound of Seth's shovel out back. Given that the snow was three feet deep, it might take him a while to reach the barn. Good thing they didn't have cows to milk.

After a few more minutes Meg heard Seth outside the

door now, clearing a broader path in front of the back door. Then he came tramping in, scattering snow, with Max adding his own. "Still cold out there! The goats are fine, if bored—much longer and they may chew their way out of the stall."

"I've got breakfast ready to go, if you think the fire's ready," Meg said.

"Let me feed Max and mop up the melted snow first."

Meg carried all the fixings into the front room. Before she could set the pan on the fire, she decided to check her messages and powered on her cell phone. Bree had called not half an hour earlier, so Meg returned the call. "Bree? How are things in Amherst?"

"Hi, Meg. Not too bad—the plows have been out already. How about at your end?"

"Seth says he's called them out, but I haven't seen them. I can't even see the road."

"So I shouldn't try to get back there?"

"Not yet. We still don't have power, and who knows when we'll have heat? Enjoy your free time—you've earned it."

"Yeah, I guess I'll just have to make do."

Meg could hear Michael laughing in the background. "I'll let you know when the roads are clear, but there's no rush."

"Well, at least you've got Seth to keep you company. Bye!"

Bree hung up before Meg could respond. When Seth came in, she told him, "It looks like Amherst has the plowing under control. I told Bree she didn't need to rush back, even if she could. Maybe she should stay there until I get this furnace problem worked out. You have any idea how long that will take?" She set the skillet on the fire to heat.

"Depends. Once the roads are clear I'll make some calls."

"Just try not to bankrupt me. My credit card is already groaning."

"I'll do the best I can. Now, about that breakfast . . ."

By the time they had finished eating, the first snowplow had gone past, making a quick detour to clear a portion of her driveway. Seth went out to confer with the driver, and watching from the kitchen window, Meg recognized John Taylor, who waved at her. He'd been so bundled up the last time she'd seen him that she hadn't gotten a good look at him. He turned out to be older than she had expected, probably in his forties, with a lean dark face, sort of like a prebeard Abraham Lincoln. Seth and John chatted for a few minutes while Meg cleaned up. Did she dare risk boiling water so she could do the dishes? How long would it be until the power was restored?

When Seth came back he said, "Good news. John says the power problem for this road is a downed line over toward town, where a tree fell on it. The rest of the town is back on line, and as soon as they break some trucks free they can fix the last wire. Figure you'll have power by this afternoon. Look, I've got to go into town and coordinate the cleanup process. Will you be okay here? And can I leave Max?"

"I'll be fine. No problem about Max, but maybe you could stop by with some more firewood later? If the furnace won't be ready for a few days?"

Seth smiled. "So you really want to keep staying here, even without heat?"

"Hey, we made it through the blizzard, and I'm getting pretty good at cooking over the fire. Once the power's back, I can shift to the kitchen. I'll be fine. You go and do what you need to do."

When he was gone, Meg turned to Max. "Well, pal, what now? You know, I think I vote for boiling a pot of water and then a quick sponge bath. If there's any water left, I might make a stab at doing the dishes. How does that sound to you?"

Max slobbered at her for a few moments, then turned and settled himself in front of the fire. Meg laughed. "Too much for you, eh, Max? Too bad." She went back to the kitchen to find a stockpot, which she filled with as much water as she could lift, then hauled it back and settled it on the coals, adding a few split logs around it. It looked stable, which was a good thing, since it would probably take at least an hour to get hot. How on earth had women done laundry in earlier centuries? It must have taken a day just to get the water hot enough. At least they'd had fewer clothes, but the downside of that was that things must have gotten pretty rank. She definitely preferred the present.

When she'd done what limited cleanup she could, Meg gave in to the siren call of the sampler. She still couldn't power up her computer, but she could take a look at what her mother had put together on the Warren family first and see if any Coxes popped up. She'd been so busy with the harvest she really hadn't had time to absorb the details her mother had so proudly assembled, beyond the barest outlines, and now was a good time to start. At least she could figure out who had lived in the house when young Violet Cox had made the sampler.

Meg had put all the Warren family genealogy information into one banker's box, which did little to distinguish it from the several similar boxes of materials she was working her way through for the Historical Society. But she'd needed the space on the dining room table to spread out her financial records. Great: now she felt guilty no matter which direction she looked, because nothing was getting finished. At least the family documents and printouts constituted the smallest stack of material.

She pulled out the sheaf of papers on top, which included a family tree, tiers of boxes showing each generation lined up. Her mother had accomplished a surprising amount in a short time, given that she had no prior experience. Meg traced the line back from the two elderly sisters she had met years ago, who had left the house and land to her mother, their distant niece. Back through their parents and grandparents, to Eli Warren the carpenter, whom Seth said had been responsible for some substantial remodeling in the house in the nineteenth century, to his father (also Eli), and his father Stephen, and finally *his* father, likewise Stephen, who had built the house. Eli the younger had been the head of household in the years around 1800, with his wife Orpha—interesting name, that—and their three children. That gave Meg a place to start.

But there were no Coxes on this chart. Meg riffled through the other papers and found no reference to any other Coxes, in any time period. So much for the easy route. Maybe a daughter? But Eli the elder had had only one daughter, according to what her mother had found, and she had married a Dickinson. Now Meg was stuck. She would have to go at identifying Violet Cox by some other route, and that would take some more research.

Her thinking was interrupted by Max, who began barking frantically and pawing at the closed door to the kitchen. "You can't be that hungry, Max. You need to go out?"

In reply Max whined and turned in circles, watching her.

"Okay, okay, I'll take you out." Meg pulled open the door to the kitchen, and Max rushed past her to stand by the outer door, quivering with eagerness. "Hang on, pal—I have to put on boots and a coat and all that stuff." He watched her pull on outer garments, whining. In a corner of her mind Meg noted that this was not his usual "I gotta go" behavior—he seemed peculiarly anxious. Since she wasn't the one who usually walked him, she wasn't prepared when she opened the door and he rushed past her, almost knocking her down. "Max, wait!" she said, afraid he'd head for the road, or escape altogether.

To her surprise he didn't bolt, but waded purposefully through the snow that all but covered his head, toward the back of the house. Meg followed as best she could. Seth hadn't shoveled here—why would he?—and it wasn't easy going, but Max seemed very determined. When she made it around the back of the shed, she found Max turning in circles again beneath the back window of one of the rooms on the west side of the house—one of the ones she never used. She didn't understand what had gotten him so excited, until she looked down and saw footprints—human footprints, made by someone wearing what she now recognized as snowshoes. She looked around quickly and didn't see anyone moving. But the footprints lead both toward and away from the house, toward the back of the property and into the woods. She followed them with her eyes as far as she could see, but there was no point in actually trying to track them—she'd never make it through the thigh-deep snow. Could it have been Seth who made them? But why would he have been at the back of the house? There was only one set of doggy-prints, from Max's recent headlong dash. No, Seth hadn't walked him here. It must have been someone else.

But who? And why?

Max, frustrated, trotted back to the cleared part of the driveway and laid his signature on a snowdrift, then turned back to her expectantly. Time to go in, she guessed. Still, why would anyone be lurking around the back of her house? Suddenly she was glad that Max was there. He was large, and he could be loud, even though in reality he wouldn't hurt a mouse.

She whistled to get his attention, then opened the door for him to go into the kitchen. She followed more slowly—and made sure to lock the door behind her.

9

Back inside, Meg made the rounds of her windows, making sure that they all were latched. That wasn't saying much, since most of the windows were held shut by antique latches, and the sashes were so loose that anyone could slip a knife in and shift a latch. It hadn't troubled her before, mainly because although her house was relatively isolated from other houses, it was still plainly visible from the street, so any intruder would have been glaringly obvious. Plus there was really nothing much to steal, apart from her laptop, and even that wasn't new. She'd already had one break-in since she had lived here, but that had been personal and wasn't about to recur.

So who was her mystery visitor with the snowshoes? And what would have happened if Max hadn't been here?

She shoved that thought out of her mind and studied the contents of her refrigerator. Feeding two people had depleted her supplies, and she had better figure on another trek to the market. Bree would be back eventually, and she would need to eat, too. Unless, of course, Bree didn't want to stay in an unheated house, not when she had Michael to keep her warm. It wasn't as though Meg needed to have Bree here during the off-season—once she had coughed up the paperwork she owed Meg.

That was essential if she was to plan for the future. Meg wasn't sure what financial results to expect, or even what to hope for. She would probably settle for breaking even in her first year, if she could figure out how to squeeze more efficiency out of her second. If there was going to be a second year. While she still had some cash in her business account, it wasn't going to last long, and Meg wasn't sure what other expenses were still outstanding. She also knew that there would be more expenses before she could expect any more income from the orchard. Her reserves were pretty thin. Bree had a stake in the success of the orchard operation, too: it was her first real job, postcollege, and it was generating her paycheck. The bigger picture was: no profit, no job, no check for Bree.

She looked out the dining room window just in time to see Bree's car slip-sliding its way into her driveway. Bree parked as far forward as she could in the cleared area, and a minute later Meg heard her at the back door, and went to meet her.

Bree was simultaneously stamping her feet and trying to greet Max, who was bounding around her feet, apparently thrilled by yet more company. "Hi, Maxie boy. Hey, down! At least let me get my coat off! Hi, Meg."

"I thought you weren't coming over?"

"Hey, I live here, don't I? The roads over toward Amherst were okay, and Michael's place gets kind of claustrophobic after a while. And he's got roommates."

"I need to dig the car out. We'll be out of food by tomorrow."

"Your car's still in the shed? I'll help you shovel it out. So where's Seth?"

"Off running the town, it seems. He's coordinating the

snow removal process, and he swears I'll have power by the end of the day. The furnace is a different problem."

"Dead, huh?"

"Looks like it. I'm sure he'd fix it if he could, but there's some major part that's just plain worn out. It's probably at least thirty years old, so it's due."

"Lousy timing, though, huh?"

"It is. So I'll understand if you don't want to stay here and freeze. Mostly I've been huddling in front of the fire with a lot of blankets. Seth's not sure when he can get around to replacing the furnace—looks like there are some other priorities out there at the moment."

"You been cooking over the fire?"

"I have." Meg felt an absurd sense of pride. "Just call me Pioneer Meg. But I don't want to do it long-term. At least when the power's back there'll be hot water and a stove. Oh, speaking of snow-plowing, have you met many of the neighbors here?"

"I don't follow your jump from plowing to neighbors, but yeah, I've talked to some of them. I even give 'em a few apples now and then."

"Have you met the Taylors from down the road? John apparently does some plowing for the town, but I don't remember seeing him before. He stopped by to talk to Seth the other day."

Bree shook her head. "Doesn't sound familiar. Everything else okay?"

"The goats are in the barn, and Seth says they're bored. That about sums up the excitement since you left."

"You and Seth okay?"

"We're good. We did some cleaning to keep warm."

"If that's your idea of a romantic adventure, I pity you."

Meg resisted the urge to stick out her tongue at Bree and retreated to the living room, as Bree headed up to her room above the kitchen. Why not take another look at the sampler, now that she had ample light? She unrolled it from her makeshift storage and carried the piece over to the window to look at it. The colors appeared a bit brighter by full daylight, and the whole had a naive charm. Now she could make out the surname for the family: Lampson. Not a name she was familiar with. Too bad the story it hinted at was so sad—first the four children died, and then the parents. Meg knew that death, especially among children, was part of the reality of the era, but it was still hard to look at. Were all those children and their parents buried in the local cemetery, along with her Warrens? Meg almost laughed out loud: how long would it be before the tombstones emerged from three feet of snow? That piece of research might have to wait until spring. Of course, she wasn't even sure the Lampsons were from Granford.

Shortly after four a snowplow dropped Seth off at the end of her drive. She met him at the door. "Are you staying, or did you just come by to collect Max?"

"If you'll feed me I can hang out a bit, but I'll head home after with Max. Hi there, pal." Seth vigorously rubbed Max's head. "I see Bree made it back?"

"She did. She's upstairs, and I hope she's working on the orchard figures. I feel like such a nag about them, but I need to know where I stand. Oh, shoot, she was going to help me dig out the car."

"I can do that," Seth volunteered.

"No, I should take some part of this, and I need the exercise. You've probably been digging all day. How was it out there?"

"Could have been worse. Could have been ice. Some limbs down, but that's to be expected. A few lines down, but no fires. Mostly people had the good sense to stay home and wait for the plows."

"If you really need something to do, you can cook dinner while I shovel."

"Works for me."

Meg donned her snow gear and headed out the back

door. It was eerily beautiful outside. The sun was sinking behind the orchard, turning the trees into stark black skeletons against the sky, and the waning light made the ocean of snow look blue. And it was definitely getting colder. Meg grabbed the snow shovel and started to make a path to her car, safely housed in the open shed. She had no garage, and no room in the barn to put her car, with both the tractor and the old pickup truck she used for deliveries already crammed in there, but at least in the shed it was under cover and had escaped the worst of the snow. Better to clear it now while the snow was still fluffy and light; if she waited until tomorrow it might start melting, and then it would be much heavier.

Thrust, lift, toss, repeat. After a couple of minutes Meg was actually warm enough to unzip her jacket. A few more minutes and she thought she could maneuver the car out, as long as she didn't mind running into a snowbank, just a little. She felt ridiculously proud of herself. She set the snow shovel against the wall of the shed and stepped back into the middle of the driveway. It was darker now, since the sun had sunk below the horizon, but the windows glowed gold.

Wait: glowing windows meant the lights were on, which meant the electricity was back! It must have come on while she was busy shoveling. And that meant she could cook, and shower—and boot up her computer. She dusted the snow off and went in the back door.

Inside Seth was busy at the stove, and Bree was leaning against a counter watching him and chatting. "Hi, Meg," she said. "Look who's cooking!"

"I told him to, while I went out to shovel. Smells great. Need help?"

Seth stayed in front of the stove, stirring. "Nope, it's under control. You rest up."

"Did you bring any more firewood?"

"Not with me, but a friend's going to come over with

some in the morning. You should be okay for tonight. You wouldn't happen to have any electric blankets, would you?"

"Uh, no. I don't like the things, and I've never needed one. But I'm getting used to roughing it. Bree, want to join me on the floor by the fire tonight?"

"I don't have to bundle with you, do I?"

Seth snickered.

"Shut up," Meg said. "No, Bree, you can bring your very own blankets. Maybe we can toast marshmallows and do each other's hair."

Now it was Bree's turn to snicker. "Yeah, right."

Meg turned back to Seth. "There was something I forgot to mention when you came in. Sometime this afternoon Max started barking like mad. I thought maybe he wanted to go out, but when I let him out, he went around to the back of the house. And I found footprints there, or more precisely, snowshoe prints, under one of the back windows. It was kind of strange—I didn't see anyone around, but you can't see that window from the street."

"Odd," Seth replied. "Did you see any tracks coming or going?"

"Yes, both, off toward the trees at the back of the property. Do you know who lives in that direction?"

"It's built up a bit over the last few years—lots of new people. I'd have to check. So you don't think it was just someone out to enjoy the snow?"

"Maybe, but why sneak up on my window? And why disappear so fast? Whoever it was must have heard Max barking and made tracks. Sorry—bad pun."

"It is. And I can't say. You didn't see if anybody tried to jimmy the window, did you?"

"I didn't look too closely, but I think whoever it was might have hightailed it away when he heard me in the kitchen. He moved fast, whoever he was."

Bree looked troubled. "I thought it was pretty safe

around here. Why would you get a Peeping Tom in this weather? And we don't use that room anyway."

"It *is* safe," Seth said. "But I don't have any explanation."

"Come to think of it," Bree said slowly, "I used to see people hanging around the edge of the orchard, back during the harvest. Just watching. They never got very close, and I didn't think about it much. Maybe they just liked to watch people pick apples. We certainly had enough lookers along the road, at peak season. Speaking of which, Meg, looks like a chunk of your fence along the road is down. Might have been the snowplows that did it. There's a lot of snow out there, and some pretty big piles."

"We can deal with it when the snow melts. I don't think anybody's going to try to steal apples at the moment. Seth, when's that food going to be ready?"

"Coming up. I'm plating now."

"Ooh, 'plating,' are you? Listen to you!" Bree joked. "You been watching those fancy cooking shows? Or are you taking lessons from Nicky now?"

"I haven't had time to stop by Gran's lately, even for lunch. But I like to learn, and I have to do something during those long, lonely winter nights." Seth set plates in front of them on the kitchen table. "Eat."

After a few bites, Bree said, "Hey, this is good. You keep on watching those shows."

Bree was right. The food was very good, and Meg was very hungry. It didn't take long to clean their plates. When they were finished, Seth stood up and said, "I'll let you two do the dishes—I need to get back to my house. Mom's coming home tomorrow, and I want to make sure her place is okay. Listen, about what you said earlier . . . you want me to leave Max here?"

Meg was tempted, but she wasn't sure how Max would fare if Seth wasn't around all night, and besides, Bree was back now. And the electricity was back, too—she could leave lights on. "We'll be fine. Can you make it home all right? It's pretty dark out there. Do you want me to drive you?"

"You've never gone snowshoeing by moonlight? You've really missed something. I'll have to take you sometime. Anyway, I've done it plenty of times, and I know the way home."

"Hey, you two," Bree interrupted, "I'm going to go upstairs and get blankets and pillows and stuff. Very slowly. You take all the time you want." She got up and pounded up the back stairs to her room.

"Tactful girl, that."

"She is. Either that or she's ducking out on doing the dishes."

"Smart, too. Listen, Meg, call me if you see or hear anything odd."

"You think I have anything to worry about? Really?"

"I don't know, but you seem to attract trouble. I can be back here in a couple of minutes if you need me."

"Thank you for the thought. Maybe it was nothing, just somebody who was curious. I certainly hope so. Are we ready to say good night, since we have Bree's permission?"

"Definitely."

Several minutes later Seth pulled away and shrugged on his coat. "Come on, Max. We're going home." At the word "home" Max leapt to his feet and waited eagerly by the door. "Night, Meg. And lock your doors."

"I will. Safe home, Seth." She watched until he and Max disappeared into the darkness and she could no longer hear the crunch of his steps, then closed the door. And locked it.

10

"Is the coast clear?" Bree said, peering down the staircase, clutching pillows and blankets.

Meg suppressed a giggle. "Yes, he's gone. So you're camping out with me down here?"

Bree clomped down the stairs, her arms full. "It's freezing up there! You know how much my windows leak? The panes have really neat frost patterns on them. If I want to wake up in the morning, we'd better stick together." She went through the kitchen and dropped her bedding in a heap on the floor in front of the fire. "Do we close the doors and stuff?"

"Yes. Lolly's already figured out the routine, and knows where all the warmest spots are. We'll build up the fire before we go to sleep, and it should last until morning, more or less. Toughen up! We're living on a farm."

"Yeah, in the twenty-first century, not the eighteenth. I like modern conveniences."

"At least we have light and hot water back. What was Amherst like?"

"Snowy, duh. Kids were sledding on the hill at the college. Looked like fun, but Michael and I stayed inside."

"You could go sledding down the orchard hill," Meg pointed out.

"What, you think I'm a kid?"

"Well, compared to me you are. You want anything from the kitchen before we settle in here?"

"Maybe something hot to drink. We could do cocoa and marshmallows," Bree said hopefully, and for a moment she did look like an eager kid.

"No marshmallows, I'm afraid, but I can handle cocoa. Remind me to tell you about what we found in a closet while Seth and I were cleaning up the house."

"Oh, you found time to clean?" Bree grinned wickedly.

"Yes, we did. Although we didn't touch your room. If you've got vermin nesting in there, you're on your own."

"They're probably going to freeze to death."

Meg smiled as she made one last trip to the kitchen, which still retained some of the heat from dinner. She filled two mugs with milk and stuck them in the microwave to heat, blessing the appliance as she did so. Yes, she did like modern conveniences, too, she thought, as she watched the mugs circle slowly in the microwave. Although the process of maintaining the orchard couldn't be much different than it was a hundred years earlier—a lot of stuff still had to be done by hand, tree by tree.

The microwave pinged, and Meg fished out the hot mugs gingerly. In compensation for the lack of marshmallows, she added a dash of brandy. Bree was an adult, and they weren't about to go anywhere. She carried the mugs back to the parlor and handed one to Bree.

"Here you go. Have you seen Lolly?"

Bree sipped and nodded her approval. "Yeah, she's under those blankets over there. We're all set. Can you imagine what things would have been like before indoor plumbing?"

"You mean the, uh, necessities? That's what chamber pots were for."

"Ick. Chalk up one more point for mod cons." She sipped again. "Listen, Meg—what you said about the footprints earlier. That was kind of scary. Why would anybody be snooping around here, especially in three feet of snow?"

"I have no idea. But if someone wanted to break in, that's the side to do it—nobody can see the back of the house, and as you said, nobody uses that room."

"Should we go check it out now? Make sure everything's locked up?"

"I guess." So Bree was worried, too? Meg was reluctant to point out how easy it would be to get in through any window in the house, but there was no point in upsetting Bree any further. "Now?"

"Better now than later." Bree stood up. "You have a baseball bat or a poker handy?"

"A what? Oh, you mean something we could use as a weapon. I have trouble imagining myself whacking anybody with a bat."

"You'd invite him into the parlor and ask him what he wants? That'll work really well. You lived in the big bad city—didn't you ever take any self-defense courses?"

"You don't have to be sarcastic. And, no, I don't have a bat or a poker, and I've never learned anything official about self-defense. How about a rolling pin?"

Bree rolled her eyes. "Isn't that what they used in old sitcoms? Why is it women don't have any useful weapons? Maybe you could throw flour in an intruder's eyes, or soapy dishwater."

"It could work. Or even a bucket of boiling water." *Oh, sure—make the intruder wait while I boil water.* "Come on, Bree—let's just do it. I refuse to believe I'm going to have to take a bat to anyone."

"All right." Bree sighed. She led the way across the hall, turning on all the lights as she went.

As Meg had predicted, there was no one there. The rooms were cold and empty. Meg checked out the single window that overlooked the backyard, but since the snow had been blowing around in the light wind all day, she couldn't even make out the footprints she had seen earlier—they were just dimples in the blanket of snow, from what she could see in the light from the window. Was she supposed to have taken casts of them? Were snowshoes like fingerprints, each unique and easily identifiable? *Meg, you're being ridiculous!* "See? There's nothing here."

Bree shook the sash and flipped the antique latch a couple of times. "Not now, there isn't," she grumbled. "At the very least you ought to put some wedges or something here so nobody can just slide the window open. Well, I don't think anybody's going to try to sneak up on us in the dark in this snow, so we might as well go to bed."

"Sounds good to me." Meg followed Bree back to the parlor, turning off lights as she went—but she left the light over the front door on.

After a final dash to the upstairs bathroom, they settled in, in front of the fire. It wasn't uncomfortable. Sure, the floor was hard, but with the lights off, the fire was soothing, casting a golden glow on the room—and hiding all the nicks and dings and frays of the cheap furniture. Lolly settled herself in the curve of Meg's body, purring.

"You ever get scared, being here alone?" Bree asked, her voice small.

"Sometimes. Mostly because it's unfamiliar—I'm not used to the noises that an old house makes. I guess I was more scared when I lived in Boston. I mean, I knew there was crime there, and I had to be alert any time I walked anywhere, especially after dark."

"You have any break-ins while you were in Boston?"

"No. I had neighbors who were robbed, but they lived on the ground floor." And she had lived on the third floor, which had given her a false sense of security. Why would a robber climb the stairs if there were easy pickings further down? And it wasn't as though she had a lot worth stealing, but how would a robber know that until he had broken in? It would have been the sense of intrusion, of violation, that would have been harder to live with, Meg thought.

Did she feel safe here? She wasn't sure. She had no near neighbors—no one to hear her scream? *Stop it, Meg!* She lived on a moderately busy street, not a dirt road in the woods, so she wasn't totally isolated. The police department was no more than a mile away, although the staffing there was pretty thin. And Bree was around most of the time. Funny how simply having another person around made her feel more secure. Would an invader be more intimidated by two women than one? She drifted off to sleep, worn out by shoveling and fighting the chill . . .

Meg wasn't sure what woke her. Too dark to see her watch, so she had no idea what time it was. The fire was all but dead, reduced to a few glowing coals. Maybe a log had collapsed, or a knot of sap had popped. She lay still, reluctant to leave the warmth of her cocoon, and listened. She could hear the wind, and it sounded as though it had changed direction. Cold air seeped through the windows.

There—a thump. At least she thought it was a thump. She might have dismissed it if Lolly hadn't reared up, her ears alert. Okay, she wasn't imagining things. Another thump, on the side of the house, the side the wind was coming from. She tried to remember what could have come loose on that side. A flapping shutter? The goats butting their heads against the barn wall, bored silly? No, they usually slept at night. She strained to hear any new sounds, but the thumping seemed to have stopped. Lolly curled herself up more tightly and went back to sleep. And so should she, Meg thought. But she lay awake a while longer, listening, hearing nothing.

The next time she woke up the room was filled with blazing light: another sunny day. She could hear the drip of water, so the sun must be melting the snow on her roof. Shoot, maybe she *should* check the attic to see if her roof was leaking, or if there were squirrels or raccoons bumbling around up there—but she really didn't want to. She had nothing stored up there, and she couldn't afford to repair or replace the roof right now, so she was happier not knowing. Living in an old house was challenging: there was always something going wrong or just plain wearing out. Although, she had to admit, many of the houses being built today were no better: shoddy materials, too-quick construction, a "slap a coat of paint on it and sell it" mentality. At least her house had been standing for two hundred and fifty years, leaks and creaks notwithstanding.

Bree wasn't in her blanket nest, and Meg could hear sounds from the kitchen. Lolly had apparently abandoned Meg in favor of breakfast. Time to get up and face the day. Meg disentangled herself from her blankets, stood up, and stretched. How much longer would she be sleeping on the floor? she wondered. A night or two was an adventure; much longer and she might be too stiff to move. How long would it take Seth to find and install a new furnace?

She made a fast trip upstairs to brush her teeth, then came down to the kitchen, where Bree was busy scrambling eggs.

"Hey, 'bout time you woke up," she said. "Sleep well?"

"More or less. Did you hear anything odd last night?" Meg helped herself to coffee from the pot, and sat down at the table. Lolly was taking a bath on top of the refrigerator.

Bree glanced at her briefly. "Like what?"

"I'm not sure. Some thumping and bumping. It was late, but it woke me up."

"Nope, I didn't hear anything. But I was kind of out of it. Besides, I'm getting pretty used to odd noises here. That room of mine, I think whoever built it kind of skimped on the construction—I hear lots of weird sounds." Bree set two plates with eggs and toast on the table. "Sit. Eat. So what's the plan for today?"

"Talk to Seth about the furnace. Check out what damage there might be from the storm. You think we can let the goats out of the barn?"

"Do I look like I know anything about goats? You can try. They'll probably let you know if they don't like the snow, and you can just put 'em back in the barn again."

"Okay. I guess I'd like to go into town and see how the rest of the world is doing. Maybe I'm getting antsy being cooped up in the house. And we need to stock up on some supplies, if there are any left at the store."

"Yeah, the people around here go kinda crazy when there's a storm. They buy up more milk and bread than they'd normally use in a month, just in case. In case of what, nobody ever says—they're all going to make bread pudding? You want me to come along?"

"What I want you to do is put together those numbers for me. This is the perfect opportunity, since there's nothing we have to do outside. And don't tell me you have to go tune up the tractor or something."

"Man, you are one demanding boss. I'll work on it. Let me add a couple of things to your shopping list first, though. Like marshmallows, if we're going to keep roughing it like this."

"Which reminds me—Seth said someone would be dropping off more firewood today. I guess we should put it in the shed. Can you supervise that?"

"I think I can handle that. You gonna wash up, since I cooked?"

"Sure."

After cleaning up the kitchen, Meg went upstairs, showered (hot water!), and dressed. She had gotten used to physical activity over the past several months, and now she felt confined and restless, stuck in the house. It would be good to get out and move.

From the kitchen she called up the back stairs, "I'm leaving now!"

Bree shouted something unintelligible in response. Meg gathered up the shopping list and her bag, rubbed Lolly's head, pulled on her boots, and went out the back door. She stopped on the steps, taking in the scene in front of her. It looked like a picture postcard: the distant trees, bare of leaves; the rolling meadow, its snow untouched; the sun in an intensely blue sky. She inhaled deeply. Yes, it was a bit warmer today, and water dripped steadily from her clogged gutters. She'd probably have some pretty good icicles later.

She made her way to the barn to check on Dorcas and Isabel, who greeted her eagerly. "Hi, girls. How're you doing? You have enough to eat and drink?" Dorcas stood up, her front hooves on the slats of the pen, and Meg scratched her head. They needed a bit more feed, and she took care of that. They probably needed some exercise, too, but she decided to wait until she came back to deal with letting them out into their pen, so she could keep an eye on them. "Bye, girls. I'll see you in a bit."

Back outside, it took her eyes a moment to adjust to the light. She checked out the house, looking for the source of the night's noise. All shutters in place. Ah—one of the downspouts from her gutters had come loose. She came closer and inspected it: the strapping at the bottom had been wrenched away from the siding, which left the downspout hanging precariously. No doubt in a wind it would bang against the house. But Meg was a bit puzzled: from what she remembered, the wind hadn't been strong enough to pull the downspout out by force, and the screws that had held it looked fairly new, and certainly long enough. The wood where they had been dislodged wasn't rotted. Why had it chosen that particular moment to come loose? She looked around her. Already the ground around the house was marked by a variety of animal prints, mainly squirrel and something smaller. Mice? Chipmunks? But there were some odd blurry tracks underlying them. More snowshoe tracks? Was she imagining things? Surely she would have noticed someone skulking around practically under the kitchen window by daylight. Had someone come along under cover of night and pulled out her downspout? If so, he hadn't tried to destroy it, which wouldn't have been hard. Instead he had left it hanging loose so it would bang against the house. Why?

Shaking her head, Meg went to the shed and cleared what snow had drifted in the night so she could get her car out. Then she backed out carefully, barely avoiding the snowbanks that lined her drive, and headed toward town.

11

Meg took her time driving to the market, respectful of the snow on the roads. At least to get there she could follow the main highway, which had been fairly well cleared, then salted or sanded or whatever they did around here. She drove slowly and carefully: she'd never had much experience with driving in ice and snow, even growing up. Luckily there were few people on the road, and most of them kept a fair distance from the person in front of them. Meg pumped the brakes a few times, experimentally, to see how quickly she could stop, and was not reassured; the road surface was treacherous. She was relieved when she made it to the market, but also dismayed that the huge mounds of snow substantially reduced the number of parking spaces available. Apparently a lot of people had felt as housebound as she had, and they had all made a beeline for the market.

She found a narrow spot adjoining one of the snow mountains and squeezed the car into it. It was a good thing that she wouldn't have to open the passenger door, because it wasn't possible. Someone at the store had made an effort to clear the sidewalks, but even so, people walking to the entrance had packed the remaining snow into icy patches. For all of that, inside the store people looked extraordinarily cheerful. Glad to be out of the house? Relieved that the worst was over? Voices seemed louder than usual, as friends greeted each other and exchanged snow stories. Meg walked past a number of conversations where people were comparing the depth of their snow accumulation—a number that seemed to keep growing the longer she listened. She shook her head: she hadn't even measured the depth at her place. Three feet? A nice round number—and more than enough.

Half an hour later she emerged with a couple of bags of essentials, after spending most of the time waiting in line for the cashier. She opted to carry the bags rather than to try to maneuver the shopping cart through the now-icy ruts in the parking lot. Despite the store's best efforts, apparently at least one person had found the footing treacherous: an older man was kneeling on the sidewalk, off to one side of the doors, and there were a few kind people clustered around him, trying to assist him to his feet. He didn't seem to need any additional help, so Meg returned her attention to trying to avoid slipping on the treacherous surface. She didn't look at her car until she reached it, orienting herself by the massive snow pile next to it.

As she rounded the back of the car to stow her groceries she was startled to see that her rear bumper was crumpled. "Damn!" she swore. How on earth could someone have run into it, protected by the snow mound? She looked quickly around, but there was nobody nearby in the parking lot at the moment, and she had no idea when it might have happened. She tried her key in the lock of the trunk, and was relieved when it opened. She dumped her groceries in and slammed it shut, then looked at the bumper again. It would have been all but impossible for someone to skid into that part of her car—unless they had wanted to hit it. But why would anyone do that? She was parked as legally as possible in the space; she had pulled as far forward as the snow would allow, and if anything, farther than her immediate neighbors. She should have been safe, but obviously she hadn't been.

She surveyed the damage. Nothing major, but probably within her deductible, for which she'd be out of pocket in any case. Should she talk to the police? The market administrators? Did they have surveillance cameras? She stopped herself at that last question: this was a fairly rural area, and they didn't worry about things like electronic surveillance. Just to be sure she surveyed the widely spaced light poles in the parking lot, and didn't see anything that looked remotely like a camera. She sighed. Not much to be done about it, except get the blasted bumper fixed, when time and the weather allowed. One more expense she didn't need right now, not when she was facing paying for a new furnace.

Without much hope she looked at her front windshield when she got into the car, and was not surprised when she saw no note from an apologetic driver. She pulled out of the space cautiously and made her way back to the main road. When she reached Granford, she surprised herself by passing the turnoff for her house and continuing straight toward town, pulling off at the driveway to the police station, half a mile before the center of town. In the neatly plowed small lot there she found a parking space easily. Inside she was happy to see the police chief, Art Preston, in the lobby, chatting with one of his officers. He looked up as she came in.

"Hi, Meg. What brings you here? No bodies, I hope?"

"Good to see you, Art. Sorry, no bodies, unless you count my dead furnace, and I think that was due to old age rather than violence. Actually I just wanted to ask a question. I was parked in the lot at the market just now, and somebody ran into the car. It's not major damage, just a crumpled fender, but whoever it was didn't leave a note or anything, and I don't know if anyone saw it happen. I just wondered what my legal liability is, or what I should tell my insurance company."

"How bad is it?"

Meg shrugged. "Cosmetic, not structural. And before you ask, yes, I have a high deductible, to keep the cost down."

Art grinned ruefully. "Then you're probably better off just getting it fixed and eating the cost. Sorry—and you didn't hear it from me. Not my jurisdiction anyway—it happened outside Granford town limits."

"I was afraid you'd say that. It's about what I'd figured."

"I'm sure Seth—" Art began.

"Can find me someone who'll give me a good deal on the repairs," Meg finished his statement for him. "I know. It just seems like everything is falling apart on me at once. Did Seth tell you about the furnace going out?"

"Maybe he mentioned it. So where are you staying?"

"At home. I've got firewood, and we got the old fireplace working downstairs. We'll be fine for a few days. I'm certainly glad the power's back, though. How's the rest of the town doing?"

"About what you'd expect. A couple of carbon monoxide scares—you know, someone turns on an old kerosene heater and forgets to open a window. We had to pull a couple of people out of a ditch, but no injuries. That sure was some blizzard, wasn't it?"

"I haven't seen many, but I was impressed. Back in the old days, did things just stop dead until it all melted?"

Art laughed. "How old do you think I am? But that's what I've heard. I gather there used to be horse-drawn plows that kind of pushed the snow to the side of the road, but I've never seen one." He checked his watch. "Well, I've got some wellness checks to make. Some of the older folk around here can't do their own shoveling, so they're pretty much confined to their houses."

"Don't make me feel guilty. Anyway, I've got groceries to take home. Thanks for the advice, even if I didn't like it. I'll see you around."

"Say hi to Seth when you see him," Art called out to her retreating back.

Meg drove home in a pensive mood. Maybe she was still a city girl, but at least she had enough strength and energy to get out of her house. Others weren't so lucky. No wonder so many older people headed south when they retired: no snow shoveling. Was worrying about hurricanes worse? Along the road to the house, she noted the stretch of chain-link fence that Bree had mentioned. Something definitely had hit it: the fencing was warped and twisted, and it looked like at least one metal post was nearly horizontal. But the snow pile shoved off the road by the plows didn't even reach the fence. Had someone skidded early in the snowfall, hit the fence, and backed out again? Right now there was no way to tell.

She pulled into the driveway to see Bree wrangling the goats. She had them both on rope leads, but being curious creatures, they were pulling in opposite directions.

Bree looked relieved to see Meg. "Hey, can you grab one of these critters? They've been cooped up too long, and now they want to go exploring. You think they've ever seen snow?"

Meg grabbed one of the ropes. "I have no idea. Will they be all right in the pen?"

Bree was tugging her goat toward the gate to the enclosure. "I think so. We can check their shed to make sure it's clean and dry, but I think they'll be happier out here than in the barn, and we can keep an eye on them from the house. Oh, and we'll have to make sure the water in their trough doesn't freeze."

"How're we supposed to do that?"

"Ask Seth. He's the plumber."

After a few more minutes of wrestling, they managed to get the goats into the pen and the gate locked behind them. Winded, Meg leaned against the fence and watched them. They were playing, running and leaping, and tossing snow in the air. They looked entirely happy in their new environment, and she wondered what they would think when it melted away.

"Did the wood come?" Meg asked.

"Sure did. All nicely stowed away in the shed. I made sure the guy stacked it."

"Did you pay him?"

"He said Seth had taken care of it, and not to worry."

"Then I guess we should take some into the house and build up the fire, keep the place warm."

"Good idea." Bree came around Meg's car and caught sight of the damage. "Hey, what happened?"

"Somebody who didn't bother to identify himself ran into it in the parking lot at the market."

"That sucks."

"I agree. And probably below my deductible."

"Did you tell the cops?"

"Yes and no. I stopped by the police station in Granford and asked Art what I should do, and he more or less said to forget it. At least that way my insurance payments won't go up. Well, let's get that wood inside."

Fifteen minutes later they had hauled a nice stack of wood, setting it by the fireplace, and Meg had added a few logs to the dying fire. "Lunch?" she asked.

"Sure, sounds good. And didn't you say you had something you wanted to show me?"

"Oh, right. But that should wait until after lunch—no sticky fingers."

"Then let's eat."

Fifteen minutes later Meg ventured into the dining room, where it was almost comfortably warm. Almost. The business papers were still stacked on the dining room table. "Bree," she began.

Bree stopped her. "I know, I know—you want those numbers. How can I forget, when I have to walk by all this all the time? *And* you keep nagging me?" She waved at the orderly piles on the table. "Show me your new treasure, and then I promise I'll get right on those numbers. Deal?"

"Deal." Once again Meg retrieved the sampler from its place on the dining room sideboard, laid it on the card table by the window, and unrolled it. "Seth and I found this in an upstairs closet. From the dust on it, I think it's been there for a long while."

"What's a while?" Bree asked, her eyes on the sampler. "I mean, two years or twenty?"

"Closer to two *hundred*, I'm guessing. There's a date on it, so we know when it was made, but I don't recognize the name of the girl who made it, Violet Cox. I don't know if she lived in this house, or it was brought into the house by someone else. And when I found it, the power was out so I couldn't check the Internet."

"Huh. So what's the story?"

"The top part seems to be a family history, one where everybody died young."

"That's kind of weird."

"Seth says it's not uncommon. A lot of people died in those days, and not in nice distant hospitals, but usually at home. Does that idea bother you?"

"You asking if I'm worried about ghosts in the house here? I don't think about it a lot. I mean, obviously somebody's died in this house sometime over two hundred years, but I haven't noticed anybody haunting it. And if I did see a ghost, I don't know why they'd have anything against me. Think a ghost would talk to me?"

Meg laughed at the idea of Bree trying to have a conversation with someone who had been dead for a century or two. "I have no idea. I think the general assumption is that they kind of pop in and out, and you can see them but not hear them. And sometimes it's cold where they hang out."

"Well, at the moment that describes most of the house, so we must have a real crowd here. Too bad they can't help keep us warm."

"So you're okay with a little haunting?"

"Sure, no problem. You going to do some research on this? Are those tombstones?" Bree pointed to the sampler.

"I certainly think so. And yes, I'm going to keep looking. I've got the time right now, and there's a lot of detail to work with."

"Maybe it's worth money," Bree suggested.

"I hadn't even thought about that. But if it comes from the family, I wouldn't sell it. Anyway, I can do some hunting online, and then maybe I can talk to Gail at the Historical Society. If she doesn't know anything about samplers, she can probably point me toward someone who does."

"So let's get started."

"Us? You've got work to do. But I'll stay here and keep you company while I check the Web."

"You mean, keep an eye on me?" Bree grinned.

"Yes, that, too."

Bree vanished up the stairs and returned quickly with more bundles of papers and several folders. Meg cringed: she could see no order in them, but at least it was a start.

"Damn, it's still cold upstairs!" Bree said. "And I hear it's going to go down to the twenties again tonight, so everything that's melted will freeze solid. Good thing you got food today."

As Bree started moving papers around she said, "Listen, about that sampler. The usual mourning stuff is urns and willows, right?"

"I think so. How do you know that?"

"That's just kind of general info—you know, weeping willows and all that? Now, on your piece you've got tombstones instead, and then one girl or woman weeping. Then there's a list of a bunch of people who were family members, and who were all dead by the time the thing was made. Right?" Bree looked at Meg expectantly.

"Yes, and that's about as far as I got. Since all these people died before 1849, if they lived in Massachusetts they may be in the online vital records. Massachusetts did a much better job of keeping records than other states did. And before you ask, I haven't had a chance to look in the cemetery to see if they're buried in Granford. It's under several feet of snow at the moment. If, on the other hand, this sampler comes from out of state, it'll be harder to trace."

"From the looks of it, whoever made the sampler was the only one left to mourn. And she was only twelve, poor kid. Sad." Bree took a last look, then settled herself at the dining room table. "I'll get to work now—and you can start digging up dead people on the Internet."

12

Seth appeared as the sun was sinking. He pulled his truck in behind Meg's car in the shed, and then went around to open the passenger door. Max jumped down, his fascination with snow apparently unabated. Seth stared at the back of Meg's car for a moment before he came to the kitchen door.

Meg opened it quickly. "What news, traveler?" she said.

"Have you been reading old books today? You sound a bit archaic," Seth said, stepping in after stamping his boots on the stoop. Max slipped past him and skidded on the kitchen floor.

"No, but I've been digging into family histories, looking for information that fits my sampler, now that I can use the Internet. Max, don't eat that—I don't even know what it is."

Seth wrestled what looked like an old sock from Max's mouth. "Any luck?"

"Not so far. I'm finding that a lot of things aren't on the Internet. For starters, it looks like the family didn't come from Massachusetts, which is going to complicate things. How about you?"

"Not bad, all things considered. Of course, we've already exhausted the Granford budget for snow removal, and it's only December. But no casualties of the storm, so far. Did the wood come?"

"It did. Bree made sure it was stowed away, and we're already using it. Any word on the furnace situation?"

"End of the week—maybe. No promises. My offer still stands, if you get tired of roughing it here and want to come over to my place."

"We're doing fine, thank you. Want to stay for supper?"

"I was hoping you'd ask. What happened to your car? Skid?"

"Nope. I was parked in the lot at the market and some idiot must have backed into me. And I thought I was nice and safe, parked next to a snowdrift. Probably whoever it was assumed it was the snow that he hit when something went crunch, and went on about his merry way. Jerk!"

"Sorry. You do seem to be having a streak of bad luck."

"Tell me about it. You want something to drink? Hot or cold?"

"Coffee would be good. I've been outside most of the day, and I'm not sure I can feel my fingers."

"Coming up." Meg mentally reviewed the food she had bought and decided on a home style chicken stew. With dumplings. She pulled out chicken, carrots, onions, and started chopping things. When the coffee was ready, she nodded to Seth. "Help yourself."

"What? You aren't going to serve me?" He stood up before she could take him seriously.

As she chopped, Meg watched him: he did look tired, and he was moving slowly, at least for him. She had the feeling that overseeing the affairs of the town under current circumstances probably meant a lot of shoveling, and she knew how exhausting that could be. "You want to take a nap or something?"

He laughed. "Don't tempt me. If I lie down I may not get up again for a while. Can you talk and cook at the same time?"

"I do believe I can. What do you want to talk about?"

"Furnace options, for a start." As Meg sliced and sautéed, he enumerated the plusses and minuses of several models and sizes of oil furnace . . . Meg found herself losing the thread of the story, but kept nodding and throwing in a comment now and then. Was it un-feminist of her to just tell him, *you decide*? Why was she supposed to know anything about furnaces? She had been a banker; now she was a farmer. Neither one included even a short course on heating systems.

She realized that Seth had fallen silent. When she glanced over at him, he was slumped back in his chair, his eyes shut. She wasn't worried that he was about to fall out of his chair, so she went on about her business, until she had set a casserole to simmer on a back burner of the stove. Now all she had to do was figure out how to make dumplings. She knew she'd seen her mother do it, so how complicated could it be? Not that her mother was a poor cook, just a disinterested one. And when was the last time she'd seen Elizabeth make dumplings? Twenty years ago? Meg realized her own mind was drifting, and got up and went to the shelf in the kitchen to retrieve an old copy of Fanny Farmer, the one with three generations of grease stains marking its pages. There had to be dumplings in here somewhere . . .

Bree clattered into the room and stopped at the sight of Seth in the chair. "Oh, sorry, I didn't mean to interrupt."

Meg suppressed a laugh. "Interrupt what?"

Bree grinned. "His nap?"

"I'm not asleep, I'm just resting my eyes," Seth volunteered, without opening his eyes.

"Yeah, right," Bree replied. "When's dinner?"

"Half an hour, maybe?" Meg said.

"Do I have time for a shower?"

"Sure." As Bree disappeared up the stairs, Meg sat down at the table with her cookbook. "Do you like dumplings?"

Seth opened his eyes. "Are you talking to me? I like almost anything, particularly if someone else makes it. Dumplings sound great."

"Dumplings it is, then," Meg said. She leafed through the book until she found the recipe she was looking for. But she still didn't get up. She was tired, but pleasantly so. The room was comfortably warm, and the chicken stew bubbling quietly on the stove smelled wonderful. Sure, she had plenty to worry about, but finding a furnace and replacing her bumper weren't going to happen in the next couple of hours, so she might as well enjoy the moment. Here, with Seth, in her own kitchen. How many generations of family members had done exactly the same thing? Although, she had to admit, few farmwives had had the luxury of sitting down, not with a hungry family and a few farmhands to keep fed.

She looked up to see Seth watching her. "This is nice, isn't it?" he asked.

She could have pretended she didn't know what he meant, but what was the point? It *was* nice. Nice to sit here; nice to sit here with him. Was this what marriage was supposed to be like? Doing nothing together—happily?

"It is. Nothing like a demanding job to make you appreciate a little rest. I guess I'm romanticizing the past, but it feels so snug here, in a warm kitchen with light and good smells. And good company. Is Max hungry?"

Seth looked at Max, wrapped around his feet. "Not yet. Why don't we just sit for a while? I'll try to stay awake."

"Sounds good. How's the rest of your family holding up? Rachel didn't have any guests when this hit, did she?"

"Everyone's good, and Rachel didn't have any bookings. I told you Mom would be back tomorrow. And so life goes on. Let's hope we don't get any more snow soon."

"Amen. Although Bree tells me it's going to get colder." Reluctantly Meg stood up and started assembling plates and silverware for dinner.

After the meal Bree went back upstairs, leaving Meg and Seth alone in the kitchen. "I should be going," Seth said.

"You don't have to."

"How's Bree going to take my camping out here?"

"She's okay with it, don't worry. You know, I don't know what I would have done without her this year—she's smart, and she works really hard. Except at record keeping, but I guess you can't have everything. I wish I could pay her more, but I'm not even paying me at the moment. At least now I have a better idea of what I'm doing, which would make next season more efficient." *If there is going to be a next season*, Meg thought again.

"Would expanding help?"

"Where to? I don't have any more land, unless you count the swamp. Wonder if there's a way to grow apples hydroponically? Bree's already talking about new stock, and what we should replace. But where?"

"Maybe you could use some of my acreage?"

She stared at him speculatively. "Wow. I mean, relationships are one thing, but sharing land? Planting trees on it? That's serious."

"You sound like a true New Englander," Seth said with a smile.

"I am one," Meg replied promptly, "and I've got the paperwork to prove it."

"That you do." He stood up and stretched. "If I'm staying, I should take Max out again, and then I could really use a shower, if Bree left any hot water."

"Go for it. After all, if the water heater goes, you know how to fix it."

As Seth and Max headed out the back door into the dark, Meg stacked up the dishes by the sink.

After a few minutes Seth came stomping back in with Max. "It is really cold out there. Even Max didn't feel like hanging out."

They made an early night of it. Meg made a quick foray into her bedroom upstairs and backed out again quickly. It had to be forty degrees there, exposed as it was with two drafty windows, and even if she and Seth managed to generate any heat between them, it probably wouldn't be enough. Downstairs again, then, in front of the fire. Seth must have read her mind, because by the time she came back downstairs he was stoking the fire. Bree had reappeared, too, and was studiously avoiding looking at them, and Meg had to suppress a laugh. How absurd was this? And how had people managed to make babies in houses stuffed to the rafters with family? People must have been skilled at ignoring things.

Maybe she was getting used to sleeping on the floor, or maybe it was Seth's arm draped protectively around her, but Meg slept surprisingly well, waking only when light from the rising sun flooded the room. Seth and Bree slept on as Meg slid out from under the quilts and blankets and tiptoed upstairs to the bathroom to do what was necessary. She sneaked down the back way to the kitchen, but Max scratched at the door, so she hurried to let him into the kitchen before he woke the sleepers. "You need to go too, Max? Hang on a sec."

Meg debated briefly about letting him go outside and take care of business, but she still wasn't sure whether she could trust him to come when she called. She sighed: taking him out on the leash meant putting on her boots and coat and facing a rather brisk wake-up. She checked the thermometer outside her window: twenty degrees, as Bree had predicted.

Max was dancing around her feet, looking anxious. "Okay, okay, I'm working on it." She pulled on the boots and coat, disentangled his leash from the collected scarves and coats, and pulled open the door. A blast of cold air rushed into the room. No, cold didn't begin to describe it: icy. Cutting. Bitter. Max tugged impatiently at the leash, and Meg stepped reluctantly outside, pulling the door closed behind her.

And stopped abruptly. On the steps outside the kitchen there lay a mangled corpse—a very dead squirrel, its guts hanging out, red blood staining the snow around it. Did blood stay red if it froze quickly? Meg wondered irreverently. Max had spotted the body and was eager to investigate, tugging hard on his leash, but Meg's stomach turned at the idea. How had the squirrel ended up on her stoop? A coyote or some similar varmint? But why would any animal have caught and killed it, then left it on her stoop? Why would any feral animal abandon its prey? Meg looked around quickly. The surface of the snow, melted by the sun yesterday, had frozen to a thick crust now. She didn't see any animal prints, but unless an animal was heavy enough to break through the crust, there wouldn't be any.

A human would have used the path.

Whoa, Meg! Why would a person sneak up and leave her a dead squirrel? That made no sense. She hadn't heard any noises outside the house last night, but she had slept pretty soundly, so that wasn't surprising. But why hadn't Max heard anything?

She shook her head in bewilderment, and stepping carefully around the squirrel, she dragged Max toward the driveway and let him do what he needed to do. By the time he was finished, Seth had appeared in the doorway and had spotted the squirrel.

"What's that about?" he asked.

"You're asking me?" Meg said. "Come on, Max, time to

go inside. I found it when I came out. Didn't you tell me there were coyotes around here?"

"Yes, but they seldom leave presents. Maybe Max has a secret admirer."

"Well, please just get rid of it. Unless you want to feed it to Max for breakfast?"

"Uh, no, I don't think so. Some local animals can carry diseases. If you can get Max inside, I'll take care of this."

"Deal." Meg dragged a protesting Max into the kitchen and shut the door firmly behind him. She could hear Seth crunching around the driveway—and the sound was clearly audible, even with the door shut. So whatever had left the squirrel had either been fairly light and quick on its feet—or had been deliberately stealthy. After all, Max hadn't alerted them. That was an unsettling thought.

By the time Seth came back, Meg had a pot of oatmeal cooking on the stove, and had laid out milk, cream, butter, and two kinds of sugar. After breakfast, Seth announced, "I'm going to check in with the plow guys, and then I'll see if I can hunt down a furnace for you."

"Bless you! Once you get hold of one, how long will it take you to install it?"

"Depends on how much ductwork I have to shift around. But probably within a day. Don't worry, a couple more days and you'll have heat again. I'll stop by later and let you know what I find out."

"Sounds good. Drive safely, it's icy out there."

"So I see. Have a good day—maybe you can track down something about the sampler."

"That's my plan."

13

After Seth left, Meg tidied up the kitchen and went back to the front parlor and the table of genealogy materials that awaited her. Bree roused herself and stumbled upstairs to wash up, and minutes later Meg heard her banging around the kitchen—she must have come down the back way to make herself breakfast. Meg busied herself with the family records.

It was such a luxury to have time to do big chunks of research. Even though she hadn't done much more than dabble in her own family history so far, she'd already found how easy it was to lose the thread of what she was pursuing, which meant that each time she sat down to work on anything she had to reconstruct where she had left things. She knew that she had a wealth of information in the sampler, but that could lead in several different and unrelated directions. She had the feeling that it was the Cox name that would hold the key, and that was where she intended to start.

She had taken digital photos of the sampler so she

wouldn't have to handle the fragile piece to examine it closely; being able to enlarge the needlework piece on-screen had helped her to decipher some of the faded numbers, and she had transcribed the family names and dates. Violet Cox had made the sampler, but the other people listed there were all Lampsons. Earlier she had spent time trying to find any of them in Massachusetts, where there were plenty of online records, but with little luck. If a woman from the Warren family had married a Cox, Meg had no record of it—yet. But the surname tickled some distant memory of hers, and she was quickly finding that persistence, and a dash of creativity, often helped to break through what looked like dead ends. Before she started searching online Meg riffled through her mother's notes again. She still marveled at how much Elizabeth had accomplished, with no experience and limited time. Obviously her mother had hidden talents that Meg had never fully appreciated. She thought she remembered . . . Yes! A note scribbled in the margin of a printout: "Cox-Warren-four sibs Pittsford." Meg stared at the notation. What had her mother meant? Apparently there was some Cox–Warren connection that had caught Elizabeth's eye, and it led to a place called Pittsford, but Meg checked quickly online and found no Pittsford, Massachusetts. She tried other New England states and found two Pittsfords, one each in New York and Vermont. The one in Vermont seemed likelier, and when she entered that in her search engine she found it was a town almost due north of Granford, and in modern terms, a three-hour drive by car. She wondered how long it would have taken by horse or carriage two centuries earlier.

And there she stalled. Vermont records were nowhere near as accessible online as Massachusetts records. She wasn't even sure what she was looking for, beyond the surname Cox, possibly linked with Warren.

"Will you quit sighing?" Bree's voice interrupted her. "I'm trying to concentrate here."

Meg laughed, then stretched. "I didn't even hear you come in. All I seem to be hitting are brick walls. I've got some vague hints of a connection to someone who might be the young woman who made the sampler, who might have some connection to some Warrens somewhere, sometime. You know, it sounds even worse when I say that out loud."

"Why do you care?" Bree asked.

"Because it's a puzzle. And because the sampler is here, in this house. I've held something that this girl Violet Cox made two hundred years ago, and I want to know how it found its way into my hands. And if I've learned anything about the people around here, it's that almost everyone is connected somehow."

"I can understand that. Of course, my family background's entirely different. I might have been born and raised in Massachusetts, but the rest of my family's in Jamaica. And my ma and my auntie keep all the relations in their heads."

"Make sure somebody writes all that information down before it's lost. You never know when you might want it," Meg said. "How's it coming?" She nodded toward the papers Bree had scattered over the table.

"Not bad, I guess. I can see progress."

"Oh, wait a sec." Meg darted back to her workspace and pulled out a piece of paper from the folder her mother had left. "My mother stumbled on this and thought I might be interested, so she printed it out. It looks like some kind of orchard accounting—from 1912."

Bree held out her hand, and Meg gave her the printout. "Cool," she said. "You know, things aren't all that different now. I mean, look at it." She laid it on the table, and Meg leaned over to read it. "It's set up chronologically through the year, and each task is assigned a cost. Fertilizing, pruning, spraying—I'd have to check what they were using a hundred years ago, 'cause they were really hitting the trees hard for a week or two there—more fertilizing. Then picking and packing, and hauling. Sound familiar?"

Meg laughed. "I guess it does. But we don't have to count horse-hours now, do we?"

"No. But you could substitute equipment costs. Amortizing your capital outlays might be the modern equivalent."

"Listen to you! You must have been paying attention in all those classes you took."

"I was an A student. I just don't like sitting still and putting all this stuff together." She held up a hand before Meg could chide her. "I know, I know—it's part of the job. I've got everything together, and now I have to make sense of it and write up a summary. You go back to your family history or whatever."

Meg looked out the window and realized that it was getting dark. Where had the time gone? "I think I'd better do something about dinner." She had some ground lamb . . . maybe shepherd's pie?

She was in the kitchen feeding Lolly when she saw Seth's van pull into the driveway. She waited until he had parked and was approaching the door before opening it, to conserve heat.

Seth hurried inside, his face flushed with the cold. "Hey, Meg. Is Bree here?"

"Yes, she's in the dining room. Why?"

"Looks like she's got a flat. Yo, Bree?" he called out.

"Yeah?" she yelled back.

"I think you'd better take a look at your back tire."

Bree appeared quickly in the doorway. "Huh?"

"Looks flat. When was the last time you drove your car?"

"Day before yesterday. It was fine then."

"I can give you a hand changing it now, if you want, before we lose the light," Seth volunteered. "If your spare's okay."

"I guess," Bree said grudgingly. "I know how to change

a tire, but this isn't exactly the best time to do it. This sucks!" Muttering under her breath, she pulled on her coat and gloves and stormed out the back door, with Seth following. They were gone for a while, and Bree was cursing openly when they finally returned. "Damn it, that tire was almost new."

"What was the problem?" Meg asked.

"A nail. A stupid nail. How the hell could I get a nail in my tire in all this snow?"

"And it was fine the last time you drove on it?"

"Sure it was. At least, I think so. The roads have been so lousy with all the ice and snow, it's hard to tell. Seth, you think it can be fixed? 'Cause I sure don't want to have to buy another one right now."

"I think so," Seth said. "A patch should do it. Want me to drop it off at the gas station tomorrow?"

Bree exchanged an amused glance with Meg. "Uh, yeah, sure, I guess. I could do it myself, you know, now that we've got the other one on."

"That's just a temporary one—I wouldn't risk that on these roads. It's no problem—I go right by the gas station. You can have it back by the end of the day tomorrow. Would you feel better if I let you put it back on all by yourself?"

Meg giggled, and Bree glared at her. "I can handle that. Thanks, Seth." She stalked back to the dining room.

Meg asked, "Are you staying for dinner, Seth?"

"Sure. By the way, I left Max at Mom's—I was making business calls today, and I didn't want to drag him along. So he's in good hands."

"Your mother's back?" Meg asked, returning to the potatoes she was peeling.

"Yup. She likes her own space. Sound familiar?"

"It does. Not only are we Yankees tough, we're independent. Sit down. Want something to drink?"

"Coffee's good."

They chatted about Meg's most recent discoveries about the sampler as Meg chopped, peeled, mashed, and mixed. Finally she dotted the top crust of mashed potatoes with butter and slid her dish into the oven. "There. Thirty minutes until dinner."

"Can I give you the good news now? I got kind of distracted by the tire problem."

She turned to face him, drying her hands on a towel. "I would love to hear anything resembling good news. What is it?"

"I've got you a furnace. I can pick it up tomorrow, and have it up and running by the day after."

"You are my hero!" Meg bestowed a sloppy kiss on him, which quickly grew into more. They broke it off only when Bree came back into the kitchen.

"Can't leave you two alone for a minute. Will there be dinner, or are you too busy?"

"Dinner's in the oven," Meg said, unruffled. "I was thanking Seth for finding us a furnace. We may have heat soon!"

"Well, then, I'll let you go back to thanking. Call me when dinner's ready." She slipped back out the door again.

"We're setting a bad example for the children, you know," Meg said to Seth. "Tell me about installing the furnace. Do I have to do anything?"

"You certainly are a romantic at heart," Seth protested.

"I'm just focused. And cold," Meg replied.

Seth sighed melodramatically. "For the furnace, no. You're keeping the oil tank, which would be the biggest problem, if I had to haul it out. The rest is really pretty simple—you'll be surprised when you see how few parts there are. After dinner I'll take another look at the ductwork and see what other supplies I might need. And I'd recommend a new thermostat, preferably a programmable one. I'd suggest multiple zones, but I don't think it would work in this house, and it would be a pain to run the wiring."

"Whatever you say."

After dinner Bree volunteered to do the dishes, and Seth disappeared into the cellar with a heavy-duty flashlight. Meg went back to her genealogy materials and stacked them neatly—and put a paperweight on them. All she needed was to have Lolly jump on the table and scatter everything she had laboriously collected and sorted. She hadn't made much progress with the Coxes. She should ask Seth—he knew everybody. Or Ruth Ferry, who was perhaps the eldest person she knew around here. Or Gail Selden. Maybe Gail had some files about local Coxes. Plenty of avenues left to follow.

Seth came back up the cellar stairs, whistling cheerfully. "Looks good. I think I'll replace the electrical line from the box to the furnace. The one you've got is Romex, and that could cause electrical fluctuations—you know, lights dimming. You noticed anything like that?"

"I did, but I thought it was just an old house problem. Like everything else. I never associated it with the furnace."

"Well, if that was the problem, this will fix it. I'd better get back and collect Max from Mom. I'll pick up the furnace tomorrow morning, and let's plan on Thursday for the installation. That work for you?"

"No complaints from me. Take care, and say hi to Max for me. I'll see you Thursday."

"Count on it." He gave her a quick kiss and disappeared into the night.

Meg turned off most of the lights in the kitchen and checked the lock on the back door. All secure against the night. Or at least, as secure as she could make it. Bree had escorted the goats back into the barn earlier, so they were set for the night. Meg went back to the dining room, where she was surprised to see Bree still hard at work. "Hey, I'm not a tyrant. That'll keep until morning."

"I'm fine—I got used to late hours at college. Except when I'm working hard physically—then I just crash."

Meg checked her watch: it wasn't even eight o'clock. What should she do? She didn't trust herself to work on the family tree—when she was tired, she was likely to miss details. Besides, that was supposed to be fun, not a chore. She didn't want to disturb Bree by turning on the television, if Bree was actually working on the long-awaited financial summary for the business. She picked up a paperback mystery she had started, and after a few pages she realized she couldn't remember what she had read earlier. She found herself staring into space, listening to the comforting ticktock of the antique clock hanging over the mantelpiece, and thinking . . .

Suddenly Meg straightened up in her chair. All the small, annoying incidents recently including Bree's flat tire: were they connected?

"Bree?" she called out.

"Huh?" Bree replied. "You want something?"

Meg stood up and went back to the dining room. "I've been thinking, and I need you to tell me if I've finally gone over the edge. I feel like I've hit a really weird streak of bad luck this past week, and I don't know if I'm being paranoid or there's something going on."

"What are you talking about?" Bree put down her pencil and focused on Meg.

Meg began ticking items off on her fingers. "Let's start with the goats—part of the pen enclosure broke and they got out, and it was only dumb luck that they headed for Seth's rather than wandering down the road. Two, I found broken glass from a smashed bottle at the end of the driveway one morning, which could easily have blown out one of my tires. Three, Seth said that someone had tried to jimmy the lock on the barn door in the back. Four, he also found one of the cellar windows open when he went down to check out the furnace—and it would have taken some force to do that. Five, I saw footprints outside a back window—and Max thought there was someone there. Six, you told me that a piece of my fence was down, and when I saw it, I didn't think the snowplow could've done it—it was too far back from the road. Seven, one of my downspouts mysteriously came loose during the night and started banging against the house. Eight, somebody ran into my car at the market. Then this morning, there's a dead squirrel smack in the middle of my back steps. And finally, your flat tire." Meg held up both hands, fingers outstretched. "That's ten separate incidents. Taken alone, any of them could be explained away. But all this has happened in one week. Taken together, they scare me. And it feels to me like they're getting more serious by the day. With that tire, you could have ended up in a ditch."

"I see what you're saying, but what's it mean?" Bree asked. "Have you pissed somebody off lately?"

"Not that I know of. Did we make any of our buyers mad? Miss a shipment? Forget to make a payment?"

"No! Nothing like that. Far as I know, everybody went away happy. Even the pickers—they thought you gave them a fair deal. You seem to be getting along well with most people in town, right?"

"I thought so, but I could be wrong. Do you think I'm crazy? Is this all just a string of coincidences?"

Bree shook her head. "I don't think you're crazy, Meg. If anything, I would have said you don't have much of an imagination."

"Gee, thanks."

"You run this by Seth?"

"No, I only put it all together now. Maybe I'm just tired. It's been a long week." Meg sighed and decided to change the subject. "But Seth says we'll have a working furnace by Thursday, so at least there's one piece of good news! I wonder if there's any sort of ceremony for welcoming a new furnace?"

Bree laughed. "Not that I've heard of, but I'll be happy to kiss it, if that helps."

"Well, I'm going to get ready for bed. Don't mind me—I hope I'm just seeing things where there's nothing to see."

"I'll be done with this part in a minute. You build up the fire, okay?"

"Deal."

14

The snap of a dying ember woke Meg out of an uneasy sleep. It was intensely dark, and very still outside. The clock over the mantel read five-something, as near as she could make out. Dawn, almost. Bree snored lightly a few feet away. The round lump that was Lolly warmed her belly. She lay listening, thinking.

She had been surprised when she'd added up the list of disturbing events for Bree. Could they really be just a string of coincidences? Sure, each one could be explained away. But all of them, in such a short time? Maybe it was a local teenager who was pulling a series of pranks on a dare: go drive some poor single woman nuts.

Meg stiffened. Was that a noise she heard? Footsteps? Near or far? She strained to hear anything, while Bree and Lolly slept on, oblivious. Another sound. It could be something as simple as ice creaking as temperatures changed. Or not. For all she knew it was a black bear foraging for food. Had she taken any garbage out lately?

She wasn't sure how long she lay there listening, but

eventually, when she heard nothing more, she drifted back to sleep, and didn't wake again until daylight. Bree was already up, in the kitchen talking to someone, and from the tone of her voice Meg decided it was Lolly. Meg pulled herself out from the tangled quilts and stretched.

Much as she relished the downtime, she had to admit she missed the constant activity of working in the orchard. It gave structure and purpose to her days. Dabbling in genealogy seemed self-indulgent and frivolous, but at the very least she thought she should finish what she could with the sampler. Maybe this would be a good day to talk to Gail Selden over at the Historical Society, if she was free.

Meg dashed upstairs to wash and dress—it was still bitterly cold on the second floor—then joined Bree in the kitchen. "You're up bright and early," she said.

"Thanks to all this snow I can't even think about doing anything outside, so I've had plenty of sleep. Look, I'm almost finished with your numbers. You mind if I head over to Michael's later? I haven't seen him for a few days."

Meg helped herself to coffee and sat down. "You don't have a car at the moment."

"Oh, s—ugar, you're right. Maybe Michael can come get me."

"Or I could take you to Amherst. I was thinking of getting in touch with Gail Selden to see if she could help me with the sampler. And since Seth can't install the furnace until tomorrow, it'll still be cold today and tonight. You don't have to stay here and suffer." Meg swirled the coffee in her cup. "Bree, did you hear anything last night?"

Bree sat down across from Meg, with a plate of scrambled eggs. "Like what?"

"I'm not sure. Footsteps?"

"Nope. You getting spooked? There are plenty of animals around, you know—raccoons, skunks, coyotes. Unless you're thinking maybe this was human?"

Meg shrugged. "I don't know. I might have been imagining things, or maybe it was an animal. Maybe whatever it was, was trying to figure out where he left that dead squirrel."

"Eew. Seth got rid of that, right?"

"He did." He'd even chipped the bloodstained ice and snow off the back steps, which was thoughtful of him. "Well, I'll be glad to get out of the house again."

After breakfast Meg decided it wasn't too early to call Gail. She had kids, didn't she? So she must be used to early days. She tracked down Gail's home number and dialed.

"Gail? Do you have a minute? It's Meg Corey."

"Oh, hi, Meg. Yes, for the first time in days I actually do have a minute. The kids are finally back in school. Another snow day and I think there would have been a murder here. What can I do for you?"

"I found something interesting here in the house, and I'd like you to take a look at it."

"Oh, cool! You going to tell me what it is, or . . . no, I'd rather be surprised. You want to come here? I can give you lunch."

"I'd love to get out, if that's okay. My furnace is dead, and it's a bit chilly here."

"You poor woman! Come over, and I'll heat up some soup. Let me tell you how to get here." Gail outlined instructions, and it turned out that she lived no more than a mile away—if you were a crow. By road it was more like two miles. "Noon work for you?"

"Sounds good. I'll see you then."

Meg debated a moment about whether to bring along the sampler or just the pictures. In the end she decided that Gail should see the real thing. Most likely the materials and the craftsmanship, which the photographs couldn't capture, would help Gail determine something about its origins.

After a few more fruitless stabs at finding anything useful on the Internet, Meg collected the sampler and placed it, carefully padded, in a box. She was afraid to fold or bend it any more than necessary, since she didn't know how brittle it might be.

"You talk to your friend?" Bree asked.

"Yes, we're having lunch. You want a lift now?" When Bree nodded, Meg added, "Why don't I give you a call tomorrow when I hope the furnace will be up and running? Maybe Michael can bring you back."

"Okay. Unless, of course, you and Seth want to celebrate? Might even be warm enough in the house to take off a few layers of clothes. And you can tell him I'll put the tire back on myself, whenever he drops it off."

Meg didn't rise to the bait. "I'll let you know what the plan is, but it's kind of hard to stop him when he wants to help. I must say I'm really looking forward to heat again. Even if the fire is nice, it really isn't very effective at heating the house. Ready when you are."

"Gimme a sec." Bree raced up the back stairs to her room, and returned in under a minute. "Let's go."

Meg picked up her coat and suited up at the back door. When she opened it, she was struck again by how cold it was, even with the bright sunlight glinting off the ice crystals that had formed on the top layer of snow. At this rate the snow would still be sitting here in April. At least her car started without any trouble, and she and Bree headed toward Amherst. The road over the mountain was reasonably clear, thank goodness, and Meg dropped Bree off in the center of town, then turned around and retraced her route, continuing this time to Gail's house, the sampler safely stowed in its box on the floor behind the passenger seat.

Gail's road, in a small residential neighborhood of twentieth-century houses, was still icy in spots. Meg pulled into her driveway, and after collecting the sampler and the notes she had assembled, picked her way carefully to the front door and rang the doorbell. Gail opened it promptly.

"Come in, come in! What a week we've had! I have to

say I was happy to wave good-bye to that school bus this morning. I love my kids, but after a few days of togetherness we were all driving each other crazy. I made lunch, and you can show me your surprise after we eat, okay?"

"Sounds good to me. I hope I'm not intruding."

"No problem. I'm happy to have some adult conversation for a change, and I'd hate to think of you sitting at home in the cold. Will your furnace be fixed soon?" Gail asked as she led the way into her sunny kitchen, where the table was nicely set with place mats and china. "I have tomato soup and grilled cheese sandwiches. Coffee?"

"Sounds good. Actually the furnace has given up the ghost, but I'll be getting a new one tomorrow."

"Handy having a plumber for a neighbor, isn't it?" Gail grinned slyly at her.

"That it is." Meg watched as Gail bustled around the kitchen, doling out coffee. "I thought the roads had been clear for a couple of days. Why'd it take so long for the schools to reopen?"

Gail sat down and ladled soup into bowls. "There aren't enough snowplows to go around. The main roads are clear, but you saw this one—the buses couldn't get through everywhere until today. The kids were happy about it, at least at first. I didn't tell them they'd probably have to make up the time at the end of the school year. So, when did your furnace go out?"

"Right before the storm, naturally, so we've been roughing it for days. Luckily the fireplace works, at least in the short run. Then the power went out in the storm, so we were really down to basics. But I can't complain—the pipes didn't freeze, and I had enough food on hand to manage."

"That's good. You said on the phone that you found something in the house?"

"Yes. We were doing a heavy-duty cleaning to keep warm. At least it kept us moving."

" 'Us'?" Gail arched an eyebrow.

"Yes, Seth and me."

"Was Bree chaperoning?"

"No, she was in Amherst with her boyfriend during the storm."

"I see." Gail giggled. "So things are moving along nicely. With the house, I mean."

"Yes, they are." Meg smiled. "This soup is great, by the way."

"Opened the can myself. Cream of tomato, and grilled cheese sandwiches. Does life get any better?"

"Works for me."

They ate quickly. Gail seemed eager to find out what Meg had brought, and as soon as they had finished, she said, "So what's your surprise? I always love these finds in old houses—and you've had quite some luck already. This should be good."

"Maybe. Can we use your dining room table?"

"Sure."

In the dining room Meg opened the box, withdrew the wrapped bundle, and spread it out carefully on the clean tabletop. She watched with pleasure as Gail's eyes widened.

"Oh, my. This is gorgeous," Gail said, leaning over to study it carefully. "It's dated," she added, almost to herself. "Silk on linen, mainly. Beautifully preserved, though badly wrinkled. Where did you say you found it?"

"Wadded up in the back of a closet."

"Some people have all the luck! I've never seen a sampler with this much detail, at least not up close, and there are some really unusual elements—I think, but I'm not an expert. The girl really tried to fit in everything but the kitchen sink, didn't she?"

"Presumably she wanted to honor her family—all of whom seem to have died by the time she made this."

"Oh, I hadn't noticed that. How awful! Of course she

would've wanted to commemorate them. Do you know anything about the family? And how the sampler got to your house?"

"That's where I was hoping you could help me. I can't find any information about any Coxes in this area, or connected to the Warren family, except for a few vague hints. Of course, I'm still pretty new at this kind of research, but they're not in the simple and obvious places."

"Ah, I see your problem. So you want me to dig around in my local records for Coxes in Granford?"

"If you would. I love how much stuff is available on the Internet, but I know there's a lot that doesn't make it there, or hasn't yet. If you could come up with at least a clue, it would be a big help."

"Sure. I love a challenge. Can I take some pictures of the sampler?"

"I already have some on my computer at home. I can e-mail them to you."

"Great. Ooh, this should be fun!" Gail stopped for a moment, and then grinned. "You know what? I know someone who would love to take a look at this. She's the textile curator at Sturbridge Village. Have you been there yet?"

"No, what is it?"

"It's what you'd call a living history museum, one of the biggest in the country. Back in the twenties, I think, there was this industrialist who started collecting New England memorabilia, and it kind of grew from there. In the thirties he and his family bought the site and started moving or creating the buildings. It opened in 1946. Anyway, the founders pulled together all sorts of old buildings from different places, and then reassembled them to look like a small town. I love the place—they've got farm animals, and crafts, and reenactors. You really ought to check it out. If you're there on a day when there aren't a bunch of school groups, you can almost believe you've stepped into the past."

Meg laughed. "After this past week, I feel like I'm living in another century anyway. But I'll keep it in mind."

"You do that—maybe we could go together. Anyway, Janice Fayerweather is something of a local expert on early needlework, and I'm sure she'd know a lot more than I do. And she'd be over the moon to see a sampler as intricate as this one. Want me to give her a call?"

"Sure, why not? Should I go there, or will she come here?"

"I bet if I send her the pictures, she'll be on your doorstep in hours. This is really a nice piece, Meg."

"Then by all means, get in touch with her. I want to know how it ended up in my hands. Oh, and I promise this won't take time away from your cataloging projects."

Gail waved a hand at her. "Hey, they've been waiting this long, they can wait a little longer. Besides, I think this sampler is much more interesting. It must be nice for you to finally have some downtime. Me, I've got Christmas and the kids to think about. But at least at this time of year people aren't looking for a lot of historical information—except you, of course. Enjoy your free time! It won't be long until the whole apple cycle starts all over again."

"Tell me about it! But I'm still trying to figure out if I've made anything like a profit this year."

"How do you think you did?" Gail asked.

"I really don't know. It's all too new. Bree's working on the numbers, but I don't think her heart is in it."

"She seems like a good kid, though."

"Oh, she is, and she's a hard worker. She just doesn't like paperwork."

"Most of us don't. I've got to finish up the numbers for the Historical Society and get them audited, according to our bylaws. At least I *know* we didn't make any money," she said wryly, "but there's still the accounting for that bequest we got this year, and I have to figure out how to handle that."

"I don't know a lot about small nonprofits—I worked primarily for city and state governments when I was in Boston—but I'll help if I can. Has the estate cleared probate already?"

"It has—it was pretty straightforward, and there was no one to contest it. And I may take you up on that offer to help. I love old records, but my eyes glaze over when I have to sort out modern ones. Oh, shoot, is that the school bus already?"

Meg checked her watch: it was two thirty. "Short school day, isn't it?"

"It certainly is. Of course, most of the sports and after-school activities are cancelled this week. Normally they'd be home later."

"I should go anyway. Thanks for your help, Gail. I'll send you the photos when I get home, and I'll let you know if I find out anything more."

"Cool. I'll see if I can find any other references for you. Hi, kids," Gail greeted her children as they burst in the door. "Boots off—now! Say hi to Ms. Corey, and then wash up and I'll get you a snack."

"Hi, Ms. Corey," they chimed dutifully, and then lost interest in Meg.

"Bye, Gail," Meg said, not sure if anyone heard her.

She drove home carefully, since the roads were still icy in shaded places, and made a detour once again at the market to fill in some missing items. The lot was much emptier this time, although the snow piles hadn't shrunk. Meg tried not to think about what had happened last time she had been there. It was close to four and already getting dark by the time she turned into her own driveway. Meg pulled into the shed and unloaded her bags, then let herself in the back door. After she had tidied up and fed Lolly, she realized that she ought to move the goats inside again. Bree had been taking care of that, but she was gone, and the weather report predicted temperatures in the teens; while the goats didn't seem to have suffered from their daylight romps, it seemed cruel to leave them outside overnight. Besides, there might be coyotes. Or something. She'd rather be safe than sorry.

She slipped on her work boots and pulled on her heavy jacket before heading outside. "Hi, ladies, how're you doing?" she greeted Dorcas and Isabel as she approached the fence. They came over to meet her, and Isabel, the younger of the two goats, put her hooves on the fence and stood up to say hello. "Nice to see you, too. Want to go inside now?"

The goats cocked their heads, curious.

"Well, you're going anyway." Meg went over to the barn and unlocked the padlock on the door nearest the goat pen. No point in opening the big front doors, even if she could, with now-frozen snow piled against them. Inside the door she flipped the switch to turn on the few bare lightbulbs hanging from the rafters, and found the rope leads dangling from a nail next to the door. By now the goats were accustomed to the routine, and they came eagerly when Meg opened the gate to the outdoor pen and stepped in. She looped the leads around their necks and guided them back to the barn, closing the gate behind her. They didn't resist; they knew that dinner would be waiting for them in the barn.

Once inside, Meg pulled the door closed—bad enough that the wind whistled through every crack in the place, without inviting it in. At least the goats had a cozy nook, surrounded by the hay bales. She tucked them into their pen, topped off their water, and poured some feed into their buckets. They dug in happily. Meg latched the gate to the pen securely, then went back to the door, hanging up the leads next to it.

When she pulled on the handle, the door didn't budge. That was odd, since she had come through it only a few minutes earlier. The lock was a basic hasp and padlock, fairly new, and she knew she'd left the open padlock hanging on its hasp outside. She had the key to the padlock in her pocket. But of course, the key was doing her no good inside the building.

She looked around. The barn dated to the middle of the nineteenth century, Seth had guessed, with various patches and additions since, including the most recent, her apple holding chambers. There was more than one door: in addition to the big ones in the front facing the house, there was one on the wall opposite the one she'd used to come in, and she knew Seth had fixed the lock on that one. She walked over to the smaller door. Yes, it was locked, as it should have been. But worse, there were several feet of snow drifted against it, now frozen into place. Ditto with the big front doors. The only door they had cleared since the blizzard was the one closest to the goat pen—the one that didn't seem to be working at the moment, and she had no idea why.

She was trapped in the barn, and it was getting dark fast.

15

Meg wanted to snarl in frustration. She knew she'd left the door unlocked. The best guess she could come up with was that something had fallen against the door while she was inside, wedging it shut. The less appealing alternative was that someone had made a deliberate effort to shut her in the barn. If somebody wanted to harass her, this was going too far. It was cold in the barn, and going to get colder. She rattled the door again, and again it didn't move. She stifled an urge to kick it, knowing it would do no good.

She stalked to the middle of the barn and studied her surroundings. Surely there was a way out of the old building. She knew the big double doors in the front were solidly blocked by snow. Back door: locked, with three feet of frozen snow against it; a single high window, too small to crawl through. Door leading toward the goat pen: no window at all. It was an old-fashioned door that hung on a track, like a traditional barn door, and was made up of solid planks of wood. It was old, but the planks were thick and still solid—too solid for her to batter her way through. That door had been working fine up until a few minutes ago. What had happened?

It was a moot point. But if the doors were no-go, how else could she get out of the barn? There were windows, of course. The problem was, the ones on the ground floor were all blocked, one way or another: the holding chambers had covered up the ones on either side nearest the front, and the ones farther back were either obstructed by equipment that Meg had no way of moving, or had been shuttered to conserve warmth—and the shutters were locked, too, also with padlocks, from the outside. When she had started keeping equipment and her apples in here, she'd made sure that the barn was as secure as possible, and apparently she had done a good job.

There were windows on the eaves at either end, twenty feet over her head. There was no ladder in the barn—the antique one that had led to the hayloft had crumbled away years ago. Even if she could get up there, she'd have no way to get down on the other side. Scratch the windows.

Meg eyed her tractor. Would it be possible to ram it against one or another of the doors until the door buckled, enough to let her slip through? Except the tractor was old and cranky, and Meg was pretty sure the rusted frame would crumple like paper if she ran it into anything. Plus, she had no idea if it would start in this weather—and the key was inside the house.

Think, Meg, think. Unfortunately she didn't like where her thoughts took her. Bree was gone for the night. Seth had said he wasn't planning to come back until tomorrow when he brought the furnace. That was at least twelve hours away. If she had her cell phone she could call someone, but it was back in the house, safe and sound—and useless.

She had electricity; she could flash the lights to attract

attention. Except the barn wasn't visible from the neighbors' houses, and the road out front wasn't very heavily traveled, especially on a cold and icy night like this. No one was likely to notice a light going on and off.

She could set the barn on fire. *Sure, Meg, that's a great idea.* That would attract attention, no doubt, but it might kill her, not to mention the goats, and would certainly make a mess of the barn, which she kind of needed. And she didn't have any matches, and she wasn't sure how she could use electrical wires to start a fire. Another thing her fine education had failed to teach her, along with lock-picking.

So what was she supposed to do? She took inventory: she was wearing a warm coat and gloves. Good. She had water, and, she reminded herself, she had apples: there were a few cases of the varieties that aged well under refrigeration, still stowed in her holding chambers. The biggest problem was going to be the cold, but all she had to do was wait until Seth arrived tomorrow, or Bree came home, whichever came first.

So, how to deal with the cold, without benefit of a heater or a fire?

The answer that came to her made her laugh: the goats. They were coping just fine with the weather. She and Bree and Seth had carefully built them a sheltered corner in the barn, so they wouldn't be subject to drafts. And they were warm-blooded animals who had to be exuding heat, and some of that heat would be captured in their little nook. Now, how could she take advantage of that?

She approached the stall carefully, and leaned over the railing. "Hi, you two." Isabel had been lying down, but she scrambled to her feet, and she and Dorcas approached Meg eagerly. "Sorry, no treats. Maybe an apple later? So, listen, do you mind if I share the pen with you?"

The goats didn't answer, but stared at Meg, their ears flicking back and forth.

"Okay, since you have no objections, let's give this a try." Meg unlatched the stall gate and slipped into the pen, latching it behind her again. It measured maybe fifteen feet square, or had before they'd lined it with hay bales for warmth, which reduced the size. Meg was glad to feel that it was perceptibly warmer inside. The goats watched her, curious. What now? She was reluctant to sit on the floor, even though she knew that Bree had replaced the straw that morning. Still . . . If she rearranged the hay bales a little, she could make herself a bench, with bales to lean against. That could work.

When Meg grabbed a hay bale, the goats backed away, startled, although they couldn't go far. "Don't worry, I'm just doing a little redecorating. I'll settle down soon, I promise." The bale came from the stack that backed against the solid bulk of the storage chambers, and Meg heaved it down to the floor, then repeated that with the one next to it. She'd reduced the floor space, but she now had a seat. Progress.

She sat down. The goats regarded her for a few moments. Then, getting bored, Dorcas turned to help herself to some feed, and Isabel lay down in the opposite corner, keeping an eye on Meg. Meg smiled at them. So far, so good. She was reasonably warm and comfortable. Now all she had to do was wait.

It was a reasonable assumption that a night in the barn wouldn't kill her, but it was bound to make her miserable. Meg pulled her jacket more tightly around herself, crossing her arms over her chest. Dorcas, after some hesitation, curled up next to her feet.

Meg wondered just what was going on. Okay, she'd been living in Granford just shy of a year. It hadn't been an easy one, but she'd made some friends, or at least she thought she had. Had she made enemies? What could she have done that would anger someone enough to inspire a harassment campaign against her? Who stood to gain by annoying her? What did they want?

And why now? Well, maybe it took a little time to get to know her—and to hate her. One of her apple pickers? She couldn't remember any animosity from any of them. Who else was there? She'd been working so hard in recent months that she hadn't had time to see many other people. And yet, here she was, sitting in a freezing barn talking to goats. *If they could see me now*, she hummed to herself. The goats' ears twitched. She smiled at them. If someone was trying to drive her around the bend, apparently they'd made a good start.

It was a long night. Meg dozed on and off, finding it hard to get comfortable on the prickly hay bales. Her hands were cold, and she tucked them under her armpits; the goats were keeping her feet warm, thank goodness. At one point she got up and helped herself to a snack of apples, washed down with some water. The goats barely stirred as she settled herself again. She listened to the barn creak and groan as the temperature dropped, sounding almost like a living thing. There were no sounds from outside, apart from the light wind. At some point she fell into a deeper sleep, under the watchful eyes of the goats.

She was awakened by the sound of a car door slamming. Seth? She felt clumsy, her feet and hands numb, as she extricated herself from the hay, and the goats, fully awake, milled around in front of her as she tried to force her way past them to open the stall gate. Finally she managed and ran to the front doors, pounding on them. "Hello? Anybody there?"

"Meg?" Seth's voice. "What are you doing in there?"

"I couldn't get any of the doors open. Come around to the side and let me out, will you?"

On numb feet she hobbled to the side door and waited impatiently as Seth fumbled with the door. What was taking him so long? She hopped from foot to foot in impatience.

Finally Seth hauled the door open. "How'd you get stuck in there?"

Meg stalked past him, and he followed, after shoving the door shut. She was cold, hungry, and really wanted a bathroom. "I came out to take the goats into the barn. Last night."

Seth hurried to catch up. "What? You've been out here since last night?"

"Yes." She didn't need her keys, since she'd left the back door unlocked last night, assuming she'd be back in a few minutes. If someone had trapped her in the barn, had they taken the opportunity to go into the house? "I left the house open."

"Then I'm going in first." Seth pushed past her and made a quick circuit of the ground floor. "No one here. Come on in." Once inside, he grabbed her arm and swung her around to face him. "Are you all right?"

"I will be, once I pee and get something hot inside me." The concern in his face melted her anger; the stress of the night bubbled to the top, and she found herself fighting tears, which Seth was quick to notice. His arms came around her, and for a few moments he just held her. Finally he said, "Why didn't you call me?"

"No phone," she said against his chest.

"You couldn't get any of the doors open?"

She reared back then to look at him. "What, you think I didn't try? There's snow piled up against the two I don't use, and it's frozen solid."

He didn't let go. "Sorry, of course. Should we worry about frostbite or something?"

"No. The goats kept me warm."

In a perverse way Meg enjoyed the succession of expressions that crossed his face. Surprise, curiosity, and finally, amusement. "You spent the night with the goats?"

"I did. They're warm, and they don't snore. We sort of nested. Listen, can I go freshen up, and then we can discuss this? Because I really want to know how that side door got stuck."

Seth finally let go. "Go! I'll make some coffee."

As she hurried upstairs, Meg noted that the inside of the house wasn't much warmer than the barn. She hoped Seth would have that fixed by the end of the day. She did what she had to do, and picked some straw out of her hair before going downstairs.

Seth had coffee brewing, and he was making oatmeal on the stove. He looked hard at her when she walked in. "You're sure you're all right?"

"Yes, I am. And I am pissed off at whoever did this."

"Did what?" he asked, returning to stirring the pot on the stove.

"Locked me in."

"You weren't locked in," Seth said. "The door was shut but not locked—the padlock was hanging loose on the outside. That pitchfork you use for cleaning out the goat pen was kind of wedged against it. I assumed it had fallen over and gotten stuck."

Meg shut her eyes, trying to recall what she had seen the night before. It had been dark . . . When had that pitchfork last been used? Bree had used it to clean out the pen, as far as she knew. But Meg couldn't remember seeing it anywhere outside the door last night. Wouldn't she have noticed? The handle was light-colored wood, and would have stood out against the weathered barn siding, even in the dim light. "Seth, I don't think it could have. Bree isn't sloppy with tools, so she would have left it in the goat shed, or inside the barn, not outside in the snow. Did you see any footprints this morning?"

"I wasn't looking, and you and Bree have been back and

forth through that door anyway. Meg, what are you saying?" Seth said carefully, dishing up oatmeal and collecting sugar and milk. "Here, eat this while it's hot."

Meg dosed her oatmeal liberally with brown sugar and added milk. "I'm saying that maybe someone knew I was in that barn, and set things up to make it look like a casual accident. Like so many of the things that have been happening lately."

"Like what?"

"Oh, right, you don't know—I told Bree about them." Meg quickly ran through the list she had given Bree—to which she could now add the mysterious jamming of the barn door. "Look, a couple of events I could accept as accidents—but there's been something every day this past week or two. I can't be that unlucky, can I?"

"If you think about probabilities, it does seem unlikely. But I can't see any reason why anyone would want to do this to you."

"Forget about probabilities—there's somebody behind this. But I can't figure out who either! Look, I had plenty of time to think about this last night, and I came up with zip. I don't know of anyone I've ticked off around here. And I don't know why an anonymous stranger would be doing this to me, unless it's some weirdo who gets his kicks by tormenting people he doesn't even know."

"Exactly." Seth thought for a few moments. "Well, assuming there is a person behind this, and not just bad karma, what do you want to do about it?"

"I wish I knew. Setting up surveillance cameras seems a bit ridiculous, and besides, some of these things have happened at other places, like the parking lot at the market. You want to tail me and keep watch? Should I hire a PI? Or a bodyguard? I'll bet there aren't a lot of them in Granford."

Seth's mouth twitched with amusement. "No, there

aren't. Look, I'll stay around as much as you want, or you can come stay at my place."

"I refuse to be driven out of my own home. Even if I did stay with you, who's to say that this person won't just wait until I come back to start up again? And Bree lives here, too. No, I want to get to the bottom of this, not just hope it all goes away."

"You want to go to the police station and talk to Art?"

"I suppose I should, just so there's an official record of this. I assume there's not much he can do, though, since there's not much to go on."

Meg lapsed into silence as she finished the very good oatmeal Seth had made.

"I'm sorry," Seth said softly.

She looked up at him. "For what? This isn't your fault. And you can't exactly protect me 24/7."

"I'm sorry this is happening to you, for whatever reason. You know I'll do anything I can. You want me to set up some bear traps?"

Meg smiled at him. "You have bear traps?"

"No, but I know where I could get some."

"Of course you do. Is there more oatmeal?"

After a second bowl of oatmeal, Meg felt almost normal. "So, what now?"

"I install your furnace, for starters."

She'd forgotten the reason he was there. "Of course! You need any help?"

"Uh, I don't think so. But if you want, you can help me carry it in."

"Whatever you say."

As Seth had predicted, Meg was surprised by how light and manageable the new furnace was. It was hard to imagine that it would really keep her entire house warm. Once Seth was happily settled in the cellar with his tools, Meg went to let the goats out of the barn again. Before going in, she studied the outside door. No marks of any kind, or at least, none that hadn't been there for a long time. Seth had tossed the pitchfork to one side, and she could see on the end of it the scars in the wood where it had caught in the metal tracks for the door. It all looked so innocent; it was so easy to believe that it had simply been in the wrong place, and fallen down at just the right angle . . . No. Her gut said that there was more than that going on. She just didn't know what.

She took a deep breath and went back into the barn to bring out the goats.

16

It was midafternoon before Seth declared the furnace operational. The process had been delayed by the installation of a new thermostat: like everything else in the house, the wiring had been retrofitted, crammed into spaces in a building that had not been planned for such exotic things, and there had been much cursing and muttering as Seth tried to fish wires through serpentine paths in the old walls.

Meg had kept herself busy during the day, mostly online, looking for information on early American needlework. The more she hunted, the more she was impressed by the piece she had found. It was no simple schoolgirl exercise. Rather, it was an elaborate, carefully planned, and beautifully executed work, and Meg was surprised by the skill it showed. Violet had been twelve when she made it—to Meg it seemed incredible work for one so young, especially since she herself had no skill with a needle and felt lucky if she could sew on a button. She smiled, though, as she wondered what young Violet would have made of a modern computer.

Meg had done as much cleaning of the sampler as she dared, given its age and fragility, but it was enough to let her read all the details. What facts did she have? Violet Cox had signed the piece, in silk, in 1798 and she had reason to be proud of her work. Since Meg knew how old Violet had been when she made it, that gave Meg a birth year for her: 1786. What wasn't clear was *where* she had made it. In Granford? It was tempting to look at the white house in the bottom panel and see Meg's own place, but all Colonials looked more or less the same. On close examination Meg had decided that the adjoining small trees, enclosed in a fence, did indeed have little dots that might once have been red, so she thought she was justified in calling them apple trees. But of course, she had learned that the majority of early New England houses had at least a few apple trees, and the other, larger trees flanking the house could be anything. Meg wondered if the tree line had been that close to the house once upon a time, or if that was merely a conventional representation.

Based on the images she had called up online, Meg could say that the mourner was a typical element, but the row of tombstones was more unusual. There was an entire genre of what was known as mourning samplers, including a group of fairly well-known ones made at a school not far from where she sat, in South Hadley, but the images there were larger and most often focused on a group of mourners clustered around a large pedestal topped with an urn, with weeping willows in the background. A sole mourner was less common, and Meg hadn't found any other images of a row of tombstones.

The verse she assumed came from the Bible: it read, "All the increase of thy house shall be cut down in the flower of their age." That was apt, if it referred to all those dead children above it.

And that was where she ran out of facts. She had plenty of questions, starting with, who was Violet Cox? How was she related to the Lampsons? And what was the sampler doing in her house, which had been built and occupied by Warrens? Meg already knew that she'd be disappointed if it turned out to be nothing more than a coincidence, but she was going to do her best to figure out who Violet was and if she was connected to the Warrens.

Finally Seth came back up the cellar stairs and sought Meg out. "I can't exactly hand you a key, but you want to start her up officially?"

"The furnace is a her?"

"You can call it 'her'—or 'it' or whatever you want. Let me show you the thermostat."

"Seth," Meg said impatiently, "I've seen a thermostat before in my life. Just tell me how to turn it on."

"You don't want complete instructions on how to program it for the next seven days?"

"No. I want heat—now!"

"Then push that arrow key. The 'up' one."

Meg complied. She waited a few moments, then said, "I don't hear anything."

"You're not supposed to. It's new, right? That old one of yours sounded like a jet engine taking off. But check the registers."

Meg walked over to the nearest floor grate and stuck her hand out. Yes, there was a steady stream of hot air rising. "Hurray! How do we celebrate warm air?"

"A kiss might be nice. And an offer of dinner. And dessert."

"All your wishes shall be granted. I am positively giddy! The house will be warm again!"

"Give it a few hours and it'll be fine. Of course, you've still got the same leaky windows and no insulation."

"Oh, pooh," Meg said. "Come here."

A few minutes later she said, "If you want dinner you're going to have to let go."

Seth backed away reluctantly. Meg opened the door to

the kitchen, and Lolly ventured out cautiously, sniffing. She sneaked up on the heating grate, and after deciding it didn't pose a threat, she settled herself on top of it, the rising air riffling her fur.

"Smart cat," Meg said. "Okay, I'm going to go figure out dinner. Oh, and I should call Bree and let her know the heat's back on."

"I'll go collect my tools and clean up downstairs." He disappeared down the stairs to the cellar once more. Meg gave her thermostat a final pat and headed for the kitchen. On the way she picked up her phone and called Bree to give her the good news.

When Seth returned, Meg was happily chopping some late pears for dessert. "Do you want something to drink? I feel like christening the furnace with champagne, except I don't have any."

"I'll settle for a beer, if you've got one."

"That I can do." She found a bottle in the back of the refrigerator and handed it to him, then returned to chopping.

After a few moments, Seth said tentatively, "Meg?"

"Yes?" she replied without turning.

"I had time to think about what's been going on here, while I was working."

"Oh?" she said.

"What happened last night, you in the barn—it could have been serious. I'm starting to think that it was a little too convenient that the pitchfork fell just the right way to jam the door."

Exactly what she had thought. "So what do we do about it?" Meg said, turning to face him.

"I don't know. Be careful, for one thing." Before Meg could protest, he held up one hand. "I know, you're already careful, but maybe you need to look harder at things. Have you noticed anyone following you?"

Meg stifled a laugh. "Uh, no, but I can't say I've been

looking. You think whoever it is, is planning all these little annoyances? Or is he just seizing the opportunities when he sees them?"

"I can't say."

Meg considered. "I do know that the incidents have been the kinds of things that are calculated to hit a woman's nerves. You know, those 'things that go bump in the night' that we all worry about when we live alone, whether or not we admit it. Nothing violent, nothing really destructive, but disturbing all the same."

"Maybe your realtor Frances is trying to force you to sell the house so she can get the commission."

"Maybe. The housing market sure has been lousy lately," Meg said.

They were interrupted by the sound of a car pulling into the driveway. A door slammed, and Bree waved at Michael as he pulled away. She hurried in, crowing with delight. "Woo-hoo! It must be sixty degrees in here! It's absolutely tropical!"

"It'll get even better. Seth promises. You and Michael have a good time?"

"Uh, we kept warm. How about you? Oh, is that coffee new or old?"

"Just made it." Meg hesitated a moment, then said, "I spent the night in the barn."

Bree stopped pouring a cup of coffee to stare at her. "Huh? Why?"

"It wasn't my idea. I went out to take the goats into the barn, and somehow the hayfork fell and jammed the door shut. Do you remember the last time you used it?"

"Yesterday morning before I left. I cleaned out the stall inside the barn, and I'm about 98 percent sure I left it inside the barn. I haven't been able to get to the hay in the shed since it snowed, so I wouldn't even need it outside."

"That's kind of what I figured. But that leaves only one other possibility."

"Someone wanted you to stay in the barn all night?"

"You got it."

"Are you okay?"

Meg smiled at her. "Actually, yes. You'd be surprised how much body heat the goats radiate."

"Ha! You jealous, Seth?"

"Of what?" he asked, bewildered.

"You've been replaced by a pair of goats. Female at that. But we can keep you around in case the heat goes out again."

Seth chuckled. "Glad to be of service, ma'am."

Bree sat down at the table. "So, you thinking that somebody's pulling these pranks for a reason?"

"It looks like it, but I have no idea why."

"What're you going to do?"

Much as she hated to make this official, Meg felt she had no choice. "I think it's time to talk to Art."

17

"Do you want to call him, or shall I?" Seth asked.

"I'll do it. This is my problem, not yours." Before Meg could change her mind, she grabbed the handset of the phone and walked into the dining room for privacy. The police chief was in his office, and she was put through quickly.

"Hey, Meg, what's up?" Art Preston asked.

"Hi, Art. Look, I need to talk to you. Do you think you could stop by the house?"

There was an unexpected silence. "Actually, I was already thinking of doing that, on my way home. There are some questions I need to ask you. Are you alone?"

"No, Seth's here, and so's Bree."

"I guess that's all right."

Meg was getting a bad feeling about his reticence. "Art, what's going on?"

"It's complicated. Look, I can be there in about fifteen minutes. Will your problem keep that long?"

"I think so. We'll see you then." She ended the call, feeling bewildered. When she walked back into the kitchen, both Seth and Bree turned to look at her. "He's coming by in fifteen minutes. He said he had planned to come over anyway. Seth, you have any idea what's going on?" Seth shook his head. "Maybe I'm just overreacting, but he sounded kind of funny on the phone. But apparently it's nothing urgent, so we'll just have to wait and see. I think I'll take a shower—I smell like goat."

"And I thought I was being so tactful," Seth said, smiling. "Bree, I brought your tire back. Want to put it back on?"

Meg was clean and dry when Art showed up. He came around to the back door, nodding at Bree, who was laboring over the tire and cursing. Did his back-door entrance mean that it was a friendly visit? Meg wondered. "Coffee?" she offered, once he'd hung up his coat.

"Please." He dropped into a chair at the table, nodding to Seth, who sat down opposite. Meg poured coffee silently, amused by the solemnity of the two men. She set the mugs down and sat between them.

"You want to go first, Art?" Meg began.

"I guess. You remember you came by the station on Monday and told me about that problem you had with your car in the parking lot in Holyoke?"

"Sure. You said not to do anything formal. Have you changed your mind?"

"It's not about that, or at least, not directly. What time did this incident happen?"

"Before lunch? I came straight to your office from there, since it was more or less on the way home."

Art nodded, once. "Did you see anything unusual in the parking lot?"

"No, except the giant mounds of snow." Meg tried to remember the setting, even while she wondered why Art wanted to know. "The parking lot was crowded—I guess a lot of people just wanted to get out of their houses after the storm. Because of all the snow, the cars were parked every which way. It was crowded inside, and I had to wait in line for a while. That's about all I remember. Oh, and when I came out I saw that somebody had slipped and fallen on the snow, but there were plenty of people helping him. What should I have seen?"

Art looked into his coffee, rather than at Meg. "Apparently there was an argument in the parking lot between a man and a woman, about the same time as your fender incident. She stormed off and pulled out in a hurry, and he headed into the store. I had to wonder if maybe one or the other had seen what happened. "

"Was the guy who slipped the same one who was arguing with the woman? Do you know who he is?"

"I do now, because he stopped by the police station in Holyoke yesterday. He's a doctor with a practice in Holyoke. It turns out he did see what happened with your car. He confronted the woman whose car hit yours and asked her what she intended to do about it, and she blew him off and left. He was going to leave you a note on the car, explaining what he'd seen, but that was when he slipped. He racked up his knee—he's close to seventy—so he wasn't able to get around for a couple of days. But he thought it was the right thing to do, to report it. He doesn't live or work in Granford, and he didn't know where you lived, so he reported it to the Holyoke police, which is where the market is. That's why I didn't hear about this immediately—not my jurisdiction. But when I did, I put two and two together. You didn't see any fight?"

"No. Did he need an ambulance?"

"Yes. The store manager brought the guy inside, and just to be on the safe side, he called the EMTs. I guess you left before the ambulance had time to get there."

"I don't remember seeing anything unusual while I was there, but I was pretty focused on getting in and out without smashing someone, for all the good that did me. Does this change anything?"

Art shrugged. "Not really. He didn't get any license plates or anything, so all we know that's new is that it was a woman who hit you, and she didn't feel like sticking around to tell you. It's nothing you can take to your insurance company. I just thought you'd like to know."

"Well, I suppose it was nice of him to try," Meg said. "Thank you for telling me."

"So, what did you want to talk to me about, Meg?" Art asked.

Meg glanced at Seth, then took a deep breath. "I think there's something strange going on here. Heck, maybe that incident in the parking lot is part of it."

He cocked his head at her. "I'm listening."

Meg ran through the list of items that she had outlined before to Bree, trying to keep her tone neutral. She didn't want to come across as a flake, and in any case she thought it was the cumulative list rather than any one incident that was troubling. She ended with the episode in the barn. "What do you think?"

"Ah, Meg, Meg . . . I know you're not the hysterical type, so I'll take you seriously. And I guess I see your point. Individually these events are minor, but taken together I can see why you're upset. When did you say these began?"

"Uh, a week, ten days ago? And there's been something almost every day."

"Did you do anything different right before this? Change anything?"

"Nope. And before you ask, I didn't tick off anyone either. Everything seemed perfectly normal."

Art sat back and contemplated the ceiling. "What do you want me to do, Meg?"

Meg reflected for a moment, then shook her head. "I don't know that I want you to do anything, Art. I guess I just wanted an official record of what may or may not have been going on—just in case someone blows up the house or something."

"Don't even joke about it, Meg," he said. "I wish I could offer you more than sympathy, but that's all I've got. You keeping an eye on things here, Seth?"

"I am. So that's it?"

"Afraid so." Art stood up stiffly. "I'd better be heading home. Let me know if anything else happens, Meg."

"I will."

Seth accompanied him out to his car, and Meg watched through the kitchen window as the two men stood by the police cruiser talking. She couldn't say she felt reassured, but at least he hadn't laughed at her fears.

"Not a lot of help, was he?" Bree said from the doorway.

"When did you come in?" Meg asked.

"Just for the end of it. I didn't think I was eavesdropping."

"Hey, you're as much affected as I am. I don't know what he *can* do," Meg said.

"So now what?"

"We keep a really good lookout anytime either of us goes anywhere. Or stays here alone. Keep your cell phone with you at all times. Hope that we can figure out what this is all about before things get worse. I think what happened last night is definitely an escalation, and I really don't want to know where this person might go from here."

"This is really weird," Bree said. "I don't even want to think about what the next step might be."

Seth came back, stamping his feet on the steps. "So nothing much has changed. Too bad the doctor didn't get a few more details, but he's not young."

"You knew him?" Meg asked, then answered for herself: Seth knew everybody.

"He's treated half the kids in Granford. After my time,

though. But he should have retired a few years ago. I think he just took on a partner or two, to ease his way out. It's hard to attract doctors to Granford."

"That's too bad," Meg said.

"It is that. All right, I'm definitely staying tonight. If whoever it is sees that you're just fine after last night, he could decide to move on to another attack. I'll go home and get Max—at least he'll hear anybody sneaking around in the middle of the night, although he might want to play with whoever it is."

Meg refrained from pointing out that Max wasn't the most dependable of watchdogs. She briefly debated asserting her independence and then rejected the idea. In fact, she'd welcome Seth's company, and even Max's. She was pretty sure she'd sleep better with Seth around. "I'd like that."

"I'll be back in fifteen."

When he'd left, Bree said, "Nice bodyguard, but he can't stick around forever. You've got to find out what's going on."

"Believe me, I'd love to. I don't need something like this to worry about. Speaking about worrying, how're those numbers coming?"

"Almost done. It's looking good. Really!"

"I certainly hope so."

While Seth was gone, Meg threw together a halfhearted dinner of spaghetti with bottled sauce. In half an hour Seth came back with Max, who greeted everyone, including Lolly, as though he hadn't seen them for months. "Should I leave him in the kitchen tonight?"

"Please," Meg said. "I'm sure he'd start chewing on the furniture if we let him have the run of the house while we're upstairs. Just make sure he knows better than to beg at the table." Meg smiled inwardly at the mental image of Max trying to cope with spaghetti.

They carefully avoided any difficult topics over dinner.

Bree disappeared first, leaving Meg and Seth alone at the kitchen table. "You look beat. You want to go up?" Seth said.

"I guess so. I didn't sleep well last night, for obvious reasons."

"I'll check the doors and be up in a couple of minutes, after I settle Max."

"Fine."

Meg couldn't even manage to stay awake until Seth returned.

18

Seth was gone when Meg awoke the next morning. She stretched luxuriantly, and then realized that for the first time in a week the room was warm. She wondered idly how efficient the new furnace was going to be. The house hadn't been built for furnaces, and the ductwork was barely adequate. She'd have to adjust to the new heating patterns of her more efficient furnace. She smiled.

Time to get up; time to face another day. Bree had said the numbers were almost done. Her dragging her heels with the financial summary was beginning to get on Meg's nerves. Was Bree trying to conceal something? Or to let Meg down gently? Was she having trouble confronting the results of her first season as a real manager? Or did she just hate math?

Meg dressed at a leisurely pace, since the room wasn't icy, and ambled down the stairs to find Bree reading the paper and eating her breakfast under Lolly's watchful eye. "Morning," Meg said, as she helped herself to coffee. "Has anything blown up in the rest of the world?"

"Same old, same old," Bree said. "I think the weather is supposed to warm up this week, though. Which means slush and mud."

"I have my trusty muck boots," Meg replied, popping a bagel in the toaster. "Do I have to go out?"

"Not on my account you don't. Just warning you. The goats may get a bit muddy, too."

Meg tried to imagine putting rubber boots on the goats and gave up. Let nature take its course. "Anything else on the agenda?"

"You mean, like your numbers? I'm on it. Today, or maybe tomorrow, I promise. You doing anything about Christmas?"

"I've been trying to ignore it. I'm not going anywhere, and I'd kind of like to spend my first Christmas in my house here. Especially now that I have a working furnace. How about you? Are you going to see your parents anytime soon?"

Bree shrugged. "Maybe in the spring. We aren't real close. I'll probably visit my auntie for the holiday. And spend some time with Michael."

"That sounds nice," Meg said. "Of course, you're both welcome here. I'm sure we could put together some kind of Christmas dinner. Are you finished with the front section?" Bree handed her part of the newspaper, and they sat in companionable silence as they finished breakfast. The tranquility was broken when the phone rang, and Meg went to answer it.

"Hey, Meg," Gail said. "I've got something for you!" Her voice was gleeful.

"That was fast. What did you find?"

"I checked the Granford Vital Records and the town records. No sign of any Coxes born here, but I did find a marriage for Violet Cox in 1805, which would be after she made that sampler of yours."

"Great! At least we know she was here. But where was she born?" Meg asked.

"I've just gotten started. And—drumroll, please—my curator friend is drooling at the prospect of seeing your treasure. Can we get together?"

"Sure—do you want to do lunch again?"

"Sounds good. And if I call Janice now, I'm pretty sure she can join us. In fact, once she saw the pictures I forwarded, she was ready to show up immediately. Why don't we meet at Gran's? Noon?"

"Perfect. See you there."

Noon found Meg waiting in the parking lot next to Gran's restaurant on the green in town. Since she'd been instrumental in bringing the restaurant to Granford, and was in a small way a shareholder, she felt incredibly proud of it, and of Nicky and Brian Czarnecki, its two young owners. Nicky was a great cook, and her husband Brian managed everything else. In addition, they'd hired several people from Granford to work there, which had further endeared them to the town. They served local food, creatively prepared, and they kept their prices affordable. All in all, it was no surprise that the restaurant appeared to be doing a brisk business, even during the week, which pleased her—and no doubt thrilled Nicky and Brian. They'd been open three months now and had made a profit each month so far. Nicky had been excited when Meg called to say that she wanted to bring a couple of guests—and why.

Gail pulled in a few minutes later. "Hi, Meg! Is Janice here yet?"

"Beats me. I don't know what she looks like."

"Oh, right. Well, why don't we go inside and keep warm? And I can start filling you in on the family history part, at least, which she doesn't care much about anyway."

"Sounds good to me. I'm amazed that you put anything together so fast. Do you know everything there is to know about Granford and its history?"

Gail laughed. "Not hardly. My family's only been here six or eight generations, while your Warrens go back to the sixteen hundreds. But I like puzzles, and this one's interesting."

They walked into the restaurant and waved to Nicky, busy with some other customers. Sitting down, Gail added, "Plus I love that sampler of yours. You wouldn't consider donating it to the Historical Society?" she asked wistfully.

"I have no idea what I'm going to do with it yet," Meg hedged. "It's pretty delicate." Much as she was fond of the place, Granford's Historical Society still had quite a ways to go before making a safe environment for anything fragile.

"Well, maybe we can find it a good home, if you don't want to keep it. Let's go ahead and order while we wait for Janice. She won't mind, and I'm starving. When I've got to get the kids off in the morning, I don't always get breakfast."

Nicky made her way over to their table. "Hi, Nicky," Meg said. "Looks like business is good."

Nicky beamed at her. "It is! We've been run off our feet from Day One, but it's a great feeling. And I've come up with some amazing new recipes. Did your folks enjoy their meal when they were visiting, Meg?"

"They did, and they're picky, so that's high praise. We're expecting one more person, but we couldn't wait to eat."

"I'll send a waitress over, and I'll keep an eye out for your friend. Good to see you, Meg. And you, too, Gail—I loved that old cookbook you found for me."

"I hope you can get something useful out of it. Oh, by the way, I'm including it, and how you're using it, in our quarterly newsletter."

"Ooh, free publicity! I love it. Enjoy your lunch!" Nicky hurried back to the kitchen.

Meg sighed. "I don't know where she gets the energy She's on her feet all day, and she never slows down. So, where were we?"

Their waitress, a middle-aged woman with a weary face

and no makeup, walked over. Gail greeted her by name. "Hi, Donna. How've you been?"

"'Bout the same. You two ready to order?"

"I think so. Meg, have you met Donna Taylor? She lives about half a mile down the road from you."

"I don't think I have," Meg said. "I haven't met a lot of my neighbors, I've been so busy until now. It's nice to meet you, Donna."

"Yeah. You're at the old Warren place—nice house you've got."

"Thank you. Wait—are you John's mother? I just met him the other day."

"Yeah," Donna said ungraciously. "What you want for lunch?"

Sandwiches and drinks requested, Gail pulled a folder out of her bag and started laying papers out across the table.

"What've you got for me, Gail?" Meg said impatiently.

"I'm getting there, and I think you'll be happy. So, we started with a name for the girl—Violet Cox—and the date on the sampler, 1798, and a register with some other people, presumably family members, right? And the piece was found here in Granford, in a house built by the Warrens and continuously occupied by them until a couple of decades ago. So either that was a cosmic coincidence, which would be no fun at all, or there's some connection to the Warren family. Right?"

"That's what I've been hoping for." Meg nodded.

"Now, you know who lived in your house in 1800, right?"

"Eli Warren senior," Meg said promptly.

"Right, and then his son Eli after him."

Meg nodded. "The first Eli was the grandson of the original owner, Stephen Warren. But all that line stayed right here in Granford, and I couldn't find any Coxes in the bunch. What does this have to do with the sampler?"

"Patience, Meg. Stephen the builder had two sons: Stephen junior, who was Eli's father, and Eleazer. Stephen's descendants stayed right here, as you know. Eleazer did, too. But he had six kids, and they *didn't* all stay. They were all born here, but then four of them don't appear again in the records." When Meg tried to interrupt, Gail plowed on. "But! There's a note in the town records that three of the sons and a daughter all removed to Pittsford, Vermont."

"What? Why? When?" Meg sputtered.

"Looks like the 1780s. As I keep telling you, the records are kind of patchy for that period, and I'm surprised I found even that much. But it was a small town then, so I guess the departure of three able-bodied men made a difference. Oh, hang on," Gail said, when Donna reappeared with their food.

She and Meg tucked into their meals, and after Gail had made half her sandwich disappear, Meg said, "So you're telling me I need to look at Vermont records?"

"Yup. I warn you, you're already getting spoiled, working on Massachusetts families. For other states there's still a lot of stuff that isn't available online. You're going to have to do some digging, maybe even head up to Pittsford."

"So you don't have a clue how and why Violet, or at least her sampler, ended up in my house?"

"You're in luck. I can't tell you the why, but I can prove that Eli Warren took her in, in 1796."

"What?" Meg couldn't believe the twists and turns this story was taking. "How on earth would you know that? The census is no help—it lists only heads of household at that point."

"It's in the Granford town records, believe it or not. The selectmen had to vote funds to cover the annual expenses for Violet Cox, payable to Eli, until she came of age or married, whichever came first. Eli petitioned for the money. Kind of a cheapskate, since he had only two kids of his own, and a house with plenty of room. To be fair, at least

Eli sent Violet to a nice school, which is presumably where she learned needlework. Maybe that's what the money went for—school fees are mentioned in the town minutes. That's as far as I've gotten, but I wanted to leave something for you to do. Isn't that half the fun? I haven't had time to track down the details of Violet's marriage yet—assuming she stayed around and married someone in Granford—but I haven't given up. Here's what I've got so far." Gail handed her photocopies of what Meg recognized as pages from the town's records.

"You've done an incredible job, Gail, in a very short time. It would have taken me a lot longer to get this far on my own."

"Well, I've got the original documents to work with—that helps. And you can see that you never would have found this on your own, because it's not published, in any way, shape, or form. That's why I have this job—that, and the thrill of the hunt."

"I can't thank you enough. I wonder why the sampler ended up jammed in the back of a closet?"

"That I can't tell you—you may never know. Maybe the old aunts your mother inherited from just kept stuff in front of the closet and never looked in the back. Nor did any of your renters, apparently."

Meg giggled. "So nobody cleaned out that closet for over a hundred years? That makes me feel a lot better!"

"Heck, the Warren ladies might not even have known it was there, or that it existed. It looks like Violet died about ten years before the elder Warren sister was born."

"Complicated, isn't it? I still need to know why Violet ended up here, and why she has a different surname. Oh, did I tell you that I finally have a new furnace?"

"Congratulations! I'm sure you really appreciate it now."

"Believe me, I do. Thanks so much for your help on this, Gail. It's one of those things that would have nagged at me. I guess I've got the genealogist's itch."

"There's no known cure for that, you know. Ah, here she is at last!" Gail waved at a woman who was headed for their table in a rush.

"Sorry, sorry—I got delayed. Hi, I'm Janice Fayerweather. And you must be Meg Corey?"

"Yes, I am."

"Sorry, we went ahead and ate without you, Janice," Gail said, "but I've got to get home in time to meet the school bus."

"No problem." Janice turned to Meg. "Gail says you've got something juicy for me to look at." Donna appeared and waited, pad at the ready. "What's good here?"

"Everything. But the sandwich special today is great," Meg said.

"I'll go with that. And coffee, please," Janice said. When Donna retreated to the kitchen, Janice said, "I guess we should eat before looking at the piece."

Gail glanced at her watch. "Oh, shoot—I've got to run. Listen, you two have fun, and I want a full report."

"Of course. I'll get the check," Meg volunteered.

"I won't argue. Good to see you, Meg! Janice, I wish we had more time. Maybe I can drag Meg over to your place one day and we'll have lunch there."

"Always good to see you, Gail, even if only for a second. We'll do that."

Gail collected her winter coat and scarf, gloves, and hat and bustled out the door, leaving Meg and Janice at the table. Janice's food appeared promptly, and she gave it the attention it deserved, but not before asking, "So, how do you know Gail?"

Meg's story of her arrival in Granford took them through the rest of the meal. When Janice had drained her cup one last time, she looked around at the now-empty restaurant. "You think they'd let us use a table so we can spread out the sampler?"

"I'm sure they will," Meg said. When Donna appeared

to clear off their plates, Meg explained what they wanted, and in short order a table near the window had been wiped down for them. Janice took another napkin and made sure it was really clean and dry.

Then she turned to Meg, with an eager gleam in her eye. "Okay, let me see it."

19

Meg retrieved the sampler and unrolled it carefully, laying it down on the table. Janice stalked around it, viewing it from all sides, mumbling to herself. "Silk on linen . . . good condition . . . interesting combination of motifs . . ." Meg watched, amused and intrigued.

Finally Janice straightened up and looked at Meg. "This is really special. How do you come to have it?"

"I found it in the back of a closet in a house my mother inherited, where I'm living now. From what Gail tells me, and what I've found doing my own family research, I think the girl who made it could be a relative, but that's about all I know. I don't know anything about samplers, beyond what I've looked up online since I found it. What can you tell me about it?"

"I think we need to sit down again."

"There's nowhere else you have to be?"

Janice laughed. "There are six other places I should be, but this is a lot more fun. It's not often something as good as this comes along. What do you know about needlework, Meg?" she asked.

"I think 'nothing' about sums it up."

"Okay, I'll start at the beginning. Fancy needlework was a pursuit of young girls who attended schools in New England, and the early nineteenth century was the heyday. There were several noteworthy schools not far from here, in Northampton and South Hadley, although I don't think your example comes from either of them. Did the maker come from around here?"

"I haven't done all the research yet," Meg said. "Were these samplers done for any particular purpose?"

"To show off the young ladies' talents, for one," Janice replied promptly. "Even in this one you can see the variety of stitches—this girl was good. And family registers were popular. They were often hung in the parlor, for public viewing, as were mourning samplers. Which, of course, means a lot of them didn't survive—sunlight is murder on needlework. Not only do the colors fade, but the materials literally can disintegrate. You said you found this in a closet? Any idea how long it had been there?"

Meg shook her head. "None. Apparently Violet was in Granford before 1800, and she lived in the house, probably until she married, so that's the most likely time frame. You're saying that being in the closet helped preserve it?"

"I'd say so. As I mentioned, there are various types of sampler. The family register form is obvious—it lists the births and deaths within one family, and sometimes, but not always, marriages. You see a lot of them that someone has started with all the births, but they never get around to filling in the rest of the dates. The top section of this sampler is a family register, but it looks as though they all died out—well, except for the young woman who made it. So this sampler is kind of a hybrid—it combines the family register with the mourning imagery. Poor Violet—she must be that sole mourner by the tombstone there. Do you know anything about the family?"

"I only found it a few days ago," Meg admitted. "Gail just filled me in on a lot of it. It's likely that Violet's mother came from Granford here, and then moved to Vermont, and that's where Violet and presumably the other children were born. Those may have been from a second marriage."

"You know, the mourning component here is really interesting. There are a lot of examples of mourning samplers, but in general the iconography is pretty standardized." When Meg looked puzzled, Janice said, "The symbolism. You're probably familiar with it without even knowing it—the tombstone or a large monument with an urn on top, combined with one or more weeping willow trees, and varying numbers of mourners drooping all over each other. I've only seen a few that incorporate individual tombstones, and this one is even more intriguing because these appear to be actual stones, rather than just a row of generic ones—you can see they're all different."

"I read about the symbolism online, but I hadn't realized that tombstones were so rare in samplers. You think I could actually find the stones?" Meg asked.

"It's possible, if you know where to look. Now, as for the rest . . ." Janice walked around the sampler again, then pulled out a magnifier. "This is really unusually fine. Incredible detail. If you look closely, you can even see apples on the trees, although they've faded a bit."

"I thought that's what they were! Could it have been made based on my house? It's a pretty standard Colonial, but the profile of that side addition looks right, and I do have an orchard near the house."

Janice shrugged. "Maybe. Remember, a lot of Colonial houses follow the same pattern, and back around 1800 everyone had an orchard, so that's not significant. But I will say that a lot of samplers incorporate houses, and often we can link the image to a particular family home, so I wouldn't rule it out. Now, take a look at the border here." She beckoned Meg closer. "This is unusually delicate and precise—see the leaves and the stamens? On the other hand, some of these flowers look almost geometric rather than organic. Of course, often these are just standardized motifs, rather than representations of anything specific. Still, it's unusual. I wonder if we could match it up with any local plants . . . looks like a vine with four-petaled flowers, and they're two different colors, maybe pink and white. I could ask a botanist who specializes in regional plants."

"You mean, that might tell you *where* it was made?" Meg asked.

"It's a long shot, but you never know."

Nicky came out from the kitchen. "Meg, you're still here! You want more coffee or something?"

Meg glanced at Janice, who shook her head. "I think we're good. This is Janice Fayerweather—Gail asked her to look at this sampler that I found in my house. Janice, this is Nicky Czarnecki, the chef-owner here." Meg pointed to the adjoining table. "Check this out, Nicky."

Nicky walked over to the other table and leaned over it to peer at the sampler. "Nice. Hey, is this your house, Meg? It has a building attached, that could be Seth's workshop."

"I've wondered about that, but it's hard to prove."

Nicky straightened up. "Well, I'll let you get back to it. Was lunch all right?"

"Terrific, as usual," Meg replied. "Thanks. See you later!"

After Nicky had disappeared back into the kitchen, Janice picked up where they had left off. "As I said, some schools can be identified based on their style, but this one's not familiar to me. I can do a little more digging, if you like—I don't claim to know everything!" She laughed. "What do you plan to do with it?"

"I haven't really thought that far. I was just trying to

figure out why it ended up in my house. Should I be worried about conservation?"

"Always," Janice said, then smiled. "You were lucky—it was protected from direct sunlight and damp, both of which can have devastating effects. So it's in good shape, all things considered. That's a start. There are a few spots on it that could use some attention, and I'd recommend a professional cleaning. Note that I say 'professional'—don't you dare try to wash it yourself, or I'll come back and strangle you with whatever's left of it."

Meg laughed in return. "Don't worry, I wouldn't dream of it. What about longer-term storage?"

Janice sighed. "I know most people want to slap it in a frame and hang it on the wall, but I wish you wouldn't. If you want it to last, it should be stored in an acid-free box with acid-free paper, and kept in a dry place. OSV'd be happy to take it off your hands," she finished wistfully.

Did she want it to be available to the public, in a collection like Old Sturbridge Village's? Meg wasn't sure. At the same time, it seemed selfish to keep it. But she didn't have to decide immediately, and she wanted to know if it had any family connections before she made any decision. "I'll keep that in mind. If I were to sell it, what do you think it would be worth?"

Janice looked disappointed. "I hate to talk about money. It depends on the condition and quality of the piece, the reputation of the auctioneers, if you go that route, the timing of the sale, the general economy, what's hot that week, and probably sunspots, for all I know. And if you know the history of the maker, it helps. The best I can tell you is, probably five figures, but low or high, I just don't know."

"Wow, that's more than I expected. I know that on *Antiques Roadshow* the owner always says something dumb like, 'It's a family piece—I wouldn't think of selling it.' I always thought that sounded fake—I figured the minute the cameras were off they asked the appraiser what he would offer. I'm just kind of intrigued by it."

Janice gave the sampler one last longing look. "Well, if you do decide to sell, will you at least let me know? It's a real beauty, and I'd love to have it for our collection. Why don't you come by the Village sometime and I can show you some of our other samplers? It might give you a better appreciation of what you have here."

"I'd love to. If you could recommend some good books or other resources on the subject, too, I'd appreciate it."

"Sure, no problem. Can I e-mail the references? And I've got the photos of it that Gail sent on, so I'll keep looking, too. I must say those photos didn't convey the quality of the work. It's a delightful piece, and I envy you. Well, I need to get back. Thanks for letting me see it."

"Thanks for making the trip, Janice. You've given me a lot of information in a very short time, and I appreciate it."

"Thanks for the opportunity to see it, and for the lunch! I'll be in touch." Janice gathered up her things and headed for the door. Meg took another look at the sampler, seeing it with fresh eyes. She'd known it contained a lot of detail, but the messages of "mourning" and "family" came through loud and clear. With some reluctance she carefully rolled it up in its towel. If it had survived in such good shape for two hundred years, she'd never forgive herself if she allowed any harm to come to it now.

When she arrived home after lunch she found Seth standing in the driveway talking to John Taylor.

"Where've you been?" Seth asked, his tone worried, when Meg approached them.

"I had lunch with Gail's friend from Sturbridge Village—she told me great stuff about the sampler. I'm sorry, was I supposed to report to you? Bree knew where I was going." She stopped suddenly and thought about what she had just said: she sounded rude. Maybe she was more distracted by recent events than she wanted to admit. "I'm sorry, I didn't mean to snap at you. I didn't stop to think that you might worry."

"And I'm sorry if I jumped on you—Bree wasn't here when I arrived, and I didn't know where to find you."

"I'm sorry—I wasn't thinking." She turned to John, who looked embarrassed by the exchange he had just witnessed. "Hi, John. Thanks for plowing the driveway. I just met your mother, at Gran's."

"Yeah, she's been working days there since it opened. Nice place. Seth, I'd better get going. Let me know when you need me. Nice to see you again, Meg." He climbed into his ageing pickup and pulled out onto the road.

Meg turned back to Seth. "You actually have jobs at the moment? The town or your business?"

"I do. That blizzard, combined with the melting that's going on now, has revealed a whole lot of structural problems to people. If we get a wet spring, I'll bet there's a run on French drain installations."

"If you say so," Meg said dubiously. "Is it supposed to be wet?"

"How should I know? You're the farmer—you tell me."

"Ha. You'd do better to ask Bree. I'm going to go inside and try to write down what I learned today about the sampler, and see if I can find a trail of my own there. Gail's been a tremendous help—she gave me some great leads on how to find out who the people in it are."

"Is there a Warren connection?"

"It looks like it, but I've got some more work to do. And I do want to keep Gail happy—why do you think I volunteered to do that cataloguing for the Historical Society? I can see that there isn't time enough in the world to upload to the Web all the information that exists, stuffed in boxes in old societies like the one here. Which means we see the barest outlines of our history, and a few tantalizing hints, but not all the wonderful details that make it human, and more real to us. Gail's lucky to have access to some of that for Granford. When you have time, I'll tell you about the sampler and how it connects to the Warrens here."

"Over dinner?" Seth looked hopeful.

"Sure, no problem. After I get done on the computer."

Meg threw together a hurried dinner. Seth's greeting earlier had startled her: she didn't expect to have to account for her whereabouts, even to him. Nor did she like the feeling that she was looking over her shoulder all the time, waiting for the next incident, not knowing what it would be or what direction it would come from. And it was absurd: she'd moved from a big city where violence was an expected part of daily life, to the peaceful countryside where she had mistakenly thought she was safe.

Bree called to say she was still at Michael's and planned to stay the night. While dinner was simmering, Meg seized a moment to check maps on the computer. Pittsford, Vermont, wasn't that far away. According to the town's Web site, there was a Pittsford historical society; when she clicked on that link, she got the impression that it was small, and there was little said about local records. Worse, the Web site said it was closed between November and April, and open only limited hours the rest of the year. Meg sighed. Some part of the answer lay in Pittsford, but she wasn't sure how she could find it, or when.

She spent some time online trolling for historic information about Pittsford, and she was still mulling over her options at dinner, when Seth broke into her thoughts. "Earth to Meg?"

"Huh? Oh, did you say something?"

"I just wanted to know if you were still in there. No aftereffects from your night in the barn?"

"Not even a sniffle. I was thinking about the information Gail gave me today, and trying to figure out how I can see if there's any relevant information in Pittsford, Vermont."

"You've lost me," Seth said.

"Oh, sorry—I haven't told you about it yet. At lunch

today Gail told me that there was a mention in the Granford records that a bunch of the local Warrens packed up and headed for Vermont as a group. Since one of them was a daughter, it's possible she married a Cox up there. And if he died after Violet was born, mom could have remarried. At least, that's the most likely scenario I can think of. Then we know from the sampler that they died in 1795, and there's another town record that says that Eli Warren took her in—and then asked the town for money. So that puts her in Granford about the time she made the sampler. Anyway, that reinforces the idea of the Warren connection, or why else would he have done that?"

"Makes sense to me. And there's more you want to know?"

"Well, actually, yes. So let's say that Violet made the sampler in honor of her mother's second family—the children listed must have been half brothers and sisters. And then everyone in the family died, and poor Violet got shipped down here to her Uncle Eli, which is how the sampler ended up in this house, most likely. We can prove that she was here. But she must have had uncles in Pittsford—why did they send her away?"

"And you think you can find an answer to this?"

Meg laughed ruefully. "Maybe that's too much to ask. But at the very least I could check the vital records in Pittsford—which aren't online. Shoot, I don't know what to do. I want an answer *now*, but it's a long drive, and the historical society there won't even be open until spring, and there's no guarantee they'll have anything useful anyway. But by spring I won't have time to do this kind of research."

"Is there a library in Pittsford?"

"Yes, of course. I was looking at the town's Web site—you know, it looks a whole lot like Granford."

"Is the library open on Saturday? If so, we could take a road trip tomorrow."

Meg grinned at him. "Let me check!" She went back to her computer and pulled up the town's Web site and then the library's, which mentioned a local history collection. Miracle of miracles, the library was in fact open on Saturdays—that would be tomorrow. Maybe there wasn't much else to do in Vermont in winter than read, unless you were into skiing? When she returned to the kitchen, Seth had half finished washing the dishes. "You don't have to do that. And, yes, the library is open tomorrow, noon to four. We can be there by lunch. But don't you have other things you need to do?"

"Nothing that can't wait. Besides, it's a good idea to get out now and then. I'll even drive—I've got four-wheel drive, and I'm more used to snow than you are. And I can guarantee you there will be snow in Vermont."

Meg wrapped her arms around him. "Thank you! I hate leaving things like this unresolved, and maybe getting out of town for a day will discourage my stalker person."

"Let's hope so."

20

They set off early the next morning. It was a blindingly beautiful New England day, the snow still pristine, save for a few animal tracks, the sky an intense and unmarred blue. Meg felt like she'd fallen into a holiday card.

She had dutifully called and left Bree a message on her cell phone, telling her where she'd be and indicating that she planned to be back the same day, but to please feed the goats and Lolly if she was late. She wasn't used to being accountable to people. Seth had called her on it, the day before, and he was right—she should have let him know, given what had been going on lately. It felt odd having someone looking out for her. But nice.

"So, where do we go?" Meg asked, once they were on the road.

"Almost due north. We follow I-91 for a while—that road runs all the way to the Canadian border. Then we veer west a bit to get to Pittsford. We should be there in under three hours. You impatient?"

"A bit. As a kid, my folks and I used to go to the shore, and even though I think it's about half the distance of this trip, it seemed like it took forever."

"We never got into the whole beach thing. Or family vacations, for that matter. You want music?"

"Depends on what you call music."

"So that's the way it is? Take a look at my CDs. Or we can talk. What is it that you're hoping to find up there in Pittsford, anyway?"

"Well, original documents that prove that Violet's mother was a Warren, for a start. And then there's something about the sampler that troubles me—all those babies dying, and then the parents, and then Violet is sent to live with someone she probably hadn't even met, when there was family nearby. Something just seems off. I'd like to know something more about the Coxes and the Lampsons. I guess I'm saying, even if there was some awful event, I'd rather know than not know. If there's any way to find out."

"Fair enough. So, we have limited time at this library, and there's no guarantee that whoever is there is knowledgeable about what you're looking for. Let's focus. What specifically do you want to know?"

"Well, I'd like to know more about the settlement of the town of Pittsford, and why the Warrens left what seemed like a decent existence in Granford to try out somewhere new. From what I can tell, the town of Pittsford hadn't existed all that long when they arrived."

"You find people in New England did that a lot back then. Hard to say whether they felt cramped, or bored, or they thought the next big thing was right over the horizon. Bunch of optimists, don't you think?"

"The men, maybe. Of course, they left all the packing and hauling stuff—not to mention taking care of the kids—to the women, who had little choice but to follow. Hubby goes haring off with his pals, looking for adventure, and Wifey trails along trying to keep the family fed and clean and healthy. To go back to your question, I'd guess that at the very least the library will have copies of whatever town histories exist. If I'm lucky they may have a genealogy section with the vital records. Or they can tell me what the historical society has and if it's worth it for me to make a second trip in the spring. And if the snow isn't six feet deep, we can go check out the local cemetery."

"I love your idea of a good time. At least you're a cheap date."

"Hey, you offered to drive."

They bantered happily for the rest of the trip, pulling into Pittsford around eleven. Meg had read the bare description of the town online, but seeing it brought home to her how much it resembled Granford, and probably hundreds of other old New England towns. Several roads converged in the center around a small green, with—no surprise—a large white church at one end. She wasn't surprised to find the library close to the green as well, along with the post office and a small town hall.

"Not much to see, is there? I hope this isn't a total waste of time," Meg said.

"Nothing ventured, nothing gained. You want to eat lunch first?"

"Sounds good to me. And I'm not picky—not that there's much to choose from."

They were lucky to find a shabby diner not far from the center of town and ate something forgettable. Meg kept one eye on the clock, conscious of the passage of minutes. Would the library actually be open? Should she have called ahead? But she couldn't have—they'd hatched this plan late yesterday, and left before the library opened today. But even if it was open, would there be anyone there who knew anything?

After lunch they drove back to the library and parked in the small lot. There were a few cars there already, and Meg felt a spurt of relief. She shoved the folder with her genealogy notes into her bag, then climbed out of Seth's car and beat him to the front door. "Twelve-o-three. Here we go!" Meg pulled open the door, and Seth followed.

She approached the central—and only—desk, heartened to see that there was a competent-looking adult woman rather than a high-school fill-in behind the desk. The woman looked up, as if surprised to see a patron. The only other people in the building appeared to be a couple of teenagers working on homework. *That would have been me in high school*, Meg reflected wryly, *hard at work in the library on a weekend.* "Can I help you?" the woman asked.

"I hope so," Meg said. "I'm looking for information about some of the families that lived in Pittsford just before 1800, and I was hoping that you'd have some town records here. I know there's a historical society, but I understand they're not open at the moment. I only got started on this search recently, so I haven't had time to contact anyone there. Do you have a local history section in the library here?"

The woman smiled. "We do, and I guess you'd have to say we share the records with the historical society. We have better storage facilities than they do, but they retain title—it's a legal thing. So you want history of the founding and the early landowners?"

"Yes, that sounds good. Are there church and municipal records?"

"Some. Record keeping was a bit spotty, early on, and like almost anywhere else there was at least one fire, so some records are gone. We have them on microfiche, if you know how to use that. I'll be happy to show you what we've got. What names are you looking for?"

"Warren and Cox, mainly, specifically a marriage between a Unity Warren and a man with the last name Cox. I'm descended from the Warren family, the branch that stayed in Massachusetts. And anything for a Jacob Lampson, too."

"Plenty of Warrens and Coxes around here. Lampson, Lampson . . . why does that name ring a bell? Anyway, why don't you let me show you our local history books, and I'll dig around in the paper files and the microfiches and see what I can find. It'll save you time." She led them to a small room at the back of the building. Its walls were lined with bookcases, and there were a couple of freestanding ones as well, which left little room for a battered oak worktable and a few chairs. "Make yourselves comfortable. I'll let you orient yourselves, and I'll be back in a bit."

After she'd left, Seth turned to Meg. "That's a good start. What do you want me to do?"

"Let's divvy up the published histories and see what we can come up with. We're looking for any mentions of Warrens and Coxes, plus information on the people who settled the town and the ones who came after them, up to 1800."

"I'm on it."

They pulled out a series of books, all but emptying a couple of shelves, and sat down to begin reading. Many of the books had been written in the later nineteenth century, and the language was rather effusive, but Meg quickly found that they provided a wealth of detail, often quite personal. She wondered how accurate the information was in those that didn't cite sources. On the one hand, the writer no doubt had direct anecdotal knowledge of the community; on the other hand, if he was writing the history late in life, his memories might have faded a bit. Still, it was valuable information, and Meg figured if she assembled enough bits and pieces, she might be able to put together a fuller picture.

More than an hour had passed before the librarian reappeared, holding several grimy manila folders and a short stack of printouts. She looked very pleased with herself. "I've got at least some of what you're looking for here."

"Oh, please, sit down. And I didn't even ask your name. I'm Meg Corey, and this is Seth Chapin. And you are?"

She sat. "Mercy Cooper. Nice to meet you. Anyway, the bare outline is this, based on what I've found in the town records: there were several Warrens who all moved here about the same time, in the 1780s. They weren't the original founders, but sort of a second wave—the Coxes were already here, part of the first wave. Even then it wasn't a very big town—maybe three hundred people? And they all married each other."

Meg laughed. "Wow, that's funny. Makes you wonder what the weddings would have been like, doesn't it? So you're saying there were four Warrens, and they all married Cox siblings, right?"

"Exactly. It was John Cox who married Unity Warren in 1785, and they had one child, Violet Cox, born the next year. Then John died, and Unity married Jacob Lampson in 1787, and they had four children, in short order. And then the kids all died young, and both parents died not long after the last child of theirs, within a couple of weeks of each other in 1795. That's the skeleton, if you'll pardon the pun."

"So daughter Violet was orphaned in 1795?"

"That's right," Mercy said.

"That's where I can pick up the story," Meg said. "She ended up living with her uncle Eli Warren in Granford, Massachusetts. I own that house now, and I found in a closet a sampler that she made after she arrived—it's dated 1798. It includes a family register and even images of what I'm guessing are the family tombstones. I wanted to know how it ended up in Granford, in my house. The head of the historical society back in Granford gave me a good deal of information from the Granford side, but it's great to have it corroborated through local records here. But that still leaves me with one big question. If all this happened in Pittsford, and Violet had plenty of relatives here, why did she end up in Granford?"

"That I can't tell you, but I'll see what I can find," Mercy said. "Could you send me a picture of the sampler? It would make a great addition to our records—maybe we could get a follow-up article in the local paper. Or at least the library newsletter."

"I'd be delighted, if you'll return the favor and send me anything else you come across. May I keep these copies?" Meg waved the slender sheaf of printouts that Mercy had given her.

"Sure—let's call it two bucks, at five cents a page. And I'll keep digging—I know there's something odd about the Lampsons, and it's going to annoy me until I remember what it is."

Meg looked at her watch, and then out the window. How much light was left in the day? "Are the Lampsons buried near here?"

"You want to see the tombstones? Yes, they should be right down the block."

Meg glanced at Seth. "Do you mind?" When he shrugged, she turned back to Mercy. "Thank you so much! I'm sorry we can't spend more time here, but I hope I can come back again. I really appreciate your help, Mercy."

"Thank you for saying so. It does get a bit boring, dealing with five-page research papers for the high-school kids, and now we don't even get a lot of them anymore, what with the Internet and that Wikipedia stuff. You've made my day—a question with some meat on it, that I could actually answer. I'll walk you out and show you where the cemetery is."

Outside the library, Mercy pointed toward the white church, then retreated back inside. Seth asked, "You want to drive or walk?"

"I think I can walk half a block, Seth. I wore my heavy boots. And I want to digest what Mercy told us. What a sad story! Poor Violet—she must have been all of ten when her mother died. And she would have seen all those babies—her half siblings—die first. I hope Mercy can find some more details, although it seems unlikely, unless somebody happened to have saved a lot of family correspondence. It does happen, but I don't know if I'm that lucky."

They started walking, their boots crunching on the frozen snow. It took them two minutes to arrive at the cemetery adjacent to the church, surrounded by a low stone wall. A single path had been cleared from the gate through to the rear. "At least we don't have to climb the wall," Seth said. "But how do you expect to find anybody? I bet we're seeing no more than half of the stones right now—the rest are covered with snow."

Meg scanned the scene, looking at the mostly slate stones, scattered like crooked teeth in the snow. After a minute she pointed. "There."

"Why?" Seth asked.

"I recognize the profile of the stones. From the sampler. See that row of five, with the big one in the middle? The profile is distinctive."

"Ah," Seth said. "So there they are."

"I wonder if the other Warrens in town put up the stone for the parents when they died?"

"Are we going in?" Seth asked.

"Of course," Meg replied.

Luckily the Lampson plot lay only a few feet from the plowed path, and the towering pines above had kept the snow from constant thawing and freezing, and it was still light and fluffy. Meg waded through the snow to stand in front of the row of stones: a large one for the parents, and smaller ones for the children. Young Violet had been scrupulous about recording the details in her sampler, and Meg counted off the children with their little stones, then moved to stand in front of the parents' stone. Seth came up behind her.

"It's been over two hundred years, and here we are," Meg said. "The story isn't over yet." She blinked back tears and looked around at the adjoining stones. "And here they all are, Coxes and Warrens. It feels kind of weird, knowing that I'm related to them, even if it's distantly."

"Are you glad you came?" Seth asked.

"Of course. It's one thing to read about these people, but it's different to see the place. Now we know that Violet was showing the real scene, not just a symbolic bunch of tombstones. We know she made the sampler after everyone died, and she must have been familiar with the family plot. How sad." Meg shivered. The sun was sinking below the tree line, and it was getting colder by the minute. "Let me take a few pictures, and then we can leave. I'll have to come back when the snow is gone, so we can see all of the stones."

Seth waited patiently while Meg snapped pictures, and then, taking her elbow, guided her back to the car. When they were settled, he turned it on and cranked up the heater to high. "You ready to go?"

"I am. Let's go home."

21

It was dark when Seth pulled into the driveway, but the kitchen lights in the house were blazing and Bree's car was in the drive. Meg turned to Seth. "Are you coming in?"

"I told Mom I'd have a late supper with her. And I'll be kind of busy this week—some people want their places shaped up in time for the holidays and all the company they expect. Why they couldn't have thought about this three months ago mystifies me, but it's business."

Meg felt a pang of guilt: Seth had downplayed how busy he was, and here she'd taken up a day of his time for her curiosity. "Thanks for today. I enjoyed the company, and I'm so glad we actually found something about the families."

"My pleasure. I'll be around—call me if you need anything."

Meg watched him pull out of her driveway before going in. After she'd hung up her coat and scarf, and pulled off her heavy boots, she called out, "Bree?"

"Be right there," Bree called from the front of the house.

Meg looked around the kitchen: it looked as though a hurricane had struck. Bree had clearly been cooking, and something sitting on the stove smelled wonderful, but apparently she had used every pot Meg owned. Bree stalked into the kitchen and immediately looked defensive. "I'll clean it up."

"Good. How was your day?"

"Not bad. As you can see, I decided to make dinner. Did you eat?"

Bree's look challenged her, and Meg was glad she could honestly reply that she hadn't. "Whatever it is, it smells good."

"Thanks. It's ready, if you want to eat now."

"Fine." Meg cleared a space on the kitchen table, transferring several dirty bowls to the sink while Bree dished up, then went to the refrigerator and pulled out an open bottle of wine. "You want some?" she asked Bree, waving the bottle.

"Sure, why not?"

She found two clean glasses and poured wine for both of them before sitting down. Bree slapped a full bowl in front of her. "Eat."

Meg dug into Bree's concoction. "Hey, this is great. What is it?"

"You sound surprised," Bree said. "I can cook. It's jerk chicken."

"I know you can cook, but this is really interesting. Family recipe?"

"Sort of. Nobody ever wrote things down, so I just did what I remembered my mom and my auntie doing. You had most of the ingredients here, except the chiles. My mom liked it hot, but this isn't, even though I added some extra cayenne. Maybe next time."

Meg sampled some more, then said, "I hope there will be a next time." After a few minutes of enjoying the food, Meg said tentatively, "No more unpleasant surprises?"

Bree met her look. "Not that I've seen. This is so stupid! If somebody's got something against you, or us, I wish he'd just come out and say so."

"I agree—but notice just how effective he's been so far, without any kind of direct confrontation. All these annoying little things, but they sure add up."

"But why? Just because he can? He's some kind of pervert?"

"I wish I knew, Bree. Seth and Art don't have any better ideas. Let's try to think about it intelligently. We'll ignore the 'why' for now and look at the 'what' and the 'how.' First, there's been no real damage. Second, the events are kind of subtle—as we've said, there's no way to prove there was a human hand involved, because any one of the incidents could have happened naturally. Third . . ." Meg stopped to think.

"Look at the 'when,'" Bree jumped in. "These things have happened at all different times—daytime, night. When we're here, or not."

"So what does that tell us?"

"That somebody is watching the house, and knows how to sneak around it. That kind of implies it's a neighbor, or someone who knows you, or us."

Meg nodded, sighing. "That doesn't make me feel much better. You think there's someone spying on us? Have you seen anyone lurking around?"

"No, but up until recently I haven't been watching. I sure do now," Bree responded.

"And yet he was still able to get pretty close to the house without our noticing." Meg suddenly felt depressed. There was nothing to get a handle on, no leads to follow. Whoever it was was doing a great job making them unsettled, if that was his plan. But she kept coming back to the "why," and finding nothing. "You want me to tell you about my day?" Meg said, feeling a need to change the subject.

"You had enough of wrestling with this lurker problem? Sure. How was your trip to Vermont? You and Seth survived six hours in a car together?"

"We did. Is that some kind of test?"

"Maybe." Bree grinned. "So, any results? Please say yes—I'd love to see somebody finding some answers to something, even if it's ancient history."

"Actually, yes. Between Gail in town here and the librarian in Pittsford, I now know who Violet Cox was, and how she came to be in this house." Meg recounted the story she had pieced together.

"That's sad," Bree said when Meg had finished. "It's a wonder anybody had kids back then, you know? So many of them died as babies, or young. I can't imagine birthing them and losing them."

"Violet's story isn't unique. I've read about families where all the children were wiped out within a week or two, from diphtheria or something like that. Imagine trying to live with that. And a simple infection could kill you, before antibiotics. What amazes me is that anybody survived into their eighties or even nineties—the one who made it through childhood must have been tough."

"With terrific immune systems, too. And then there were wars, where you lost your kids and might not even know about it for months, if ever. Or wives whose husband sailed off and never came back."

"How did we get on this morbid subject?"

"Hey, you're the one who visits cemeteries for fun, and you even drag a date along. But things are better now, right? We've eliminated a lot of diseases, medicines have improved, doctors know a lot more than they did. We're lucky."

"That we are."

Later, Meg was getting ready to close up the house and go upstairs when she remembered she wanted to ask Mercy to look for anything additional about the Lampsons. She switched on her computer and shot off a quick e-mail, thanking Mercy once again for providing copies of the Pittsford vital records, and asking if she could expand her search just a bit to include the Lampsons. In exchange Meg attached digital photos of the sampler, and sent it off. She wasn't sure what she was looking for, but she had a feeling that she hadn't found everything there was to know after only a few hours in Pittsford. So many questions, so little time!

She knew that Violet had come back to Granford, and had lived with Eli Warren's family. Had she stayed in Granford when she married? The relevant censuses for the right time frame would list only male heads of household, but she had a date and a name. She jotted a sticky note to herself, to check the 1810 and later censuses in the morning and see if Violet and her husband had stayed around.

When Meg went out to feed the goats the next morning, the air felt warmer, much to her surprise. She still wasn't familiar enough with New England weather to know if there was a thaw coming, but it would be nice if some of the snow would go away. *Ha*! she said to herself, silently. At this rate they'd be pruning apple trees while wearing boots. Or maybe snowshoes. She made a mental note to herself to ask Seth if she could borrow a pair to try out. That was a skill that might come in handy.

The goats were happy to see her, as usual, and butted her affectionately as she led them out to the pen. "Yeah, I know—you think just because I slept with you, that we've taken this relationship to the next level. But I'm not that easy." The goats gave her one last quizzical look, then headed for their food. Meg looked around: everything seemed to be where it was supposed to be. Nothing broken, nothing dangling. No mysterious footprints.

She felt restless. She stuck her head in the back door.

"Bree, you need anything from the store?" Meg called out, and received a garbled reply that she took as a "no." "I'll be back in an hour or so." She went out to her car, but before getting in she walked around it. All tires intact. The road muck on the fenders wasn't disturbed. She thought she could probably get in safely. The car turned over on the first try, so nobody had tampered with the wiring. Should she check for a bomb underneath? *Meg, you're definitely paranoid!*

She pulled out of the driveway and headed toward the highway. But, she realized, she really wanted to talk to Violet. Yes, she knew Violet was dead, and had been for at least a hundred and fifty years. But if she and her husband had stayed around, as Gail had implied, then Violet's mortal remains shouldn't be far away, and if there was any spirit component of hers left, maybe it hovered nearby, or at least visited now and then. Unfortunately she didn't have Violet's married name, but how many Violets could there be buried there, in the right time frame? Would the tombstones be legible, even if they weren't under a foot or two of snow? Did Violet even have a tombstone, or had her family been too broke to afford one, or had someone just added a line to her husband's stone, assuming he was buried there, too? But even as she wondered if she was supposed to find a single tombstone in a snowy cemetery based purely on some unlikely psychic connection, Meg found herself turning off the highway onto the road that led to the cemetery. It was on her way—wasn't it?

The old Granford cemetery lay no more than a mile from Meg's house, along a two-lane road that led off the highway. She had forgotten how little traveled the residential road was, and she drove slowly down the single plowed lane between two massive snowbanks. Luckily there was no other traffic on the road, since it might have been a tight fit if she had had to pass anyone. She stopped the car, leaving the engine running, and scanned the cemetery.

The end of the cemetery nearer to the highway held the oldest burials; a second section had been opened farther back, perhaps a hundred years later. The grave markers in the older part marched in more or less orderly rows parallel to the road, the later ones perpendicular. She'd been here more than once before, but she'd never seen it under snow. The land was flat, and the wind had scoured much of the snow away, but then sent it drifting erratically around the stones. She knew where "her" Warrens were, in both the older and the newer sections, but she'd never looked for families not somehow connected with her. Of course, there were connections she was still discovering, and the list kept growing.

She jumped a foot when a voice said, "You okay?" A man had approached her car, and she hadn't even heard him coming. This was what she called being wary? *Stupid, Meg, stupid.* Before she could panic she realized she recognized the man, and cranked down her window a cautious couple of inches. "Hi, John. Yes, no problem. I was just thinking about looking for something in the cemetery. I know, it's kind of a weird time of year for it, and I hadn't thought how hard it would be in the snow. I guess I'll have to wait. What brings you here?"

"I'm in charge of keeping the paths clear. There are people who visit their loved ones no matter what the weather."

Now that she looked, Meg could see that there were several paths that had been recently shoveled, although mainly in the more modern section. Meg knew from past visits that there were no paved paths leading among the eighteenth-century tombstones. "I can understand that. But what I'm looking for is pretty early, so I guess I'll have to wait until the snow melts."

"Feels like it's warming up—maybe a couple of days'll do it. I'll get back to work, long as you're all right."

"I'm fine, thanks. I'm going now." She put the car in

gear and continued along the road again. Meg watched in the rearview mirror as John remained observing her, until she turned a corner at the end of the road.

She shook herself. Here she'd wanted Art to take her seriously about all these maybe-threats, when she wasn't doing it herself, even after Seth had lectured her about it. What on earth was she thinking, stopping by a deserted cemetery on the spur of the moment? When nobody knew where she was? If there was a stalker—still an "if"—she couldn't do things like that. Okay, she'd met someone she knew, but it could have been anybody. What if it had been someone who wanted to do her harm? She shivered. Murdered in a cemetery—what a tale that would be!

In a chastened mood Meg hurried on to the market.

22

Meg returned home restocked with supplies, and after stashing them in the kitchen, she sat down and checked her e-mails. She didn't expect to hear from Mercy before Monday, but Gail had replied, and her e-mail read, "I think I've got Violet's marriage record now. She married Abiel Morgan, but I don't have access to my records right now. There aren't a lot of Morgans in Granford. I'll confirm in a day or two and get you a photocopy."

Hurry up and wait, as usual, Meg fumed. She did some mental math: if Violet had been born in 1786, she would have been in her sixties in 1850, which was the first year the federal census had listed all family members and not just the male head of household. So if she looked online for a Violet Morgan in Granford, she might learn a little more. She clicked through to the appropriate Web site and held her breath as she entered the information. Bingo! There was a Morgan household headed by one Abiel Morgan, with wife Violet, in 1850. No children listed in the household, but they were probably long out of the house, and Meg didn't feel like wading through all the other Morgans in town just to satisfy her own curiosity. She pulled up the 1860 census and found Violet living alone, so Abiel must have died in the intervening years. In 1870 she was living with another family, with a different surname—a married daughter? Had there been sons? She couldn't tell from the earlier censuses. In 1880 there was no sign of Violet, which wasn't surprising. Gail had already said that she knew Violet had died before the Warren sisters who had owned the house were born.

At least Violet had lived a long life, unlike the rest of her close family. Abiel was listed as a farmer during his lifetime, as were most people in Granford in the nineteenth century. Meg felt obscurely pleased: now at least she knew who she was looking for the next time she visited the cemetery, whenever the weather permitted.

She was surprised to see Seth's van pull into the driveway, followed shortly by the pickup truck she recognized as John Taylor's—he was certainly getting around today. But John wasn't alone: she could see someone else in the passenger seat. Meg ambled out to say hello.

Seth and John were talking when she approached. "Hi, John," she said. "We meet again." When Seth quirked an eyebrow at her, she explained, "I drove past the cemetery on the way to the market, and John stopped to make sure I was okay."

Meg was amused when John hung his head and kicked at the snow. She almost expected him to say, "Aw, shucks, ma'am, it weren't nothin'." Instead he said, "We don't get too many people passing along that road, except the ones who live there. I didn't want you to get stuck."

"Hey, I appreciated it. But if you take care of the cemetery, you'll probably see a lot more of me there. I've got plenty of ancestors buried there."

"We do get a lot of people looking for ancestors, but

mostly in summer," John said. "I'm not interested in all that family history stuff—don't have the time."

A woman with a baby climbed out of the truck and called out. Meg guessed she was in her thirties. She was dressed for the weather, although she wore no hat and her fine blonde hair was pulled back carelessly. "You gonna be long, John? Eli really needs a clean diaper."

"Almost. Hey, Jenn, come over and meet Meg—she's the new owner here."

Jennifer didn't look too excited about the idea, but she came over, balancing the baby on her hip, and stuck out a hand. "Hi, I'm Jennifer, John's wife. And this is Eli. I guess we're neighbors."

Her tone wasn't exactly enthusiastic, Meg thought. "Nice to meet you, Jenn," Meg said. "I'll probably be seeing more of John, if he's working with Seth. Hi, Eli." Meg waggled her fingers at the baby.

Meg was no expert, but Eli looked to be no more than two. He was blond like his mother, and he regarded Meg with a blank stare. Meg smiled at him, but Eli didn't return the smile.

"You have kids?" Jenn asked.

"No. It's just me and my housemate, Bree. Have you met her, John?"

He nodded. "Jamaican girl, right? I've seen her, but not to talk to. She works in the orchard, doesn't she?"

"She *manages* it," Meg corrected him. "I'm kind of new to farming and orchards. I can't pay her what she's worth, so I give her free room and board, which is why she's living here."

"John, come on," Jenn whined, jiggling the baby.

"Okay, okay. Seth, you want to go over the schedule for the week?"

"Sure. It's inside." Seth led John into the barn extension that held his office, leaving Meg and Jenn standing awkwardly in the middle of the driveway.

"How old is Eli?" Meg asked.

"He's one. Well, sixteen months," Jenn said curtly, and didn't volunteer anything more.

"You have other kids?"

"No."

Meg gave up trying to make conversation. "Well, it was nice to meet you, Jenn. I've got some things to do inside."

Jenn didn't seem heartbroken by her departure. From the kitchen window Meg watched as Jenn climbed back into the truck, then honked the horn several times. She certainly was impatient. Hadn't Seth said that John had lost his job? Jenn should be happy that he was finding even odd jobs at the moment. Maybe she was just stressed out, or embarrassed. John and Seth emerged from the barn, and John joined his wife in the truck and did a k-turn before heading off down the road away from town.

Seth knocked at the back door, and Meg went to let him in. "Was it something I said?" Meg asked.

"You mean Jenn's attitude? Don't take it personally—she's having a hard time. But John's a good guy, and a hard worker."

"Didn't you tell me their child was sick?"

"Yeah. Poor Eli. It's some kind of neurological thing. They don't talk about it a lot, and I don't like to pry."

Maybe that explained his lack of responsiveness. "That's a shame. You want some coffee or something?" Meg asked.

"No, I've got to run."

"But it's Sunday!" Meg protested.

"Yes, but the big box stores are open, and I've got to get my supplies together for this week. What the heck were you doing over by the cemetery?"

"Looking for Violet. I know, I know—kind of stupid, since I didn't even have her married name at the time—I guess I thought I should be drawn to her mortal remains by some psychic connection or something. But even I should know it's pretty deserted over there. I ran into

John there. Is that one of those municipal jobs you were telling me about?"

"Yup. Actually it works out well for everyone. The town can't afford to hire a full-time maintenance crew, so we pay him hourly on an as-needed basis, and maintaining the cemetery is one of those intermittent things he does. He needs the work, and we need the work done. We asked him to keep the main paths clear."

"Lousy time to be looking for work. Anyway, when I came back Gail had emailed me to say that Violet married Abiel Morgan here. I checked the censuses for Morgans, trying to figure out if Violet stuck around, and I found only one family with that name, so I should be on the right track. I think she and her husband lived out their days here in Granford, but I haven't figured out which kids were theirs. Does the name ring any bells with you?"

"Not offhand. But you do know that almost everyone in this town is related somehow?"

"Including me, apparently. I guess it keeps surprising me. It's a wonder my great-grandfather ever escaped the place."

"We let people out now and then—but we can't afford to lose much more of the population. Well, I've got to get moving. See you later!"

Back inside, Meg wandered aimlessly, tidying the kitchen, and then drifted into the dining room, where Bree was sitting surrounded by piles of paper.

"Just the person I wanted to see," Bree said, looking smug.

"You're finished?" Meg asked.

"Rough version, at least. You want me to summarize? Unless you're too busy right now."

"Bree!" Meg checked to make sure she was joking.

"Just kidding! You've been bugging me for weeks. Here." Bree handed Meg a single sheet of paper. "This is the simple version—I'm still tweaking the details, but this'll give you the big picture."

Meg scanned the page, willing herself not to go straight to the bottom line, which was . . . small but positive. She looked up at Bree. "We made money?"

"Yes, ma'am, we did. Not a lot, but not too shabby for the first year. Let me go over some of the details."

As Bree started reviewing the numbers and her calculations, Meg was surprised by her own reaction. Sure, she had a background in financial analysis, and she recognized the parameters that Bree was outlining for her. But at the same time, she had no way of knowing whether the results in individual categories were good or bad.

When Bree had wrapped up her short version, Meg said slowly, "So let me get this straight." She started ticking off points. "We paid competitive salaries this year, but we'll have to go up a bit next year?"

Bree nodded. "Maybe 5 percent."

"You've figured in capital depreciation?"

Bree snorted. "That antique tractor?"

"Well, it was a capital expenditure. So was building the storage chambers. I'll have to review the IRS regulations. How much of the gear and containers will we have to replace next year?"

"Maybe 20 percent. That's about normal."

"Did you figure in mileage for deliveries?"

"Yes."

"Insurance costs?"

"Yes."

Meg thought for a moment. "What would you change, going forward, to optimize our marketing?"

"I'm not in any hurry to figure that out. This year, nobody knew who we were. I'll bet they knew the apples and the trees better than they knew either of us. Next year they'll know what we're offering, and that we can deliver what we promised. We'll probably pick up some more orders, maybe 20 percent."

"All right. What about new tree stock?"

"We could add some trees on the north end, but you know that they won't bear for a few years."

"Seth offered to lease us some of his land, long-term, if we wanted to expand in that direction."

"Oh ho!" Bree said. "That's talking serious commitment."

"I know. I told him I'd think about it." Meg looked Bree squarely in the eye. "So what's your professional assessment?"

"Looking at this as a business? I won't sugarcoat it—it's not terrific, but under the circumstances it's not bad. You're paying me a pittance, and you're not taking any salary yourself at the moment. That's not a great long-term plan. But you've got good tree stock, you've established relationships with your vendors, and I'll bet you've learned a heck of a lot. Right?"

"That's the truth."

"Then I think this is a good outcome," Bree said triumphantly.

To her dismay, Meg realized she wasn't sure how she felt about it. She'd been waiting for these results for weeks, and now that she had them, she didn't know what to make of them. What had she expected? A five-figure profit? That was unreasonable and she knew it. She knew the trouble small farmers faced—she should be ecstatic just to be in the black after her first year. But did the results justify all the hard work she—and to be fair, Bree, too—had put into it? Could she see herself doing this in ten or twenty years' time?

"You don't look very happy, Meg," Bree said. "Do you know how hard it is to make a profit at all in this business? And you—we—pulled it off on the first try."

"I know, and I really appreciate all you've done, Bree."

"So what's the problem?"

"I'm weighing the profit against the amount of work it took to make it."

Bree stood up abruptly, her eyes cold. "So you're just dabbling in this, to see if you like it? And if it's too hard, you're just going to walk away?"

Bree's anger startled Meg. "No, that's not what I meant. Hey, you know I want to see this work. I've enjoyed the work, even the sweaty physical stuff, and I've loved learning something new. But I need to believe it's a good business decision to keep going. And I need to decide that now, before I invest too much more energy into it."

Bree regarded her for a long moment. "Well, let me know what you decide. If I'm going to be looking for work, I'd rather know sooner than later." She stalked out of the room and went up the stairs.

Meg continued to sit, staring at nothing, shocked by Bree's vehement reaction. She had disappointed Bree—that much was clear. And Bree had done a terrific job. So why wasn't she happier with the outcome? What the heck did she want from her life? If there were some cosmic guarantee that she could keep on doing what she had done for the past year, and that costs and income would keep pace with each other, would the return on her investment of energy be enough? It was honest work, if hard. Did she want to go back to city offices and endless number crunching?

And what was forcing the decision? She had come to love the house, cold and drafty and decrepit as it was. She liked the town, and she was beginning to make friends. And then there was Seth . . . was he part of the problem? Their relationship seemed to be moving forward in fits and starts. They were both busy people, and she'd told him from the beginning that she wasn't ready to jump into anything right away: she'd been burned by her last relationship, and she had wanted to focus on learning the business, seeing if she could make it work. Well, she was definitely over Chandler

Hale, and apparently the business was solid, if not highly profitable. What was she waiting for?

Bree came clomping down the stairs. "I'm going over to Michael's," she said curtly.

"Bree, I'm sorry. I didn't mean to rain on your parade."

"Yeah, whatever. I'll be back tomorrow." Bree pulled on her jacket and hat and slammed out the back door. Meg heard Bree's car start up and watched as she pulled out of the driveway. She took a deep breath, then picked up the phone.

"Seth, are you busy?"

23

Seth had still been in his office next door, so he appeared a few minutes later. "What's up?" he asked, as he hung up his coat. "You sounded upset."

Meg struggled to find an answer and chose to duck the question. "You want something to drink?"

"Sure. Beer if you've got it. Stay there—I know where to look." He went to the refrigerator and pulled out a bottle. He knuckled Lolly's head before turning to Meg and leaning against the refrigerator. "You didn't answer my question."

"I know." Might as well get straight to the point. "Bree finally finished working the numbers for the orchard operation," she said.

"Are they bad?"

"No, we actually made a profit. A small one."

"That's great! So what's the problem? Because you don't look exactly happy."

His smile should have warmed her, but it didn't. "I don't

know." Which was the absolute truth. She wanted to be happy—didn't she?

"Do you want to talk about it?"

"Yes, I guess so." Meg sighed. "After she gave me a summary, Bree got mad at me and left in a huff because I guess I didn't seem enthusiastic enough for her. I can't blame her. I should have realized how important this was for her. I mean, it's her first job, and she's worked really hard, under difficult conditions, and then I go and blow her off. Could you pour me a glass of wine?"

Seth complied, handing her a full glass. Meg took it from him and downed a healthy swig. She realized that Seth was watching her. "What?"

"I'm worried about you. You get what should be good news and it makes you depressed. Did you expect something different?"

She shook her head. "I don't know what I expected. For so long I was focused on getting through the harvest—just surviving, I guess. I don't think I had any specific expectations. What's worse, *I* don't really understand why I'm not happier."

"Agriculture isn't easy—you must have figured that out by now. You shouldn't expect too much. *Any* profit is good these days."

"I know that, at least in my head. I grasped how hard it all was about the third week in the orchard. I don't know what's wrong with me."

"Well, you're stressed out," Seth said.

"Why do you say that? This is the easiest time I've had since I arrived. In fact, I keep looking for things to do, which is why I've been sucked into all this genealogy stuff, and figuring out the sampler. I'm getting plenty of rest, and probably eating too much."

"Well, there was the furnace going out on you, and a major blizzard. And then this harassment business. It's a lot, coming all at once."

Meg laughed bitterly. "I'm not even sure if this so-called harassment is anything more than a series of coincidences. Maybe my karma is misaligned, or there's a full moon this week. Things happen. It doesn't mean there's anyone behind them."

"And if there is?"

"Seth, we've been over this before. I have no idea why anyone would have a grudge against me. I haven't seen anyone doing anything suspicious. Maybe I'm just being overimaginative, now that I'm not perpetually exhausted."

Meg held out her now-empty glass, and Seth refilled it without comment. Lolly jumped down from her perch on the refrigerator and started winding around Meg's ankles. "Oh, right—you want food." Meg stood up and found a can of cat food in a cabinet and spooned out half of it on a plate, which she set on the floor. Without looking at Seth, Meg said, "You're not saying much."

"I'm not sure what you want me to say. It sounds like this is something you have to work through in your own head."

"And here I was looking for a father confessor and kindly counselor."

Seth held out his hands in protest. "Were you? Meg, what do you want from me? If you want advice, I'll give you advice."

"I haven't asked for advice."

"Then why am I here?" Seth asked.

Meg opened her mouth to answer, although she wasn't sure what she was going to say, when she was startled by the sound of breaking glass, followed by a distant crack. Seth threw her to the floor, landing on top of her, and she realized that the window over the sink was now *in* the sink and all over the floor, and cold air was rushing into the room.

"What was that?" she managed to say from under Seth's weight.

"That," Seth said, his voice tight, "was a rifle shot. Which just blew out your window. Did you see anyone outside?"

"What, just now? No, I was looking at you. I guess nobody can say I was imagining that." The reality of what had happened finally caught up to her: that had been a bullet, and it could have hit her, or Seth. She began to shake.

"Stay there," Seth ordered, and stood up, keeping away from the gaping hole that had been the window. He moved to the back door and looked out cautiously. He didn't move for several moments, then he came back to the kitchen. "No one out there now, that I can see."

"You think it was a hunter?"

"If it was, he's an idiot. You never fire a shot without knowing where your target is, and what lies on the other side. Which in this case is houses—including yours. That shot could have hit you. I'm going to call Art—he needs to know there's some damn fool out there shooting carelessly."

Meg picked herself up off the floor, avoiding the pieces of glass. "What about the window?"

Seth was fishing in a zipped outer pocket for his cell phone. "Let me call Art first. I think I've got some plywood that would fit." He stalked into the dining room to make the call.

When he came back, Meg asked, "Is this hunting season? Because I *have* seen deer up in the orchard. They like the fallen apples."

Seth snapped his phone shut. "Art's on his way. The state hunting season runs from October through the end of December, and it's still open. But any hunter is supposed to have a hunting license, so there'd be a record. That doesn't mean somebody isn't poaching. Or it could be someone after coyote—there are a lot of them around now, and they're getting to be a nuisance. But how can anybody be so stupid?"

"I hadn't even realized," Meg said. "Is that my land, beyond the meadow?"

"Part of it is, to the other side of that stand of trees. Technically, it's illegal to hunt without the owner's permission anyway. Apparently whoever it was didn't know—or didn't care."

Meg shivered, and not from the cold. Who could be thoughtless enough to shoot a rifle without knowing what lay beyond? Assuming it was a mistake and not something worse. "Is there a lot of hunting around here?" She knew she was just making conversation, because she didn't want to think about what had just happened.

Seth shrugged. "Some. Maybe a little more this year because people are strapped and they want the meat. You ever eaten venison?"

Apparently Seth was making conversation, too. "Not that I can remember," she said. She took a breath. "We'll need to clean up this glass. You said Art's coming?"

"Yeah, he'll be here any minute."

Meg found a dustpan and brush and had begun carefully sweeping up shards of glass from the floor when Art's cruiser pulled into her driveway. Seth went out to meet him, and together they studied the window. Then Art turned 180 degrees and looked at the distant tree line, as Seth pointed. As Meg watched them, she realized that hunting—and the dangers that hunting represented to her—had never crossed her mind. She had never even held a gun, and the last time she had shot a bow and arrow had been in summer camp a couple of decades earlier. She couldn't imagine depending on bagging a deer to feed a family, although she had heard that there were areas where deer posed a real threat to crops and needed thinning. Meg had noticed a few deer now and then, but how big could the population be? This part of town was moderately built up, although there were still plenty of open fields and woodlands. How much space did a deer need to hide and to forage? More things she didn't know.

A few minutes later Seth brought Art into the kitchen, and Meg greeted him. "Hi, Art. You look tired. Can I get you anything?"

"Yeah, thanks, coffee would be great. Sorry this happened. I know most of the guys who hunt around here, and usually they're careful."

Meg chose her words carefully. "Do you think this was an accident, Art?"

Art looked at her. "You don't? You thinking about that other stuff you told me about? Because this is in a different league, if you don't mind my saying so. Someone could have been hurt."

"I know. Believe me, I'd rather think it was an accident, even if it's a stupid one."

Art looked around the kitchen. "Where were you when it happened?"

"We were standing on either side of the table here."

"Would you have been visible from outside?"

"You mean, from that distance?" Seth asked. "We weren't right next to the window. It was light outside. And the land slopes down to the marsh there. So I wouldn't swear that anyone could see us standing in the kitchen. You agree, Meg?"

"I guess." She'd never looked at the house from that angle.

"So it could have been a very careless hunter," Seth went on, "or maybe someone who didn't plan to hit anyone, just make a mess and scare us. Which he did, damn it."

Meg looked at Seth, and then at Art. "So it's part of the same pattern, just more serious? Intimidation?"

"Maybe," Art said. "Let me take a look at the bullet. You see where it went?"

It took the three of them a couple of minutes to locate the bullet, partially embedded in the plaster wall. Art took a penknife and pried it out. "Twenty-two caliber. Not very big. Could have done some damage to you, but probably not from that distance." He slipped it in his shirt pocket. "Look, I'll investigate, check for footprints before I lose the light. Ask around. I'll let you know if I get any other reports of hunters, legal or otherwise." He stood up wearily. "I'd better be going. Sorry it had to happen to you, Meg. See me out, Seth?"

"Bye, Art," Meg said. She watched the men leave the house and stand in the driveway talking. At least Art couldn't tell her she was imagining things this time—that bullet was very real. She shivered in the air from the broken window.

When Art left, Seth came back and said, "I'd better get something over that window. You sure you got all the glass?"

"I think so."

He looked at her critically. "Are you okay?"

"I don't know, honestly. I don't know what to think—whether this was a stray bullet or somebody is really trying to get to me. You tell me."

"Meg, I don't know what to say. I've lived just over the hill all my life, and I can't recall any incident where someone was hurt by a hunter around here. You haven't heard any other gunshots?"

"I'm not sure I'd even recognize them. I'm a city girl, remember? And I lived in a nice neighborhood in Boston where we didn't hear a lot of gunfire. I'm more likely to assume it's just a backfire." Meg sighed. "You want dinner?"

As she started her dinner preparations, Meg realized how much time she spent looking out the window over the sink, now that she couldn't. Seth came and went, measuring and cutting a sheet of plywood, then screwing it into place, making the kitchen dark. Meg began to feel claustrophobic. At least it hadn't been one of the antique windows; the sink window was some later generation's plate glass installation, from some past kitchen remodeling, and she had to admit she preferred it for the light it provided.

When dinner was ready she dished up two bowls and all but slapped them on the table. "There. Food. Let's eat."

Silently Seth found forks and napkins, and sat down at the table across from Meg. "Meg, we kind of left that earlier conversation about the orchard unfinished. What is all this about? Are you looking for a reason to bail out on Granford, this house, this whole thing? Am I supposed to tell you that I'm sorry your business is doing well? Is that what you want to hear?"

In spite of herself Meg smiled. "It sounds ridiculous when you put it that way. I'm mad because I didn't fail? Yeah, that makes sense." She paused to eat a few forkfuls of her dinner. Seth was still watching her. "What?" she said.

"Are you waiting for me to say something like 'I'm madly in love with you, and I want you to stay here forever with me, the orchard be damned'?"

Meg looked up from her plate, startled. She'd never even thought about that. "Are you? Madly in love with me? Slightly in love with me? And I'd still need to make a living. I don't want anyone to pay my way."

Seth stared at her for several seconds, his expression unreadable, and for a moment Meg wished he would break out of that calm and rational mode—get angry, or at least respond with some emotion. In the end Meg held up a hand. "This is definitely not the time for that conversation. For the record, I am not trying to force some sort of commitment from you. I don't do that."

"I know. I'm sorry, Meg. Look, you've had a hard year, and I haven't wanted to push too hard . . ."

She interrupted him. "And I haven't encouraged you, either. I know myself well enough for that—I knew I couldn't deal with a new place and a whole new profession and a new relationship all at once. Seth, I don't know how I would have made it through this past year without you. But a lot of that has been just because you were there. A problem came up, and you would have been there anyway, as plumber or neighbor or selectman, whether or not it was me who was involved. It's been easy to avoid looking too hard at 'us,' whatever that might be. And honestly, I don't know what I want from you. I don't know what I want from this place. Damn." She shut her eyes, mostly to hold back tears. Why did she feel this way? "I should be happy," she whispered.

"Meg," Seth said helplessly.

Meg opened her eyes. "If you want another cliché, I'll give you one: it's not you, it's me. You're one of the greatest guys I've ever met."

"But?" he asked.

"As I keep saying, I don't know what I want. I expected to be happy if the orchard was in the black, but now I'm just confused. And I've got to decide whether I want to keep going with it, or walk away now while I still have other options."

"And I don't fit in the equation anywhere?"

Meg realized that she sounded as though she was putting the orchard ahead of him. That seemed awfully cold. Was she trying to push him away? And why? Was she really that afraid of commitment, to a person, a place, a way of life? She meant what she'd said to him, but she'd been skirting around the term "love." Did she love him?

"That's not what I'm saying, Seth. I mean, it's not a package deal, you and the orchard, and it's not exactly either-or. I can't see giving up the house and the orchard but being together with you, whatever form that might take. But I can't see telling you to get lost and then staying on here, with you in my backyard all the time, literally. And I don't want to do that, either."

Seth was silent for several seconds, and then he stood up. "I need to go. I think you have to make up your mind what you want, and I don't want to make that more difficult for you. You know I care about you, and I want to find out where that takes us, but that's a choice that has little to do with your business decision about the orchard."

Meg stood up as well. "Seth," she began, hating that she sounded so helpless.

Seth put on his coat and pulled open the back door. "Let me know what you decide." He disappeared into the night, shutting the door firmly behind him.

Meg remained standing in the middle of the kitchen, her mind in turmoil. In the space of a few hours she had managed to tick off her business manager and her . . . Seth. They were both good people; she did care about them both, and what they thought of her. Worse, she needed them. So what the hell was she doing? And given Seth's tendency to take care of everyone and everything, the fact that she had managed to drive him away after what had happened this afternoon spoke volumes about how upset he was.

Mindlessly she cleared up the dishes, checked the dead bolt on the back door, turned off lights. She drifted into the dining room, but she had no interest in looking up Internet information about dead people. Although, she had to admit, dead people were a whole lot easier to deal with than living ones. Or maybe she was just lousy at dealing with living ones, period.

In the front parlor, she looked around. Not much had changed since she had moved in nearly a year earlier. She was still living with the same crappy furniture she had inherited, mainly because she hadn't had either the money or the time to do anything about it. The old wooden windows still rattled and leaked cold air. She hadn't done anything about them either, for the same reasons. Ever since spring she had been focused on getting in the harvest, challenging herself to see if she could pull off something difficult, with no experience. Well, she had done it. So why wasn't she happy?

Postpartum depression, Meg? All that anticipation—the end result could hardly help but be an anticlimax. *So you managed to do what farmers around here have been doing for as long as this land has been settled: bring in a crop. Big deal.* And because she had been so focused on that one goal, she had put off thinking about what she would do after. She had deferred that decision with a lot of "we'll see's." She had once prided herself on her clear thinking and her decisiveness, and yet she'd been waffling about this for almost as long as she had been here.

She sat down in one of the shabby armchairs, and a heat-seeking Lolly jumped into her lap and curled up. *One more obligation to worry about*, Meg thought. Lolly had been abandoned once; could she do it to her again? Was a cat the only thing she would take away from this whole experience?

All right, Meg—think! Fact one: she had proved she could run the orchard, as long as she had help, and make a profit. She could support herself, even though there might be up or down years. Raising any kind of crop was uncertain. It was also hard work. Could she live with those?

If she was going to stick around, there were things that absolutely had to be done. The roof wouldn't last much longer, and the house sorely needed painting. She had to pay for the new furnace. And, as Bree had pointed out, she wasn't even pulling a salary for herself, and at some point she was going to have to buy clothes and a new car and maybe even furniture. How far would that slender profit stretch?

And there was Seth. Meg knew she had personal issues with intimate relationships, which was probably why she hadn't had many. Knowing it and doing something about it were two different things. It would be nice if either she or Seth had been overwhelmed with blind passion and made imperious demands: *I love you! I want you! Marry me!* Did she want to marry Seth? Did she want to marry anyone?

Or did she want to walk away from him? Go back to Boston, or somewhere else, and start a new life—again?

That idea brought a twist to her gut, and Meg almost smiled. *Look, an honest emotional reaction, Meg.* Did she love him? The answer was a definite "maybe." Should she tell him? She shied away from that. *Not until I'm sure.* Which could be about the same time that hell froze over. *What are you so afraid of, Meg? Of making a mistake? That's part of being human. You can't sit on the fence forever. People won't wait forever for you to make up your mind. Life moves on.*

Meg stroked Lolly, who remained oblivious to her mistress's inner turmoil. "I guess I should go to bed, eh, cat? Come on." She picked up Lolly, who protested sleepily, and headed up the stairs, turning off lights as she went.

She awoke sometime in the middle of the night, in the pitch dark. Had she heard something? Animal, human? She lay still, listening. Nothing, or at least nothing identifiably human—just the usual creaks and groans of an old house, ancient trees swaying in the slight wind, a lone car on the distant highway. Lolly slept on. Damn it, these harassment incidents were getting to her—making her see or hear or suspect things that weren't even there.

And then Meg got mad—gloriously, indisputably mad. She didn't need this kind of aggravation, not on top of all the rest of the mess of her life. She couldn't keep ignoring the events: real things were happening, and someone was making them happen. If somebody around Granford had a problem with her, she wanted to know who, and why. She was not going to let this faceless someone drive her off her land, or deprive her of her satisfaction in what she had accomplished. It was time to go on the attack and figure it out.

Even with that resolution in mind, it took her a while to get back to sleep—but at least now she had a plan.

24

Meg woke late the next morning—if late could be considered any time after the winter sun came up—and the first thing she remembered was her righteous anger from the middle of the night. Did it hold up in the light of day? Damn straight it did! If she could clear up this one part of the mess of her life, it would make it much easier to sort out the rest. And she owed both Bree and Seth an apology. They had done nothing but try to support her, and she was whining and moping. She had no right to inflict her self-centered indecisiveness on other people. *Get over yourself, Meg!*

She was downstairs fixing breakfast for herself when she saw Bree's car pull in. Bree stopped short of slamming the car door, but barely. She stormed toward the house and came in the back door, throwing her jacket at the hook on the wall, and saying a curt "Morning" before turning toward the back stairs.

"Bree, wait! Please!" Meg called out.

Bree turned reluctantly to the kitchen and faced Meg,

her expression belligerent. "What? I'm not staying around—I just left too fast yesterday to take any clothes along."

Might as well get right to it. "Bree, I want to apologize for yesterday. You gave me good news and all I could do was complain. It wasn't fair to you. You did an outstanding job this year, and any success here is largely yours."

"So, what? You'll write me a nice letter of recommendation when I go looking for a new job?"

"No, that's not what I'm saying. Although I will, if that's what you want. But I don't want you to go. *I* don't want to leave." There, she'd said it. How did it feel?

It felt good.

Bree still looked wary. "You're saying you want to keep working the orchard? With me?"

"Yes, that's what I'm saying. Can we sit down?"

"You got coffee?"

"Of course."

Bree finally noticed the boarded-up window. "What the hell happened here?"

"A stray bullet, yesterday."

"You're kidding!" Bree looked hard at Meg. "You're not kidding. Was it aimed at you?"

Meg shrugged. "No way to know, but probably not. The consensus is that it was a sloppy hunter. Art came by, so he's got a report."

"Why are you so calm about this? Somebody shot at you!"

"They missed. And maybe it was accidental. What is it you want me to do? Look, can we talk about the orchard?"

Bree helped herself to coffee and sat at the table, and Meg refilled her mug and joined her.

"I don't know what I was expecting," Meg began. "Maybe I thought you'd tell me we'd been a fantastic success and doubled the profits from any previous year." She ignored Bree's snort. "Maybe I wanted to prove to those people back in Boston that I could succeed quite well without them. I know I had to prove it to myself."

"Okay," Bree said. "And?"

"Well, that was my problem, not yours. If I'd been thinking rationally, I would have realized that a modest success was all I could hope for, given all the strikes against us, like my total lack of experience, and the fact that we had to build the holding chambers for the apples, and buy equipment, and set up new contacts with vendors. Not to mention all the other dramas we had to deal with."

Bree smiled grudgingly. "Yeah, and I was pretty new at this, too."

Meg nodded. "You were, but you handled yourself really well. You did all the hiring, and you kept things on track. Tell me, were you dragging your feet on the numbers because you weren't sure what you would find?"

"Maybe. I don't know. But I had a lot riding on this, too, you know. It mattered to me as much as to you."

"I know, and I'm sorry if I didn't acknowledge that. All I can say is, I was kind of overwhelmed for most of the year, but I want you to know that I'm proud of the results. And of you, and even of myself. So, are we okay?"

Bree sat back in her chair. "Just to be clear, you're saying you want to go forward with another year, at least? Same terms? Or, maybe I could get a raise?"

"You tell me—you ran the numbers."

"Huh." She thought for a moment. "We should probably pay the pickers better before I take any more. But we can see." She stood up. "Thank you, Meg. For trusting me, and for giving me this chance. And for being willing to pitch in and do the grubby stuff. I think we *should* be proud of ourselves." She hesitated. "Uh, we don't have to hug or anything, do we?"

"No, I'm good. And thank you, too, Bree. Are you still going back to Michael's?"

"Sure. Gotta seize the day when we can. You tell Seth the good news?"

"Kind of, but I guess I was giving him the same mixed signals I was giving you. We left things . . . kind of unsettled. I don't think I've been fair to him either."

"Nope, you haven't," Bree said promptly. "The guy's in love with you, and you keep putting him off. How long you think he's going to hang around? He's prime merchandise—somebody'll come along and snap him up."

"Bree! And I haven't put him off, not exactly. Well, sort of. But you're right—he deserves better, and he's been very patient."

Bree snorted again. "You got that right—he's a saint to put up with you and all your waffling. Okay, I'm leaving, as soon as I throw some clothes together. Go patch things up with Seth."

"I will," Meg said to Bree's retreating back. She sat sipping her coffee, trying to figure out what to do next. Growing up, her family had gone out of their way to avoid confrontations or sticky emotional situations. She'd heard things from her mother during her recent visit that had never been mentioned before. But avoidance was not an answer, even if it cut down on unpleasantness. Or deferred it, because somewhere down the line there was usually a price to pay.

Would the price of her waffling be losing Seth? Bree was right: he had been a saint. She had wanted time and space to decide whether they could have a relationship, and he had granted her that. But he wasn't going to wait around forever for her to decide that the time was right. There was never a perfect time. You took what life handed you, you dealt with it, and you moved on. Okay, so in the past few months life had handed her a lot of manure, but she'd come out of it stronger. Maybe Seth was the prize at the bottom of the box. But now she had some fences to mend with him.

Before she could worry the idea to death, Meg stood up,

grabbed her coat, and headed out for her car. If there hadn't been snow on the ground, she would have walked over the hill to his house, which might have burned off a little nervous energy. As it was, she had to take the long way around to reach his place. She pulled up beside the side door, climbed out of the car, then knocked.

It took him a minute or two to answer, and when he opened the door he looked sleep-rumpled. And surprised.

"May I come in?" Meg asked. She realized her heart was pounding.

Silently Seth stepped aside to let her in, his eyes never leaving her. She turned to face him. "Seth," she began, and then realized she had no idea what to say. She had a better idea what to do: she closed the distance between them and, grabbing his head, kissed him, hard. He didn't respond at first, but when she didn't retreat, he gave back as good as she gave.

Until she finally managed to take a step back and look him in the eye. "I'm sorry. I'm an idiot. And I hated the way we left things when you walked out last night."

"Okay," he said cautiously.

Meg waited for him to add something, and when he didn't, she realized that she wasn't finished, and he knew it. "Seth, I haven't been fair to you. Maybe this past year hasn't been the best time to fall in love—or maybe it was, because there was so much stuff going on that I didn't have the energy to put up defenses. But I can't stand the idea of hurting you—or losing you."

His mouth twitched in a half smile, and he pulled her to him again, and held on. "You have no idea how long I've been waiting for you to figure that out," he said to the top of her head.

"Yeah, that's what Bree said," Meg said into his chest.

"What, you talked this over with Bree before me?" he said, in mock dismay.

"Well, she showed up this morning, and I had to apologize to her. God, I've been an annoying prima donna, haven't I? Thinking I get to call all the shots, and not considering other people. I'm sorry."

"You already said that."

"I know, but I thought I should get some practice. Look, I think I love you, but I don't have a lot of experience in this area, so you'll have to bear with me. Is that all right?"

"I'm good with it. I know I love you. I have since, oh, February, I think."

"Oh, Seth . . ." She really had nothing to say to that, so she grabbed him again, and picked up the kiss where they had left off. This time it didn't end as quickly.

25

"You want breakfast?" Seth called out from the kitchen.

"I ate at home, but I'm hungry again. Sure," Meg said, coming down the stairs.

"French toast all right?"

"Of course. Can I just sit and admire your efforts?"

"Great."

As she watched him move efficiently around his kitchen, Meg said, "You know, I had a kind of epiphany in the middle of the night last night. I woke up around four and I was trying to figure out whether I'd heard something that woke me up, and if it was my mystery prowler."

"Was it anything?" he said, beating eggs in a bowl.

"I don't think so. But I realized I didn't want to live my life jumping at shadows and worrying every time something creaked. Which happens a lot."

"Old houses do that. So what's your solution?"

"I want to do something about it."

Seth dropped egg-soaked bread into a hot, buttered pan. "Like what?"

"Well, the majority of the incidents have happened around the house, right? So I think we need to set up some sort of watch system—make sure someone is home at all times, but not obviously, you know?"

"I did suggest security cameras."

"And they're still absurd. Besides, they'd be too obvious. Can't we just use our eyes? There are three of us, if I enlist Bree. Surely we can manage to keep an eye on things for a few days? And nights?"

"Maybe. Are you figuring that we need to watch the area between the house and the barn, primarily? My shop overlooks that, too."

"True. I know it's a kind of vague plan, but I'm not sure what else to do. Wait until somebody really gets hurt?"

"No one has yet, although that shot came pretty close. And I can't say that whoever it is won't up the ante. But what I still don't get is what he wants."

Meg sighed. "I have no idea, other than to drive me nuts, which he seems to be doing. That's why I want this to stop—I don't want someone I don't even know to dictate how I live my life. I don't want to give him that kind of control over me."

Seth set a plate of French toast in front of her, and handed her a bottle of maple syrup. "Before you ask, yes, it's local, from Parker's on the other side of the highway."

Meg made approving sounds as she sampled the syrup. "This is good stuff. Do I have any maple trees I could tap? Seriously, though, do you have any better ideas about what we can do?"

"Nope," he said, sitting down with his own plate. "You've done the right things, and informed the local authorities, who are helpless. They don't have the manpower to keep watch on your place, and even if they did, the person—

assuming it's a local person who's paying attention—might just lay low until they went away. I guess it's up to us."

"So you'll help?"

"Of course. But I've got a full schedule this week, so it may not be easy to stay awake all night."

"We'll work it out. Thank you, Seth. It makes me feel better just to be doing *something*. I'm tired of being anxious all the time."

After finishing the unquestionably delicious French toast, Meg stretched and stood up. "I should go. I'm sure you've got work to do."

Seth collected the dishes and deposited them in the sink. "I do. I'll be right behind you. Meg?"

She wrestled her arms into her coat, then turned to face him. "What?"

"If you hadn't showed up this morning, I would have been at your door. But I'm glad you came to me."

Meg smiled. "So am I. See you in a few."

She drove home feeling ridiculously pleased with herself. Was that really all it took? Saying *I'm sorry*? As she had told Seth, she hadn't had a lot of practice. Not that she believed she was never wrong, but she'd seldom tried to explain or defend herself. Maybe she'd always hoped that the people who cared about her knew what her true intentions were and forgave her automatically. Or maybe that was the mother of all rationalizations and she was just too insecure to say the words. Well, she'd changed a lot in her life; she could change this, too. And look at the results!

Her "watch and wait" plan might be rather vague, but it was better than doing nothing. If someone was targeting her, for whatever reason, she wanted to identify the person—and ask him why. No one had the right to disrupt her life like this. Not now, when she should be happy, or at least content. She'd accomplished something with the orchard and her home, and she wanted to enjoy that. She'd earned that.

As he had promised, Seth pulled into the driveway in his work van a few minutes later. He waved as he got out, but he headed directly toward his office at the back. Not long after Meg heard another vehicle, and looked out to see John arriving. Seth came out to greet him and they conferred, although Meg couldn't hear what they were talking about. John nodded a couple of times, and they both started loading supplies into the back of his pickup truck, then they both pulled away. Business as usual. It was, after all, the start of a new workweek—and Meg felt rather lost without some work to do. What had farmers done in winter, in the old days? Mended things, no doubt. Sharpened their tools. Done what interior repairs they could.

Bree had put the goats in their outdoor pen before she left, and Meg wandered out to say hello to them. They looked happy and healthy—although Meg wasn't sure she would recognize an unhealthy goat. Would their hair fall out? Would they refuse to eat? Mope in the corners of their pen? Bleat constantly? Well, at the moment they were doing none of the above, so Meg hoped they were all right. "Hi, Dorcas, Isabel. What's new?"

They both looked at her briefly and went on munching hay.

Meg leaned on a fence post. "I know how you feel. Kind of dull these days, isn't it? Spring should be a lot more interesting. Plus you can spend more time outside then. You should be active, right?" Meg knew she missed the sheer physical activity that the orchard demanded. "Uh, you haven't seen anyone lurking around, have you?"

Dorcas and Isabel ignored her. It was a silly question anyway. How did she expect goats to identify a prowler? If they bit someone, could forensic evidence link the goats' teeth to the culprit? Maybe she should train them as watchgoats.

Meg was surprised when an unfamiliar car rattled its way into the driveway, though when she walked toward it, she recognized John's wife Jenn as the driver. Jenn opened the door and stood in its lee, out of the wind. Baby Eli was strapped into his car seat in the back. "Is John here?"

"He was, but he and Seth went off a little while ago. They didn't say where they were going."

"Damn. We must've got our wires crossed—I thought he said he'd be around this morning. Eli's got a doctor's appointment, and John's got the checkbook."

Jenn didn't look well, Meg thought. Her pale hair needed washing, and her eyes and nose were red-rimmed, as if she had a cold. Her jacket was far from new, and whatever stuffing it had was limp and defeated. "Are you in a hurry, or do you want to come in for coffee?" Meg asked.

"Oh, no, you don't have to . . ."

"Please. I'm kind of at loose ends now that the harvest is over, and I'd love to have someone to talk to. Besides, we're neighbors. And I have Seth's number—maybe John's with him, or at least he knows where he is. I can give him a call."

Jenn sniffed. "I guess. The doctor's appointment isn't until eleven. You don't mind if I bring Eli, do you?"

"Not at all. Unless he's allergic to cats. But I've only got the one."

"That's okay. We've got three." Jenn went around to the other side of the car and started disentangling a sleepy Eli from his car seat. Meg went back into the kitchen to put a kettle on to boil. Jenn rapped on the door a couple of moments later.

"Come on in. Is coffee all right, or would you like something else?"

"Coffee's good." With a practiced move, Jenn shrugged off her jacket without letting go of her son. With one hand she slung the jacket over the back of a chair and sat down, settling Eli on her lap. He pointed at Lolly, once again curled up on the top of the refrigerator. "Gah!" he said.

"Yeah, baby, that's a cat. You've got a great house, Meg."

"Thanks. Have you been inside before?"

"No, but I've been driving past it most of my life—I grew up in Granford. Good thing you got rid of some of those lowlifes that were living here before."

"The renters?" Meg measured coffee, then poured hot water over the grounds. "Why?"

"They were bringing down the neighborhood. You're lucky they didn't trash the place."

That was something Meg had never considered. Sure, they had ignored some needed repairs, and left behind some seriously shabby furniture, but it had never occurred to Meg that renters would want to do real damage. "I guess I am. My mother left all that to the local law firm, who found a real estate firm to handle the rentals."

"Your mother, she's the one who inherited?"

"Yes, she did, although now we own it jointly. I must say, it was a real surprise to her when the Warren sisters left it to her. We're pretty distantly related. What do you like in your coffee?"

"Milk and sugar, if you've got 'em."

"Of course." Meg set her sugar bowl on the table and pulled a carton of milk out of the refrigerator. "Here you go. You want me to hold the baby—Eli, right?—while you fix your coffee?"

"You don't have to—unless you want to?"

Did she? Meg's experience with small children was limited. "Sure." Meg held out her arms, and Jenn deposited a rather damp Eli in them, who promptly stuck a finger up Meg's nose. She gently removed it, asking, "You said he was sixteen months old? Is he walking yet?"

"Some. Mostly he crawls. Don't you, sweetie?" Jenn cooed at Eli. Eli turned his head toward his mother but otherwise seemed content to stay in Meg's arms. Jenn added two spoons of sugar and a healthy dollop of milk to her mug and stirred.

"He's so blond," Meg said, looking down at the top of Eli's head. "He must take after you."

"I guess. Hey, you got anything to eat? We kind of missed breakfast."

Meg recalled belatedly that John was out of work, so food money was probably tight. "Toast, muffins?"

"Whatever."

Jenn held out her arms for her son, and Meg handed him back, then went to the refrigerator to explore. "I've got some leftover coffee cake."

"Sounds good."

Meg pulled the coffee cake out of the refrigerator and set it in the microwave to warm up, then found plates, knives, and butter. When she turned back, Jenn was wandering around the kitchen, studying the details, bouncing Eli in her arms. "How old's this place?" she asked.

"I figure it was built around 1760, with some changes maybe a hundred years later."

Jenn nodded. "Our place is maybe fifty years old. And a lot smaller."

"I don't remember which house it is," Meg said.

"Small, white asbestos shingles, green roof, one-car garage. Easy to miss. It's actually John's mother's place."

"Does she live with you?"

"We live with her. She helps with the babysitting, so I can get out now and then."

Meg noticed that the coffee cake had disappeared quickly from Jenn's plate. "She works at Gran's, right? I met her there this week. Can I get anything for Eli?"

"No, he liked the cake." That was evident from the abundant crumbs he'd scattered down his front and on the table. Jenn extricated her wrist and checked the time. "Can you call Seth, see where John is?"

"Oh, sure." Meg found her cell phone, hit Seth's speed dial number, and handed over the phone and busied herself with washing their few dishes while Jenn talked.

When she was finished, Jenn handed back the phone. "Thanks. John's gonna meet me at the doctor's office. I'd better go or we'll be late. Thanks for the coffee, Meg. Come on, Eli—bye-bye time."

"Here, let me hold him while you put on your coat," Meg volunteered.

"Thanks." Jenn handed the baby back to Meg.

Meg and Eli contemplated each other silently for the few seconds it took Jenn to pull on her coat. He certainly was a placid child, Meg thought.

"He's sure no trouble," Meg said.

Jenn took him back. "Yeah, he's Mommy's little sweetie."

Meg opened the back door for her. "Nice to see you, Jenn. And you too, Eli." Meg waved at Eli. Eli just stared at her. Maybe she had no knack for babies.

She watched Jenn buckle her son into his car seat again, and pull out in a cloud of exhaust—obviously the car could use a tune-up. Which they probably couldn't afford.

Entertaining Jenn and Eli had used up maybe half an hour. It wasn't even time for lunch. The goats were taken care of. Now what? With a sigh, Meg acknowledged that she'd probably be forced to do some of that dreaded housework she kept deferring. Maybe she could make curtains—or order them online, since she hadn't used her sewing skills since she was a Girl Scout. So she should go measure windows and decide which curtains really had to be replaced.

But first she called Bree on her cell phone. "Bree? Were you planning to come back tonight?"

"Uh, maybe. Why?"

"I'm hatching a plan to identify our mystery stalker, and I want to talk to you and Seth about it. I'll make dinner."

"Uh, sure, okay. See you sixish."

26

Meg had massacred an army of spiders, and her windows were cleaner than they had been since she had arrived. She was basking in the glow of virtuous satisfaction as she chopped parsley. Seth had agreed to join them for dinner, and was due to arrive any minute. Bree returned first and came bounding in. "Hey, you need any help?"

"No, I've got it under control. Thanks for coming back—I didn't mean to cut into your time with Michael."

"He's cool with it. He had some stuff he had to do, anyway. It's not like we can't stand to be separated, you know."

Did she know? Bree's love life was her own business, and Meg didn't pry. She liked Michael. And a small part of her was glad that Bree wasn't rushing into any kind of serious relationship; she'd rather Bree concentrated on the business, at least for now.

Bree helped herself to a soda from the refrigerator. "Besides, I want to hear what you're planning."

"And I want your input. This all started when I realized

in the middle of the night that I'm tired of sitting here waiting for the next bad thing to happen, without doing anything about it. I think it's time to turn the tables."

"Good for you. I'm with you."

Seth's van pulled into the driveway, and a few moments later he knocked at the back door. Meg went to open it. "Hey, you don't need to knock."

"Just being polite."

"Bree's here."

"I know—I saw her car. So I can't ravish you on the kitchen floor?"

"Save that for later."

Bree was watching them with amusement. "Hi, Seth. I guess you guys made up, huh?"

Meg looked at Seth, and they both smiled. "Uh, yeah," Meg said. "Seth, help yourself to something to drink. I'll finish cooking." As Seth fished a bottle of beer from the refrigerator, she added, "I was surprised to see Jenn here today. She said Eli had a doctor's appointment but John had the checkbook. You said their baby was sick? He seemed fine today. What's the problem?"

Seth shrugged. "I don't really know. John doesn't talk about it. I get the impression it's something chronic, though. I wish I could hire him and give him health insurance, but I don't have the work, at least not at the moment. He signed up with the state program, but even that's hard to afford. Lousy situation all around."

"It's sad. And I'm pretty sure Jenn was hungry when she was here. I offered her some coffee cake and it disappeared in under a minute. She said they're living with his mother?"

"That's what I understand. She's been widowed for years, so I guess it works out for all of them."

Meg dished up dinner and set plates on the table. "Okay, let's eat, and then we can plan."

They talked about trivial things through dinner and

while they cleared away the dishes. Meg put a plate of cookies—another product of her free afternoon—in the center of the table, filled coffee cups, and sat down. "I feel like I should say, 'the meeting will come to order.' Bree, you take notes."

"You're kidding, right?"

"Yes, I'm kidding. Okay, Seth and I were talking this morning—"

"Bet that's not all you were doing," Bree said, grinning, her mouth full of cookie.

"Shut up." Meg glanced sidelong at Seth, who was studying the depths of his coffee—and smiling. "So as I told you both, I was thinking last night and I realized I want to do something about this. Seth pointed out that there's nothing the police can do to help, at least until some major crime is committed, and we don't want to wait for that."

"No way," Bree said. "But what *can* we do?"

Seth spoke up. "We've already ruled out using electronic devices—too complex, too expensive, and probably too obvious. So Meg thinks we use human eyes. We start by making sure there's somebody here 24/7. We stay alert."

"And we set a trap," Meg interrupted. When Seth cocked his head at her, she went on, "No, not a physical trap. We just make it look like no one's home, then wait and see if this person takes advantage of it."

"And how long are we supposed to keep doing this?" Bree asked, looking skeptical.

"I don't think we'd have to wait too long," Meg said. "Look, these things seem to have started happening less than two weeks ago. Assuming that was the beginning, then there's been something almost every day since. So, bottom line—this person is moving fast and keeping up the pressure."

"If we knew 'why' we'd have a better chance of knowing 'who,' " Seth said quietly.

"I agree," Meg replied, "but I've racked my brains and I can't come up with anything. You've lived here all your life, Seth. Any ideas?"

Seth sat back in his chair and rubbed his hands over his face. He looked tired. "No. It would be nice if it was an outsider, wouldn't it? I know—they don't know you, and they'd have no reason to target you. But at the same time I can't think of anyone in Granford who would have a grudge against you—that's what makes this so hard to figure out."

Meg nodded, then resumed, "Can we set up a schedule, so that at least one of us is here and awake at all times? I can cover a lot of it, since I don't have anywhere I have to be right now. But not twenty-four hours a day! I can plan any errands I have to do when Bree will be here. Seth, what can you handle?"

"Not much, at least during the day. I've got a couple of jobs going, but they're scattered, so I'm moving from one to the other. Night's better, but I can't promise I'll stay awake. Bree, how about you?"

"I don't need much sleep—I can probably cover the late shift. How about this: we ditch the cars somewhere else and then sneak back? So it looks like the place is empty, but it's not?"

"Good idea, but let's start tomorrow night. I have to make some plans first. Oh, by the way," Seth added, "the weather report says it might snow again."

"A lot?" Meg said anxiously.

"Not like the last time, just a normal winter snowfall."

"Will that make a difference in our plans?"

"Maybe. Snow would make it harder to see anyone, but then they would leave footprints, at least for a short while—so at least you'd be sure you're not imagining things. Let's just play it by ear, okay?"

"Okay, I guess," Meg said, stifling a sigh. She really

wanted to get started, because she wanted the whole thing to be over. "Bree, will you be around tomorrow?"

"I can be. So, how do we pull off hiding my car?"

"You can leave it at my place," Seth offered.

"And then I can come and collect you there," said Meg.

"Ooh, do I get to hide under a blanket in the trunk?"

"Only if you really want to." Meg laughed. "It's pretty dark late in the afternoon, especially if it clouds over, so if you leave by four or five, you can sneak into the house."

"Why not the barn?" Bree asked.

"What?" Meg replied, startled.

"I could spend the night in the barn, like you did. We've got built-in goat-heat"—Bree flashed a smile—"and if I was out there, it would spread us around, give us different views, better coverage. You bring me back and I sneak into the barn, and lay low for the night. You got any night-vision goggles?"

"I do not! Wouldn't you be kind of bored with no light and nothing to do out there?"

"I'll figure something out."

Meg turned to Seth. "Does that make any sense?"

"Maybe," he said. "She's right—it would expand the area we could watch. She's got windows in a couple of the doors, but she'd have to keep patrolling. But if it's late, I think anybody moving around outside would be pretty obvious and she'd hear. Nobody can be completely quiet."

"If you say so," Meg said, unconvinced. "This person has managed to sneak up on us before, even while we were in the house."

"But you weren't paying attention," Seth said.

"Okay, say Bree settles in the barn after dark. What about us?"

"You can drive over to my place, and we'll walk back."

"In the dark?"

"Meg, I've been walking around here for most of my life. It'll be fine. I'm not asking you to do it alone."

Meg wasn't reassured. "Then how do we sneak into the house?"

"The door from the shed. Wear dark clothes. Leave the door unlocked and the lights off—Bree will be watching until we get back. Then we can spell each other through the night."

Meg sat back and looked at Bree and Seth. The idea was solid, but as they laid out the details, it sounded more and more ridiculous. She was pretty sure she would sound like an elephant blundering around in the dark, even with Seth to guide her—not the best way to avoid detection. But what other alternatives were there? She couldn't think of any.

"I guess that's the best we can do. So, Bree, we'll trade off during the day tomorrow and do whatever we need to do, then you'll drive to Seth's and I'll collect you there and sneak you back."

"Hey, that means the place will be uncovered then," Bree pointed out.

"I can try to stop by after five, and wait for you to come back, Meg," Seth said.

Meg nodded. "Okay. Then you leave, and Bree hides in the barn. Then I'll leave, and you and I will come back overland. Should we write a script for this?" Meg received blank stares. "I mean, shouldn't we have some kind of dialogue, in case anybody's watching? Like 'So you're going over to Michael's and you'll be gone all night, right, Bree?' "

Bree laughed. "And my line is, 'Yes, Meg, I will be gone until tomorrow. And yourself?' "

Meg countered, " 'Indeed, Bree, I plan to go over to Seth's house and stay there all night. I shall feed the cat and the goats before I leave, but I will not be back until morning.' "

"You two are nuts," Seth said, smiling. "I don't think

anyone would be close enough to hear you, but if it makes you happy, go for it."

Bree bounded out of her chair. "Well, I'd better rest up for our big day—or should I say night?—tomorrow. I'll leave you two kids alone." Before Meg could say anything, Bree had disappeared up the back stairs to her room. Leaving the last of the dirty dishes, Meg noted.

"You want help cleaning up?" Seth asked.

"No, don't worry about it. You've already put in a full day of work. Seth, is this crazy?"

"Odd, maybe. But I understand that you want to do something, and I don't think this will be dangerous. And I'll be around to keep an eye on things."

Meg swatted his arm. "Oh, yes, I need a big strong man to protect me. But seriously, you don't think there would be any violence, do you?"

Seth studied her face before answering. "Maybe I've lived around here too long. The people I know in Granford aren't violent. My gut feeling is, if this person had wanted to do any real harm, either to you or to your property, he would have by now. It would be too darn easy to set fire to the barn or shoot your goats when they were outside."

"Seth!" Meg was appalled at the thought, but realized he had a point.

"I'm just saying that he could have, but didn't. And believe me, if I thought you were truly at risk I wouldn't let you out of my sight. Seriously, I don't think destruction is the point here. I think this is intended to keep you on edge."

"This jerk is good at that, damn him, whatever it is he *is* doing. I just hope this doesn't take too long—more than a couple of nights, anyway."

"Amen to that," Seth said, standing up slowly. "I'd better be going. Tomorrow's going to be a long day."

Meg stood up, too, and went to him, wrapping her arms

around his waist. "Thank you for going along with this. It may be silly, but . . ."

"I don't think it's silly. I think you're defending your home, which is pretty primal. I admire you for trying, whether or not it works. Nobody can say you don't have guts."

"Yeah, I'm a gutsy broad." She kissed him hard, then shoved him away. "Go home and get some sleep. You're going to need it."

"Yes, ma'am. See you in the morning."

Meg cleaned up the kitchen, locked up, and went to bed, trailed by Lolly.

The next morning the sky was heavily overcast. Maybe the forecasters were right about snow. Should they defer their plan to trap a . . . what? Harasser? There should be a better word. "Nemesis" sounded a bit too strong, invoking overtones of fate and angry gods. "Gadfly"? Not serious enough. "Persecutor"? "Tormentor"? Nothing felt right. But Meg still wanted an answer, an identity for the shadowy figure who'd been dogging her for a couple of weeks now.

Bree was sitting at the table drinking coffee and reading the paper when Meg came downstairs.

"What are they saying about the weather?" Meg asked, filling her own mug.

"Snow, maybe four to six inches. No big deal."

Meg wasn't sure whether to be relieved or disappointed. She sat down. "You have any new thoughts about our plan?"

"Not really. I agree with you, in principle—but I'm not convinced that what we're planning will flush him out. If he's smart he'll see right through us and just wait for a while."

"I know." Meg sipped her coffee. "I'd still like to know what set him off, and why he's in such a hurry. Why now?"

"Fewer people around? When we were picking, there were always people coming and going, and one of us was home most nights."

"True, but that makes a person hanging around here all the more obvious now. No, I think there must have been something that triggered this, but I can't figure out what it could be. What happened around Thanksgiving?"

"Got me. We finished the harvest, went to Rachel's for Thanksgiving dinner."

"Maybe somebody thought we took their place at Rachel's dinner? She's one good cook!"

"Agreed. But bugging you after the fact doesn't change anything. Seth have any jealous ex-girlfriends?"

"Not that I know of. I can't imagine his ex-wife is involved in this. You think someone else has set her cap for him and is trying to drive me away so she has a clear field?"

"Boy, are you mixing your metaphors."

"You know what I mean."

Bree nodded. "Yeah, I do. And no, I don't think that's it."

Meg giggled. "Well, I'm out of ideas. Look, I've got a couple of small errands to do this morning. What are you up to?"

"I'm going to catch up on my reading—it's a real treat to have enough time for it."

"Good for you. Just keep your eyes and ears open, will you?"

"Always do."

After breakfast Meg went out to the car. The air felt heavy. Could one smell snow coming? Maybe if she hung around in Granford long enough she'd learn to recognize it. She got into the car and headed toward the nearest mall: new socks, some nicer underwear—she giggled at that thought—and a stop at a pharmacy were on the top of the list.

Two hours later she was headed back toward Granford, but on a whim turned off on the road toward the cemetery. No one was following her, and she was going to stay alert, just in case. The last snow had more or less melted, except where it had been piled deep, and if there was more coming, she didn't know when she'd have another chance to locate Violet Morgan, née Cox. Maybe it was a bit odd to stop by and visit someone who had died more than a century earlier, but Meg thought it was only right to introduce herself if she was digging up all of Violet's dark secrets.

Once again, there was no other car in sight on the road by the cemetery. Meg pulled as far over as the surviving snow piles would permit, climbed out of the car, and headed for the central gate. John had been right about winter visitors: even now Meg could see new flowers—garish plastic ones—on some of the newer graves. People did stop by regardless of weather. That made her feel a little better. After all, Violet was a relative of a sort, and Meg was here to remember her. She picked her way through the rows, looking for stones in the style popular in the mid-nineteenth century: not the old slate slabs, but more likely white marble.

Gail had said there were a few Morgans in Granford, and Meg wondered what the odds were that she'd find any of them. She wandered aimlessly for a bit, and almost cheered out loud when she finally spied a tall stone for Abiel Morgan, and directly under his name, "Violet C. Morgan, beloved wife." It was too cold and damp to sit on the ground, so Meg leaned cautiously against a tombstone in the next row. "Hello, Violet."

The wind whistled through the trees bordering the far side of the cemetery, and a raucous crow took flight. Otherwise, silence.

Meg was glad not to have an audience. "I found your sampler. It's lovely—you did nice work. I don't know how it stayed hidden for so long, but I'm glad to have it. I live in the house you once did, with your Uncle Eli." Meg looked around, at the other, later tombstones flanking Abiel's central one: more Taylors. "Looks like some of your kids stayed around—that must have been nice for you, to have close family nearby."

The wind was picking up, and while it might not have been below freezing, the dampness made it chilling. Time to wrap this up. "Well, Violet, I'll be back again, I'm sure—in better weather. It was nice to meet you."

Meg retraced her steps to the main path, and then decided to make a small detour and say hello to Lula and Nettie Warren, the sisters her mother had inherited the house from, at the far end of the newer section. When she reached them, Meg said, "Hi, ladies. You know, if you'd been taller, you would have found a nice surprise in one of your closets. Well, I just wanted to say hello, and let you know that the house is looking good."

OK, enough craziness for one day. If the good citizens of Granford could see her now, talking to lumps of rock in the snow . . . As Meg made her way back toward her car, her eye was caught by another stone, this one much newer granite, with the name John B. Taylor 1940—1972 at the top. John's father, Donna's husband? He'd died so young. No spouse was listed on the stone (which would make sense if this was Donna's husband), but below John's name were two others: Megan Taylor, Sean Taylor. Both had been born in the late 1990s—too late to be John's own children—but both had died before reaching age five. Meg shivered, not sure whether from the cold or from what she was seeing.

There had to be a story here. The children's dates of death were different, so it wasn't some sort of tragic accident. But what natural cause killed children so young in modern times? Meg had no idea.

And were these children related to her neighbor John Taylor? She didn't want to think so. It would be heart-wrenching to lose not one but two children so young. And

Seth had said Eli was sick; he hadn't looked particularly sick when Meg had seen him, even held him—but he had been on his way to a doctor's appointment. Jenn had said Eli was their only child . . . but was it too much of a leap of logic to assume that the children in the cemetery here were related to Eli? Maybe even deceased siblings? That wasn't the kind of question Meg could exactly ask someone she didn't know very well. But maybe Seth could tell her. Meg filed the question away for future thought, and headed back to the house. Right now she had a trap to set.

27

The sky was gray and heavy as Meg drove home, and the clouds seemed lower than they had been earlier in the day. When she pulled into her driveway, she stopped to check the mail. Bills, a few early Christmas cards, and at the bottom of the pile was a thick Express Mail envelope. Meg was surprised to see that it had come from Mercy at the Pittsford Library. Mercy must have been very eager to have assembled and copied information for her so quickly—after all, Meg had been there only three days earlier. And it looked like Mercy had paid for the speedy delivery herself; no doubt her library, like many, was facing a budget crunch. Mercy must have believed that this was important, and Meg was intrigued.

When she came through the back door, Meg called out to let Bree know she was back.

"What took you so long?" asked Bree, thudding down the back stairs.

"Am I late for something? I stopped by the cemetery on my way home."

"Oh, well, of course—I should have guessed," Bree said sarcastically. "I thought I'd squeeze in lunch with Michael, since I'm busy tonight."

"You haven't noticed anything suspicious since I left?"

"Nope. I might have seen a fox over on the other side of the meadow, but that's been the high point so far. No calls, either."

"I'm going to be here the rest of the day, so you go have a nice lunch. But be back before dark, okay?"

"Can I tell Michael what's going on?"

Meg considered briefly. "I guess. It's unlikely that even if he did talk about it around Amherst, our perpetrator would get wind of it. Unless, of course, it's Michael who's behind all this. He wants to put you out of a job so he can spend more time with you?"

"Ha! We see plenty of each other now, and we're fine with it. But you just keep thinking. Heck, according to that logic, maybe Seth wants you to move out of this house and into his."

"Nope, not happening. My, aren't we independent?"

"Sure are. See you later!" Bree pulled on her coat, grabbed her bag, and went out to her car. As she closed the kitchen door behind her, Meg was both amused and saddened to see Bree walk all the way around the car, just as Meg had earlier, to make sure everything was all right. Apparently it was, because Bree got in, started the car, and pulled away, waving as she passed the back door.

Leaving Meg alone in the house. Should she feel worried? She was surprised to find that she wasn't. Seth had been right: if someone truly wanted to do her harm, they could, quite easily. They hadn't, at least so far. Yes, the events were intensifying—and that gunshot was unsettling. But it hadn't hit anyone, and Meg chose to think that was because it hadn't been aimed at anyone. In any case, as she had told Seth, she didn't want to live in fear, looking over her shoulder all the time, especially when she didn't even know what—or who—she was looking for. So she was going to do something about it, and that felt good.

Meg looked at the pile of mail where she had left it on the kitchen table, tempted by Mercy's envelope. No, she would eat first and then settle down with it. Anticipation was a good condiment.

After a hasty lunch—she could only wait so long, after all—Meg cleaned up, then took Mercy's envelope into the dining room. The temperature was comfortable, so the furnace and thermostat were working as they should, which was good news. She opened the tear-strip on the envelope and pulled out a stack of photocopies, at least a half-inch thick. Mercy had also printed out a long note, attached to the top of the stack.

Meg—

After you left I started digging through our files and I hit pay dirt. I gave you the bare outlines of the Cox-Warren story, but there was a lot more, that I'm sending to you here. I knew the name Lampson rang a bell! What I found was a transcript of a nineteenth-century diary that was in our family history section. The transcription was made maybe fifty or sixty years ago by a member of the library board—who as you will see was a lousy typist. The original dates to around 1825, based on internal evidence.

I only knew about the diary because we're working on a special event for the library, to raise money (hint, hint), and we figured we'd better give the public something juicy to draw them in. So I enlisted some students and sent them snooping in the files for anything we could use. You'd be surprised at how much they came up with, and the Lampson story was pretty interesting.

I'll let you see for yourself.

Her curiosity piqued, Meg turned to the copies. She skimmed through the whole stack quickly, then went back and started reading the particular sections that Mercy had marked. The transcriber had obviously had some trouble deciphering the original handwritten document, but the basic story was clear enough. The writer of the diary had been a child when the events she described had happened, and it was possible that her memory was cloudy—or exaggerated. Still, it must have been a juicy scandal in its day, one that was passed down in whispers over the years, becoming a warped piece of local mythology.

What the author of the diary had written was that Unity Cox, née Warren, had been driven mad by the deaths of her younger children in quick succession (except, of course, future sampler-maker Violet), and when the fourth and last Lampson child died, Unity had killed her husband and then herself. According to the diary, the public story was that Unity had blamed her second husband for breeding sickly children, since Violet, her only child by her first husband, was clearly healthy. Meg paged back: earlier references in the diary made mention of the children's illnesses and deaths, in matter-of-fact language. But it hadn't been disease that killed the parents, but violence. Murder, then suicide. Had Unity left a note?

Mercy's bounty didn't end there. She had enclosed copies of some church records, and a single-line item from 1796 recorded the recommendation that the orphaned Violet Cox be sent to a distant relative, in order to escape the taint of her mother's acts. Yet another page turned out to be a copy of a Pittsford selectmen's report, where a corresponding entry allocated money to send Violet to live with an uncle in Massachusetts. That had to be Eli Warren. That explained why Violet hadn't stayed in Vermont: she would have been forever branded by the scandal of her mother's last deeds. Instead, she had been shipped back to Granford, where Eli had taken her in and seen to it that she received a decent education. So the sampler had been made when the awful events were relatively recent—Violet's last act of remembrance, perhaps, before she had moved on with her life. How much had she known—or seen?

Meg sat back in her chair, stunned. Poor Violet. Violet had to have watched her half siblings die, one after another. It was a wonder that she'd had the courage to have children of her own, after what she had experienced.

And yet, these were modern times, and Meg could easily see other interpretations. Perhaps the explanation of the town fathers had been a polite fiction. Had Unity abused her own children? Maybe it hadn't had a name back then, but had she suffered from such a thing as Munchausen's syndrome by proxy? Unity had wanted the attention and sympathy of the community upon the deaths of her children? And had Unity killed her husband, and then herself out of remorse? Or maybe Jacob Lampson had been the one responsible for killing his children, and Unity had finally gotten fed up and killed him, and then inflicted her own punishment upon herself, leaving poor Violet to fend for herself? Or had Violet had a hand in their deaths? Surely Violet couldn't have killed her own mother?

Meg sat back and closed her eyes. Well, she had asked for it. Any of these scenarios made it more understandable that the many other Warrens in Pittsford had washed their hands of Violet. But there was no explanation that did not carry a heavy freight of pain and anguish all around. At worst, Violet had been a murderer; at best, she had had to witness all the deaths, wondering if either her own mother or the only father she had ever known was behind them.

Could Meg trust what amounted to centuries-old gossip? Not necessarily, but the cold facts remained: six people had died in Pittsford, and Violet had been exiled to Granford.

Mercy was definitely going to get a contribution for the library fund from Meg. From a genealogy standpoint this kind of intimate personal information was priceless. Meg had to share it with someone, and Gail was the logical person. Meg checked her watch—it was just past two, so her children should still be at school. She picked up her cell phone and dialed quickly. "Gail? It's Meg. You have a minute?"

"Hi, Meg. Yes, I've got . . . twenty-two minutes until the little monsters are dropped off. I'll bet they're hoping for another snow day tomorrow. What's up?"

"I didn't get a chance to tell you, but Seth and I drove up to Pittsford over the weekend, and talked to the librarian there. She confirmed most of what we had guessed—the Warren brothers and one sister all moved to Pittsford together, and they all married Cox siblings."

"Oh, that's cool! But I take it there's more?"

"Yes. Unity Warren Cox's husband died, and she remarried a Jacob Lampson. They had the four kids listed on the sampler, and they all died young. Unity and Jacob died shortly after, and Violet was sent to Granford."

"So what've you got that's new?"

"I'm getting there. I just got another stack of copies from the librarian in Pittsford, and I've got a much better idea why Violet was shipped here."

"And? Sorry to rush your story, but the clock is ticking," Gail said.

"I know. So, part of the new information was a diary written by a Pittsford woman from the early nineteenth century. She claims that Unity was driven over the edge by all the deaths, and she killed her husband and then herself. The town thought Violet would be better off somewhere else, away from all that scandal—that's when they sent her back here to Eli. It's in the town record. What's worse, there are hints that the children didn't die naturally."

"Oh, wow, how sad! Poor Violet, to have lived through all that."

"I know. And then in a way she relived it by making the

sampler. Heck, maybe she's the one who wadded it up and hid it."

"Oh, dear. But, Meg, do you have any idea how lucky you are to have this much information? It's called serendipity. Some genealogists are blessed with it. Congratulations, you seem to have the knack! Look, the kids'll be home any minute. Maybe we can plan a lunch later this week and you can fill in the details. Talk to you soon!" Gail hung up.

Meg checked her watch—it was already darkening outside, and as she watched, a few flakes of snow began to drift lazily toward the ground. She had better get dressed for skulking tonight. The weather hadn't stopped their lurker last time, Meg realized, remembering the tracks in the snow under her back window. In any case, Bree would be home soon, and they would have to begin their absurd charade. Meg could only hope it would do some good.

28

Bree walked into the kitchen at four thirty and announced, "Michael thinks we're nuts."

"Why?" Meg asked. She was running late, since Seth's window repair person had shown up earlier in the afternoon and replaced the window. She hadn't even thought about dinner yet.

Bree shrugged. "I'm not sure he believes that any of this is real, and if it is, then we're being stupid to think we can handle it ourselves. What if this guy gets violent?"

Meg sighed. "We've been over this before. Do we have to wait until somebody is hurt—or worse—before we can do anything about it? Would it be better if he killed someone? Just so that we'd be really, really sure something was going on?"

"I'm just reporting what Michael said. I didn't say I agreed with him."

"I notice he didn't volunteer to come along and protect you."

"Michael does not believe in violence," Bree replied

primly—then laughed. "I think he's a wimp. But, no, he didn't offer. So what's next?"

"You want something to eat in the barn? I can pack you a picnic or something."

"Oh, great—just me and the goats, and a few sandwiches."

"Don't forget the apples. Seriously, you should eat something. It's going to be a long night."

"Yes, mother," Bree replied, but she went to the refrigerator and studied the contents, pulling out some containers of leftovers. "When's Seth coming over?"

"Anytime now. So, you eat, and then we'll drive over to his place and leave your car, and I'll sneak you back in my car. Don't forget to leave the barn door unlocked before we go—we want you to get inside as quickly as possible, just in case someone is actually watching. And dress warmly—it's cold out there. How's the snow?"

"Not bad. Those big fluffy flakes aren't a problem, really." Bree stuck the leftovers into the microwave and pushed some buttons.

"I got some additional information from Mercy, the librarian I talked to in Pittsford," Meg said. "She found a diary that explains why Violet ended up here. It's a sad story—I'll fill you in when we've got more time."

"Yeah, right, whatever," Bree replied, clearly not interested, which didn't surprise Meg. Fifteen minutes later, Bree was ready to go, bouncing with eagerness. She didn't appear at all intimidated by the idea of spending the night in a cold and drafty barn, waiting for some unknown assailant to show up.

"You sure you'll be warm enough?" Meg asked for the third time.

"I'm good, really. I've been living around here for most of my life, and I haven't lost any body parts to frostbite, right? So let's just do this thing. You remember your lines?"

"What, we're really going to do that?"

"Can't hurt, can it?" Bree grinned at her, clearly into her role.

Meg stood in the doorway, watching Bree march toward her car, suitably bundled up, laden with food, and, Meg hoped, something to entertain herself with in her backpack. "When will you be back?" she called out, feeling ridiculous.

"Tomorrow morning sometime. Have a nice evening," Bree replied, more loudly than usual and speaking slowly and clearly.

"I'll be at Seth's, remember," Meg dutifully gave her reply.

"Oh, right. Then I'll see you when I see you. Don't do anything I wouldn't do," Bree said, sounding surprisingly natural. "Bye!"

Step one accomplished. Now Meg had to wait a few minutes before heading over to Seth's to pick up Bree. Seth's van pulled into the driveway a minute after Bree had left.

"Right on schedule," Meg said.

"I've got some stuff to drop off, and I need to pick up some house plans." He came close and kissed her, then said in a low voice, "So what's your excuse for going out now?"

"Liquor store?" she replied in the same tone.

"Perfect."

Meg raised her voice. "Shoot! I forgot to pick up a bottle of wine for tonight at your place. You're busy—why don't I just run and get some now?"

"Good idea. I'll see you later at my house, then," Seth said. In a lower voice he added, "You know, we're lousy at this."

"Tell me about it. Do you really think anyone is watching?"

"I don't know. Go."

Meg, feeling foolish, went inside to collect her coat and keys. Might as well actually go to the liquor store: while drinking was definitely not on the agenda for tonight, maybe by tomorrow they'd have something to celebrate.

Seth had already vanished inside his shop, turning on more lights than usual, when Meg pulled out of the driveway. The detour to the liquor store took no more than fifteen minutes, and then Meg headed over to Seth's house to collect Bree. She found her sitting in her car, reading by the car light.

"About time!" Bree said, getting into Meg's car.

"Seth's at my house, and we followed our silly script. I had to go to the liquor store to make my story convincing."

The drive back took no more than two minutes, and when Meg arrived home, she was happy to see that Seth had pulled the van up close to the front doors of the barn and was unloading what looked like large boxes of plumbing fixtures. It would be easy for Bree to slip inside unnoticed. "You ready?" Meg asked her.

"Let's do it!"

In the lee of the barn, Bree slipped out of the car and headed quickly for the door. Her dark clothing blended well with the night, and the swirling snow camouflaged any movements. If Meg hadn't been looking, she wouldn't have noticed anything. Seth came out of the barn, sliding the big doors shut behind him, then slammed shut the van door. He walked over to Meg's car, and she lowered her window. "See you in a bit," he said.

"Right. I'll bring the wine."

He ducked in for another quick kiss. They were certainly doing their part to convey the impression of an amorous couple looking forward to a romantic night—at Seth's house. At least no one watching would think they were planning to sneak around in the dark setting a trap.

Meg went inside and tried to look busy as Seth left the driveway, headed for home. Step two accomplished: Bree was in place. Meg fed Lolly and tidied up aimlessly. How many lights should she leave on? If they were supposed to slip back into the house unnoticed, fewer would be better. But she always left some lights on, the evenings she wasn't home, didn't she? It was a gesture more symbolic than practical: anybody could open one of her aged windows in about a minute, with no special tools. But it made her feel better to come back to a lighted place. In the end she compromised, leaving on the light over the front door, but not the one in the back; leaving on a bedroom light; and one in the front parlor. She debated briefly about leaving on one over the sink in the kitchen, until she realized that they were supposed to come in through the back, and that light would make that difficult. She gave Lolly one more pat, then headed out into the night.

At Seth's she came in through the kitchen door. He was waiting. "I guess we're committed now?" Meg said.

"Unless you want Bree to be really, really annoyed at you, I'd say so. By the way, I filled Art in about our plan, off the record. He can't approve what amounts to vigilantism, but he'll come if we need him."

"Before or after the fact?"

"Look, if we see someone who's acting suspicious, we call him. We don't have to try to stop this person, but we do have a legitimate complaint if there's a prowler. We do not try to do something brave—or stupid. Let Art deal with it."

"How anticlimactic. So we sit in the dark, waiting for someone to show up, and if we happen to see anyone, then we call the cops. And if we aren't careful—or lucky—the sneak will be long gone. By the way, where's Max?"

"What, you think he'd be any help? He'd probably bring the guy a chew toy and want to play. I left him with Mom."

One less thing to worry about. "Should we go?" Meg asked.

"Might as well. Look, when we get there, we go in through the shed door, right?"

"Yes. I left the light off in the kitchen, so it will be dark."

They stepped outside into swirling darkness. Meg

waited a moment for her eyes to adjust—Seth had turned off the outside lights, as though they had retired for the evening, expecting no additional visitors. The snow blew in her face, and she settled her knit hat more firmly on her head. At least there wasn't much accumulation yet. She'd walked this path before, but never under these conditions. *Think of your ancestors, Meg!* They must have done this regularly. Did churches hold evening meetings, a century earlier? Did local citizens walk, rather than riding or hitching the horse to a carriage? Did they use lanterns, or would it have been easier to see in the dark, or to trust the horse's sense of direction?

She stumbled over some unseen clod and Seth caught her arm. "You okay?" he asked.

"Sure. I love wandering around in the dark for questionable reasons. Sounds like the story of my life."

"We can still call this off. Just pull Bree out of the barn—unless she's gotten really chummy with the goats."

"Hey, they're nice enough, once you get to know them. No, I want to go through with this. Or is this one of those Too-Stupid-to-Live things you read about in bad novels? Should we know better? At least we did try to involve the authorities, instead of just insisting that we could handle it ourselves. Art didn't say no, did he?"

"Not in so many words. I'm pretty sure he wishes he could do more to help, but he hasn't got the manpower, and he can't commit what he does have to something as vague as this."

"So here we are. How far do you think sound carries, under the circumstances?"

"Not too far, with this snow. Are you worried about it?"

"I don't know. Maybe. We don't know what direction this person might be coming from. I mean, the road's kind of obvious."

"It's not likely anyone is coming through the meadow. It may be frozen, but the footing's pretty uneven."

"I guess that's good, since that's one of our blind spots—Bree can't see out the back of the barn easily. So that leaves the back end of the property—and this way, the direction we're coming from. Maybe we should shut up?"

"Good idea."

They trudged on in silence, until Meg could see the lights of her house glowing in the near distance. She stopped for a moment, listening, watching, but she couldn't hear or see anything. The barn looked dark, so Bree wasn't reading by flashlight—or if she was, she hid it well. "I guess we're going in," Meg whispered. "Should we split up?"

"I'll go first." Seth headed toward the house, and Meg hung back for half a minute. His dark-clad figure disappeared quickly, and she felt a moment of panic. It was all but impossible to see anyone, friend or foe, under these conditions. Maybe they should have waited for a better night. But it was too late now. Or was it? They could still call in Bree and just get a good night's sleep and think about it in the clear light of morning. What had sounded like a good plan in the warmth of her kitchen turned out to be entirely different when Meg was standing in the middle of a snowy field in the dark.

But the first step was to catch up to Seth. Meg started moving again, placing her feet cautiously, and then slipped into the shed. Seth was waiting for her by the door, but she couldn't read his expression. She reached out and pulled open the storm door, then the inner door, congratulating herself on remembering to oil the hinges. They moved soundlessly, and she led Seth into the dark kitchen. He shut the doors.

Step three accomplished. They were inside the house, and undetected as far as they knew. Now all they had to do was wait.

29

Meg listened hard but heard nothing out of place. She jumped when there was a sudden thud, quickly explained when Lolly appeared and wound herself around her ankles, pleased by the unexpected company.

"Now what?" she whispered to Seth.

"Are you okay keeping watch for a while, while I get some sleep?"

"I guess. What am I supposed to do? Stay put? Patrol through the rooms?" Meg had an absurd vision of herself crawling from room to room, popping up to peer out a window now and then, most likely with Lolly pacing alongside her.

"Yes."

Meg sensed rather than saw his smile. "You're no help."

"What I meant was, you can stay in one place, but get up and check outside the windows every now and then. It'll keep your circulation going, if nothing else."

"Got it. You want to go upstairs?"

"I'm good for now. We can wait together, at least for a while. Let's hope this person has an early bedtime."

"Where should we sit?"

"You left the lamp on in the front room."

"Yes, that's what I normally do when I'm not here at night. I wanted to stick to my usual pattern, in case somebody really has been watching."

"I'd say we could sit there, but if we moved around we might throw shadows, which would give us away. How about the dining room?"

"If we can sit on our coats. The floor in there may be historically correct, but it's not soft."

"Good thought."

They stripped off their outer garments, then scrambled their way across the kitchen floor into the dining room, settling themselves with their backs against a wall. For once Meg was glad she wasn't overburdened with furniture—there was plenty of room to stretch out their legs.

"Is it okay to talk?" Meg asked in a whisper.

"Probably. I don't think anyone outside could hear, even if they were standing under the window. Is there something you want to talk about?"

"Mercy from Pittsford sent me a packet of stuff—I got it today. I'm trying to figure out what it means."

"How so?"

"Well, the key information comes from an old diary, and there's stuff in there that could be gossip, or could be fact—it's hard to say now. But the gist of it is that after all the Lampson children and then the parents died, the town elders thought Violet would be better off somewhere else. I may be reading too much into it, but I wonder if they thought she had something to do with the deaths? Or maybe knew something she wasn't supposed to?"

"Like what?" Seth asked.

"I haven't thought this through, so I'm kind of guessing here. Violet was the eldest child, but she never knew her own father. Mom remarried quickly and started having more kids, and the last one—or two, actually, since they were twins—were born in 1791, when Violet was only five. And all the children died, the last one in 1794. And then the parents died."

"Meg, I think it's great you've memorized all this information, but what's the point?"

"The diary writer claimed that Unity was driven to kill her husband, and then she killed herself. The language the town used was kind of vague, but implied a scandal, bad enough to think that removing Violet from the only home she'd ever known was a good idea. It fits. And there's more. The writer of the diary said all the children were 'sickly.' Do you think the mother had something to do with it?"

"Like a case of Munchausen's? She liked having the kids, but not raising them?"

"I wondered about that. Did that kind of thing happen back then? But Violet lived. What if Mom thought the weakness in the other kids was her husband's fault? She'd borne one healthy child by her first husband, and the evidence was right there in front of them, but all the offspring of the second died early. Wait! The line on the sampler, remember? The Bible quote: 'All the increase of thy house shall be cut down in the flower of their age.' Violet was describing her family."

Seth yawned. "If you say so. But things like that happened back then, for lots of reasons. What's your point?"

"Where's the scandal, then, if everybody died a natural death? What I think happened is that after the last child died, Unity just lost it. I mean, what mother wouldn't, after watching four of her children die in the space of four years? It's like a dose of postpartum *plus* postmortem depression, and it was too much for her. Poor Unity, driven mad with grief, kills her husband, and then herself—while Violet watches the whole process. And the town thought Violet would be better off far away from Pittsford, and sent her here. Unity would have known that Violet would be cared for, by one or another of her relatives."

"So, what now then? You want to exhume Unity and Jacob and check for—what?"

Meg swatted Seth's arm. "No, that's ridiculous. But I am curious. *How* would Unity have killed her husband and then herself?"

Seth yawned again. "I assume you're going to tell me?"

"Poison would be the easiest for her. There were plenty of plants available to any housewife in those days. I can't see a woman shooting her husband, waiting a day or two, then shooting herself—and surely there would be a mention in the records somewhere. If it had been a shooting the town probably would have labeled it a 'tragic accident.' "

Seth didn't answer, and after a moment or two Meg realized he was snoring lightly. It was too dark to see her watch. She nudged him gently.

"Huh?" he said.

"You're falling asleep. Why don't you go upstairs and take the bed? I can wake you after a few hours."

"Sorry. Come and get me if you see or hear anything, okay?"

"Sure. Now, go."

Meg watched as Seth struggled to his feet, then moved surprisingly quietly into the hall and up the stairs, avoiding the light cast from the single lamp in the front parlor. When she heard the bedsprings creak upstairs, she stood up and tiptoed into the dark kitchen. Outside it was lighter only because of the falling snow reflecting the light from the front room, and she could barely see the far edge of the driveway. Great night they'd picked for a stakeout. There could be an elephant standing in her driveway and she wouldn't know it.

Would the snow keep her stalker at home, or would he take advantage of the cover it provided? What would be the next logical step in the progression of nuisance events?

Worse, would this mystery person graduate from nuisance to something more serious? What form would that take? Meg stared out into the odd half darkness, straining to see anything.

She went back to her post in the dining room, and it didn't take her long to realize she was bored. How did the police do this kind of thing? She couldn't read, she couldn't boot up her laptop, because either would cast light where there shouldn't be any. All she could do was sit and think. Not that there wasn't plenty to think about. One: her business could be called a success, which was good news. What would she like to see for it going forward? Did it make sense to expand her operations—plant more trees, thinking of the future? If so, what kind, and how many? The heirlooms were selling well, but would they be by the time new trees were bearing? Or should she stick with the tried-and-true best sellers?

How long would Bree be willing to stick around? She was smart and hardworking, and Meg knew she would never have survived this first year without her. Would she want to move on at some point? What kind of track record would she need to make the jump to the next level? What the heck *was* the next level? Where was Bree's relationship with Michael going? Or maybe it didn't have to be headed anywhere—maybe they were just enjoying the moment, with no strings. He seemed like a nice, earnest young man—Meg smiled inwardly at her use of "young," since Michael was less than ten years younger than she was—and his interests and Bree's were compatible. Was that going to be enough to carry them through?

And what about Seth? What did she want from him? What did she expect? She'd told him she loved him, and it was true. But where did they go from here? Maybe now, with the harvest under her belt, and a niche in the community—and some friends—she could give their relationship the attention it deserved.

She sat in the dark, listening to the light wind wrapping itself around the corners of the old house—and occasionally sending a gust down the chimney, whose damper didn't quite close—and the light tapping of snowflakes against the windowpanes. At least it didn't sound like ice, which was a good thing. Poor Bree, stuck out in the barn with only the goats to keep her company. Not that Lolly was much of a companion, curled up in a snug ball in a nearby chair. Meg dozed off . . .

To be awakened by an unholy and unnatural racket. Pulse pounding, Meg tried to sort out what was happening. Was that an air horn? The goats were bleating, and there were crashes coming from the barn. Obviously Bree had encountered someone and had sounded the alarm. Meg stumbled to her feet, hampered by the fact that one of her legs had gone to sleep, and lurched toward the kitchen door. No need for secrecy now. She jammed her arms into her coat, pulled on her boots, grabbed a flashlight, and hauled open the door—to be met by a swirling mass of snow. It didn't matter—the noise from the barn continued unabated, and she knew the way. She waded through the snow—which had already lived up to its "six inches" forecast—and dragged open one of the big doors facing the house. She fumbled briefly for the light switch beside the door, then turned it on—to a scene of chaos.

Bree was standing in front of the goat pen, whose gate was open, which explained why Dorcas and Isabel were darting around the interior. Meg quickly slid the barn door shut behind her to prevent them from escaping. Bree was wielding a piece of two-by-four like a baseball bat, squared off against . . . Jenn Taylor? Who was clutching the hayfork, pointed straight at Bree.

Meg took a step into the barn. "What the hell is going on?" she demanded.

Bree grinned, her eyes never leaving Jenn's weapon. "Looks like we have a visitor. How'd you like my air horn? Kids around here use them at football games." Bree didn't appear at all rattled by this midnight confrontation with an armed attacker.

"Very effective," Meg said. "You probably woke up the entire neighborhood. Jenn, what are you doing here? Put that thing down!"

Jenn's glance darted briefly toward Meg before returning to Bree. "She went after me first."

"Well, of course I did! What are you doing skulking around the barn in the middle of the night?"

"What are you doing *in* the barn in the middle of the night?" Jenn countered.

"Looks like I was waiting for you," Bree said. "You thought it would be empty, right? What were you planning this time?"

"Bree, did you call Art?" Meg said sharply.

"Sure did, soon as I spotted her."

Meg started when she heard fumbling at the big front doors. Then one door slid open behind her and Seth stepped in, closing it behind him. He came up to stand alongside her. "He's tied up with an accident over on 202. We're on our own for now," he said quietly to Meg, then more loudly, "Jenn, what's this about?"

Bree waved her lumber. "She came in carrying this, but she dropped it when I surprised her with all that noise. You thought the place would be empty, right, lady? Well, we're onto you now." Bree glanced at Seth again. "She grabbed the fork once I got hold of the two-by-four."

Jenn was trying to watch everyone at once, her eyes darting around like a trapped animal's. "Jenn, put that down, please," Meg said. "We aren't going to hurt you, we just want to talk."

Jenn looked at Meg full on then, and Meg nearly took a

step back, so strong was the hatred in Jenn's eyes. It wasn't clear whether Jenn would have cooperated, but then Dorcas came up behind her and nudged her, and Jenn turned on the goat in a fury, and raised the hayfork.

"No!" three voices yelled in near unison, as everyone moved to stop her.

30

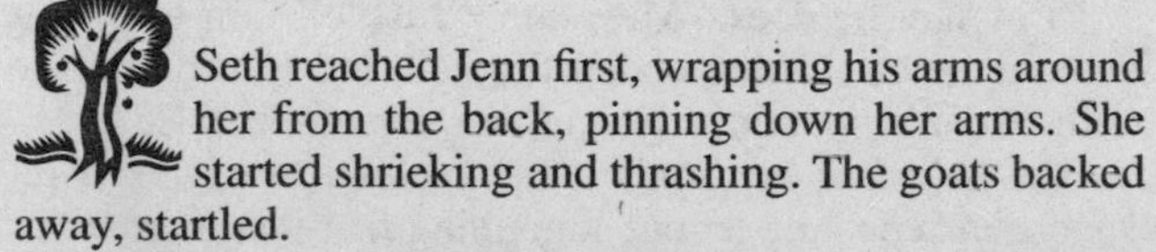

Seth reached Jenn first, wrapping his arms around her from the back, pinning down her arms. She started shrieking and thrashing. The goats backed away, startled.

"Will somebody get the damn hayfork away from her?" Seth shouted, ducking the sharp tines.

Meg and Bree exchanged glances. Bree nodded once, then approached cautiously. She swung the two-by-four and batted the fork's wooden handle, forcing it out of Jenn's hands. Meg rushed forward to pick it up and move it out of reach, then rounded up the nervous goats, one at a time, and herded them back to their pen. The gate securely latched behind them, she turned to face Jenn. "What the hell are you doing here?"

Jenn just glared at her.

Seth looked at Meg over her head. "Maybe we'd better get John over here—he can probably calm her down, get her to explain."

"What's the number?" Bree asked. As Seth rattled it off, Bree punched it in, then handed the phone to Meg.

Meg waited through three, four rings, until someone finally picked up. An older woman—Donna? "Mrs. Taylor?"

"Yes, this is Donna Taylor. Who's this?" the woman said, her voice sleep-clogged.

Meg ignored her questions. "Is John there?"

"No, he's gone out. I'm here with the baby. Can I take a message?"

Why was John out somewhere at this time of the night? Meg looked at Seth and shook her head briefly. "Could you tell him that Seth Chapin needs to talk with him, right away?"

"All right. Seth Chapin, you said? That's the man he works for sometimes, right? John must know the number."

"I'm sure he does," Meg said. "Just tell him to call as soon as he can." Meg ended the call and turned back to Seth. "John's not home. His mother's home with Eli."

The sound of her son's name seemed to trigger a response in Jenn: she let out something that was a cross between a sob and a snarl, and struggled harder. Seth, caught unawares, lost his grip, and before anyone could move, Jenn darted toward the back door, which apparently was how she had come in, and disappeared into the snow. Seth followed quickly, but returned less than thirty seconds later. "Lost her. Can't see a damn thing out there. I'll try to get hold of Art again, now that we've got a more serious situation here. Bree, are you all right?"

"Sure. I was ready for her. Don't know what she thought she was going to do with that two-by-four, though."

"You're lucky it wasn't anything worse. Meg, give me Bree's phone a sec." When Meg handed it to him, Seth retreated to a corner and turned his back.

Meg looked at Bree. "You didn't tell me that you had an air horn."

"You didn't ask. I came prepared—I've got all sorts of stuff in my pack. Got you out here fast enough, didn't it?" Bree looked almost gleeful now.

Meg didn't see any point in mentioning that if Jenn had brought a gun, nothing would have been enough to get help in time to do any good. "It did. Did Jenn say anything to you?"

"Apart from the 'What are you doing here?' kind of stuff? Nope. I assume she expected to be alone out here. You think she's been behind all this?"

"I don't know. I wish we hadn't lost her. And where's she going to go? She really wasn't dressed warmly enough to stay out in weather like this. She could just walk home, but she's got to know that's the first place anyone would look for her. But I have no idea where else she could be headed."

"Art's going to send a car to the Taylor house," Seth said, his call completed. "Here's your phone, Bree. Art's headed here—the accident on the highway was mainly a fender bender, people sliding in the snow, and they don't need him there. Why is it some people around here never figure out how to drive in snow?"

"Hey, I'm as guilty as anyone—it takes practice. Can we go inside? It's freezing out here," Meg said. She led the way across the drive and into the house, and the others followed. Inside, Meg shook her snow-covered coat before hanging it up, then went to make coffee. If Art had been out in the cold sorting out traffic problems, he would probably need it. She knew she needed something hot, now that the adrenaline of the confrontation with Jenn was ebbing.

The coffee was ready by the time Art arrived at the back door. He stomped his feet on the stoop, then stepped inside. "Can't leave you all alone for a couple of hours without you getting into trouble. Seth gave me the basics, but you all want to explain now? And should I be putting together a search party for Jenn Taylor?"

"If she hasn't gone home, I'd say yes," Seth said grimly. "She lit out of here in a hurry."

"Her mother-in-law said she was watching the baby," Meg volunteered. "She didn't know where John had gone."

"Great. People wandering all over in the dark, in the middle of a snowstorm. Well, my guy Hanson's down at the Taylor house, so if anybody else shows up there he'll let me know. Okay, from the top: what happened?"

Meg set a mug of coffee in front of Art, then sat down and gave him the details of the plan they'd hatched and how they all came to be hiding out, waiting for the mystery harasser. "Bree stayed out in the barn, to give us eyes on that side. Seth and I took the house. Seth was upstairs asleep when Bree signaled the alarm."

Art swiveled to Bree. "What happened in the barn?"

With evident relish, Bree recounted what had happened while she waited in the dark. Meg was impressed that Bree had waited until Jenn had come in through the back door—that is, when she was fully committed to what had to be breaking and entering. If Bree had spooked her by moving too early, Jenn could have disappeared into the night without being seen. "And then Meg showed up, and Seth maybe thirty seconds later. Seth got Jenn under control, sort of, and I got the pitchfork away from her. But when Meg called her house and found out that John wasn't there, and Mrs. Taylor was alone with the kid, Jenn just freaked and got away."

"And here I thought this was a peaceful town," Art said, rubbing his eyes. "Okay, Jenn broke into the barn, so that's a crime. Then you confronted her with your noisemaker, and she panicked and dropped the two-by-four. Then she grabbed the first thing she could, which was the pitchfork. Did she threaten you?"

"Maybe. Kinda," Bree replied. "But it sure looked like she was going to go for Dorcas—that's when we all jumped her."

"Dorcas the goat?" Art shook his head in disbelief. "And then she freaked out and ran out into a snowstorm. What a mess." Art's walkie-talkie blatted; he listened a minute then signed off. "No sign of Jenn at the Taylor house, but Hanson's going to stay there. You tried John's cell, Seth?"

Seth shook his head. "He doesn't have one—he can't afford it these days. I would have given him one for work, but he wouldn't accept it."

"Damn stiff-necked Yankees," Art muttered. "Guy's clearly got a bunch of problems, but he won't take help when it's offered. So we can't track him, and if he's not home, we have no idea where he could have gone, and he doesn't know his wife flew out of here like a bat out of hell. Just great." He drained his coffee mug and stood up stiffly. "Well, I'd better make some calls, see if we can find Jennifer Taylor. You available, Seth?"

"Of course. Why don't we split the list of calls?"

"I'd appreciate it."

Seth and Art went toward the front of the house, presumably to call searchers. Meg wondered idly if Seth had everyone in town on his phone's contact list. How many people would it take to find Jenn—especially if she didn't want to be found? But she wouldn't leave Eli for long, would she? Meg felt both tired and keyed up, and Bree looked twitchy, as if she wanted to move. "You think maybe Jenn was going to rig up some kind of booby trap in the barn?"

Bree shrugged. "No idea. There's plenty of stuff out there already, if she wanted to fake an accident or something. If she's really the one behind this. You think so?"

"It looks like it, but it's hard to say. I barely know the woman—I only met her a week or two ago. Why would she be doing this?"

"Got me. Maybe she doesn't need a reason, if she's hearing voices or something. Maybe God told her to sacrifice a goat for some reason."

"Don't even joke about it," Meg said sharply.

Art and Seth returned and started pulling on their outerwear. Art said, "Thanks for the coffee, Meg. You'll let me know if she comes back this way? Or if John shows up? We've both got our cells."

"Of course," Meg said.

"Lock your doors," Seth added, as he and Art went back out into the dark. Shortly after that a couple of cars and a pickup pulled into Meg's driveway, and men started climbing out, clustering around Art for their orders. As Meg watched, they split up into teams of two and they all vanished into the snow.

Meg looked at the clock on the microwave: one o'clock in the morning. Even Bree looked like she was drooping. "I have no idea what to do now," Meg said. "There's no point in us bumbling around out there—I'd get lost in a minute."

"Agreed," Bree said. "You think she'd sneak back into the barn?"

Meg shrugged. "I don't know. It might be smart, but I don't know if she's thinking straight. You were thinking it could be something like schizophrenia? Or . . ." Meg recalled the tombstone in the cemetery, and those lost children. Hers? Would that be enough to threaten Jenn's sanity? Or the prospect of losing Eli, too, if he had whatever had killed the other children?

And wasn't that a lot like what she had suggested to Seth, about what Unity might have done in Pittsford all those years ago? Was there some connection?

Meg jumped when there was a pounding at the back door. She and Bree exchanged a startled glance, and Bree looked around the kitchen quickly. For a weapon? All the traditional women's weapons were there at hand—kitchen knife, rolling pin, cast iron skillet. Would either of them be able to use them?

This was ridiculous. Meg stood up and strode to the back door, to find John Taylor standing on the stoop, shivering. "Is Jenn here?" he shouted through the door.

Meg looked at Bree again, who was standing with her hand on a skillet on the counter. Bree nodded cautiously, and Meg pulled open the door. "Come on in, John."

She waited until he had come in, shutting the door behind him while he stomped snow off his boots and shook his coat.

"Is she here?" he demanded again.

"No, but she was earlier. Have you been home yet?"

"No, I've been looking for her for a couple of hours. I fell asleep in my chair at home, and when I woke up she was gone, and Ma wouldn't say where or why. But I think she knew." He looked awful, his hair dripping with melting snow, his face white, save for his reddened nose. "Why?"

Meg sighed. "John, you'd better sit down. I'll get you some coffee, and then we have a lot to talk about."

John allowed Meg to lead him to the kitchen table, and fell heavily into a chair. He nodded once at Bree but didn't speak to her.

Wordlessly Meg filled a mug with coffee and handed it to him, then she sat down opposite him at the table. Bree maintained a wary stance a few feet away, although she had put the skillet down on the counter next to her within easy reach.

"John, do you know why Jenn was here?"

"No, do you? Look, I don't really have time for this right now. I need to keep looking for her."

"John," Meg said gently, "the police are already doing that. You should stay here in case she comes back, so everyone knows where to find you."

"The police? What've they got to do with it?" He started to rise, and Meg laid a hand on his arm.

"Jenn was acting kind of odd when she left here, and she

didn't go home—the police checked, and they have someone waiting there. You'd be better off if you stay here." Meg glanced at Bree, trying to signal that she should let someone know that John had reappeared. Apparently Bree got the message, because she nodded once and slipped out the kitchen door—carrying the skillet, Meg noted. John was so absorbed in his own misery that he didn't even seem to notice her disappearance.

"I'm so tired," he said. "I can't do this anymore."

"Do what, John? Does this have to do with Jenn?"

"Jenn, me. Losing my job. Eli. My mother. Do you know, there isn't one damn thing in my life that's going right? And I'm supposed to be the strong one who keeps it all together. I just can't do it anymore."

When Meg looked at John again, she realized that the melting snow was now mixing with tears, running down his face. "I'm so sorry. I wish there were something I could say that would help, but there's no easy fix for your problems."

"I don't want your pity, or anybody's. Sorry—that sounds kind of rude. Thank you for not throwing a bunch of fake sympathy at me. I get plenty of that from people. 'It's all for the best.' 'What doesn't break you will make you stronger.' It's all bullshit. I don't deserve this, and Jenn doesn't either."

"Is this about Eli? And . . . your other children?"

John's head came up abruptly. "You know about them?"

"A little. And I've made some guesses. Can you tell me about it?"

Bree slid silently back into the room, and nodded. Meg took that to mean that help was on the way, not that she was sure she needed help. She didn't think she had anything to fear from John Taylor.

"Nobody else in town knows, or at least *I* didn't tell them. I know people talk. But maybe I've been wrong. It's not like I ever did anything wrong, and Jenn didn't either.

We fell in love, we got married. We couldn't have known . . ."

"Known what, John?" Meg said quietly.

"About what those kids had, what Eli's got, that's going to kill him."

31

And then the pieces came together for Meg: Unity and her daughter Violet, who had married in Granford. All the dead children. "It's hereditary, isn't it?"

John stared into his coffee mug, clutched between his hands, and nodded. "There've been a lot of kids around here who died before their time. They start out fine and healthy, and then they get sick and die. I remember that from when I was a kid, but nobody talked about it."

"And nobody knew why?"

John shrugged. "There's a name for it. But the end's the same, no matter what they call it. I thought maybe we could get away from it if we moved away from Granford, but it didn't make any difference."

Meg tried to make some sense out of what he was saying. John and Jenn had lost two children, and Eli was headed down the same path. There had to be a medical explanation.

He went on, almost talking to himself. "I grew up around here—down the road. Jenn did, too. We met in high school, we fell in love, we got married. Normal, ordinary stuff. We had kids, Megan and Sean. Then Megan got sick, and nobody knew what the problem was—she had fits, she had breathing problems. She died when she was almost four, and we never got a good diagnosis. Jenn was pregnant with Sean by the time they figured out what it was. It's called Batten Disease. There's no cure."

"Oh, John," Meg said softly. "How awful. They're buried in the cemetery here, aren't they?" Was that why he was so willing to maintain it? To stay near his lost children?

"Yeah. We were living in Springfield, but Ma bought the plot when Dad died, and that was the only place we had for them. We didn't come back here to live until I lost my job. Ma had the house, so we moved in with her."

"How did Jenn feel about that?" Meg asked.

"She was okay with it. I couldn't find work anywhere, not full-time, and she couldn't work because somebody had to take care of Eli. Ma's been working steady at the restaurant, but she doesn't make much." John looked directly at Meg. "We didn't mean to have Eli—it was a mistake. We knew before he was born that he'd never make it. And Jenn won't let him out of her sight most of the time. That's why I was surprised that she left him with Ma, to go out in this kind of weather. You said she was here? Why?"

Meg hated having to make John's life even more complicated, but she had to know. "John, someone's been pulling pranks on me lately—letting the goats out, breaking small things. Bree found a nail in one of her tires. And then someone shot out my kitchen window. Do you know anything about that?"

His bewildered look was convincing. "You think Jenn had something to do with all that?"

"She broke into my barn tonight. She didn't expect to find Bree in there, waiting. She tried to attack her, and then she ran out and disappeared. That's why the police are looking for her. Would she be likely . . . to do harm to herself?"

John looked grim. "Not as long as Eli is alive. Me, I don't matter to her anymore. I don't blame her—I've screwed up almost everything I've done."

Meg realized that there was a question she had never asked. "Has Jenn's family lived around here for long?"

"What?" John seemed startled by the non sequitur, but he nodded. "They settled here like two hundred years ago. She's proud of that. Wait—are you telling me that what Eli's got has something to do with her Granford ancestors?"

"I think so. By any chance, was Jenn's family name Morgan?"

John stared at her as though she was crazy. "How did you know that?"

Meg shook her head: this was not the time to explain. "It doesn't matter. The point is, it's not your fault. It's not anybody's fault. The only thing you're right about is that you have rotten luck. I'm so sorry."

Meg looked up to see a car pulling into her driveway, now completely filled with vehicles. This one was a police cruiser, and as Meg watched from the kitchen window, an officer she didn't recognize climbed out, then opened the back door for Jenn Taylor, who was clutching Eli. Donna Taylor climbed out of the other side of the car. The officer herded them all to the back door, and Meg had it open before he had time to knock.

"Ma'am," he said, "I've called the chief, and he's on his way. May we come in?"

"Of course." Meg stepped back and collided with John, who shoved past her to grab Jenn's arms. Meg backed farther into the kitchen while John, Jenn, and the other woman were sorted out by the officer. Jenn looked the worse for wear: her lank hair was wet, her face pale. Her coat was soaked, but she refused to relinquish her hold on Eli, who was squirming and whining.

Meg went to make more coffee. It looked as though everybody was going to need it.

32

Five minutes later Jenn, John, and Donna Taylor were seated around the kitchen table with steaming mugs. Bree had retreated to one corner, and the young officer was standing stiffly in another, keeping an eye on all parties. Jenn had a towel draped around her shoulders; Eli was sitting on her lap. John had pulled his chair as close as possible to hers. Finally Art and Seth emerged from the darkness and came in the back door.

"Hanson." Art nodded to the young officer. "Hello, Jenn," Art said with surprising gentleness. "We were worried about you."

"She turned up at the house maybe fifteen minutes after you went out to search," Officer Hanson volunteered. "You said I should bring her here, right?"

"That's fine. John," Art greeted the other man. "Is everybody okay?" When he received nods all around, Art sat down and said, "Jenn, you want to tell us what this is all about?"

Jenn's stony expression didn't change, and she remained mute.

"What were you doing in Meg's barn?" Art prodded. No response. "Are you responsible for what's been happening to Meg for the last couple of weeks?"

Donna Taylor spoke, her voice hoarse. "That was me. Jenn didn't know, before."

Meg felt a weird mix of emotions: elation that she hadn't been imagining the whole string of events, horror that her neighbors—whom she didn't even know—had been harassing her. Before Art could say anything, Meg asked, "Why?"

"You don't deserve it." When Meg looked blank, Mrs. Taylor looked as though she wanted to spit. "This place. You have no right to it."

Meg looked around the group, more and more confused. "What are you talking about? My house? My mother inherited this place. We share the title to it." Meg glanced at Art, who nodded slightly; apparently he was going to let Mrs. Taylor keep talking.

"John and me, we took care of the old ladies. John was in high school when we started, but he helped out with the outside chores—kept the gardens neat, the lawn mowed. Painted the place, summers. Oh, they paid him, but not near what he could have made somewhere else. Me, I looked after the inside of the house, as much as those old biddies would let me. They hated admitting they were getting old! And, damn, they were cheap! Still wanted to put up preserves every year, and they couldn't lift more than a couple of jars at a time, so I ended up doing all the work."

This still wasn't making sense to Meg. "And you thought they'd leave the place to you?" she guessed.

Mrs. Taylor twisted in her chair to face Meg directly. "Why not? They didn't have anybody else. They'd outlived everyone, the spiteful old hags. If it hadn't been for us, the state would have put them in a home somewhere, because they sure as hell couldn't take care of themselves. And then they died, and the lawyer says they left the whole lot to somebody we'd never heard of. Who never even had the decency to show up for their funerals."

"That was my mother. But she didn't even know they'd died! Nobody told her until the will was read."

"So you say. Then we hoped she'd up and sell the place—I mean, she never showed her face in Granford. What did she want with a run-down farm? I figured I'd make your life miserable and you'd give up and go back to wherever you came from. Stupid, huh?"

Donna was right, Meg realized. Her mother hadn't bothered to do anything with the farm—she'd just collected the rent for years on end until Meg had decided to move in last year. "You wanted to buy this place?" Meg asked.

John was staring at his mother with fascination. "Ma, you never said anything to me about this! Besides, how could you have bought it?"

Donna turned to her son. "John, I own my place free and clear, and I had some money put by from when your father died. I could have done it. I wanted to, but it never went up for sale. I've been waiting ever since."

"But, Ma, you could have told me," John protested. "Maybe we could have worked something out, made an offer to the lawyer or something. Why'd you wait so long to say anything?"

"It didn't matter, when you were in Springfield. And then you started having troubles with your babies, and I didn't want to bother you with it."

Finally John sputtered to life. He jumped out of his chair, and the law officers in the room stiffened to alertness. John ignored them and paced back and forth a few times. "Let me get this straight. You wanted this property. You had the money to buy it. But other things got in the way, like . . . the babies dying. So did something change all of a sudden?"

Jenn spoke for the first time. "It started when we lost our insurance, John. When your extension from the job ran out, and we had to go on the state plan." She turned to Meg. "There was this new drug that looked real promising, but the insurance won't cover it because it's still experimental." She looked again at John. "Your mom thought this was our last chance. She thought if she could make Meg here leave, maybe it would all work out and we could have a chance for something better."

"You knew about this, Jenn?" John looked like he wanted to cry, trying to process everything at once.

"No, John, not until tonight. She didn't tell me, honest. And, God help me, I wanted to help. I'm sorry, Meg. You've been nice to us. I didn't mean to do you any harm."

John seemed to be having trouble processing Jenn's words.

"You never said anything to me! Why didn't you talk to me?"

"What, and make you feel worse? I know it's not your fault you lost your job. I know you've done everything you could to find another one. I'm grateful to your mother for taking us in—at least we have a roof over our heads and food to eat. But that won't make any difference to Eli." She hugged him tighter, drawing another squawk from him.

"And getting this farm would?" John asked.

"At least you could work it and earn a living! You'd have some self-respect, and maybe we could have a couple of good years before Eli . . ." Jenn swallowed a sob.

Art cleared his throat. "I'm sorry, but I have to interrupt. Meg, you've told me about a number of things that have happened here, but the only serious ones were the accident in the parking lot and the gunshot."

"Hey, what about my tire?" Bree protested.

"All right, we'll include that. Donna, were you responsible for those?"

Donna glared at him. "You gonna arrest me?"

"You want to lawyer up?"

"I can't afford a lawyer, Chief, and you know it."

"You can have a court-appointed one, if you need one."

"Bunch of second-raters. Hell, I'll tell you. The only thing I feel bad about was that problem with Doc Murphy."

"You were the woman he was arguing with in the parking lot?" Art asked.

Donna nodded. "I followed Meg there. I figured if I bumped her car, did a little damage, nobody there would notice—everybody was bent on getting into the store and getting home again. And I almost pulled it off, except Doc Murphy saw me do it. Damn do-gooder. I knew who he was—he's been Eli's doctor for years. I don't think he recognized me. He was the one told Jenn about that new drug, but there wasn't the money for it. So he saw me back into the car, and he comes over and tells me I have to report it to someone or other. I hightailed it out of there, but I never heard anything more."

"He reported you, but it was a couple of days later," Art said. "And the rifle shot? Was that you?"

"I didn't hit anyone, did I?"

"Did you use your rifle?"

Donna nodded. "John senior's old .22. John had it for years. But he taught me how to shoot it, back when we were first married. I'm a pretty fair shot. If I'd wanted to hit somebody, I would have." She turned to Meg. "I'll pay you for the window, and the car repairs."

Art looked at Meg, and she wondered what message he was trying to send. All she knew was that she was confused and tired. It was going to take her a while to make sense of all this. She realized that Art was talking again

"Donna, John, Jenn—look, it's late. I'm going to trust you all that you aren't going to pack up and leave town, if I let you go home now. I need to consider what charges, if any, should be brought against you, and I need to talk to

Meg about what she wants to do. Will you promise to go home and stay there, so we can sort this out?"

"I'll make sure they do," John said. "Meg, Seth, I apologize for whatever trouble we've caused you. Now, if you're willing, I'd like to take my family home."

Art canvassed the room. "Hanson, you can go. Thanks for your help. John, you take care of your family. I'll talk to you all tomorrow." He waited until everyone had cleared out, leaving Meg, Seth, and Bree gathered around the table. Then he dropped heavily into a chair. "Damn, why don't I ever get simple problems?"

Meg sat, stunned with a kind of secondhand grief. She had done nothing to bring this on herself, and yet she felt guilty. Her mother had put this property out of her mind, cashed the rent checks, and now Meg was paying a price for it. That wasn't fair. But neither was the bad luck heaped on the Taylors. If she had found herself in the same position, how would she have acted? "Art, does it make a difference if I press charges?"

"Meg, my brain is so addled that I'm not even going to try to answer that. I'll say, maybe. I think we'll all be in better shape tomorrow." He stood up. "Seth, thanks for your help. I'm glad nobody ended up hurt. You all get some rest and we can talk later. I'll call in anybody who's still out searching and tell them to go home."

Seth escorted Art to the door, then shut it firmly after him. He leaned against the doorframe. "I sure didn't see that one coming. I don't think John knew anything about what his mother was up to. Which doesn't mean he won't feel guilty about it." He straightened up. "I should go."

Meg roused herself to ask, "Do you have to?"

"You don't need protecting anymore, you know."

"I know. Just stay—please?"

Bree stood up, too. "All right, you old fogies, I'm going to bed."

"And so are we," Meg said.

* * *

Meg awoke still exhausted the next morning. Once again Seth was already gone—didn't the man ever sleep? She reviewed the scene in the kitchen: what an unholy mess. That poor family! In a way she was relieved that the small acts of harassment hadn't been directed at her personally—it wasn't like she had antagonized or offended anyone. She'd merely been in the way of Donna Taylor realizing her dream. It wasn't even a big dream, just a hope of having a decent place for their family, where they could make a modest living and enjoy whatever time they had left with Eli. In a town they regarded as home. But Meg realized that she had the same long history with Granford as they did, except that her family had been absent for a few decades. At what point did one become an outsider? One generation? Several?

No way could she press charges, compounding their misery. She hadn't lost much compared to what John and Jenn had suffered.

But something still nagged at her. The Taylors had lost two children to this illness she had never heard of. Unity Warren Cox had lost children as well. Were the two events connected, and was there some way to prove it? Apart, of course, from the devastating grief any family would feel as they watched one after another of their children die. If it was in fact a hereditary illness, as Meg had guessed, and Unity Warren had shared it, there was a chance that she carried it, too. Should she be thinking about the risk to her future children, should there be any? That made it pretty personal.

Meg jumped out of bed and headed for the shower. She needed to do some more research.

After breakfast, armed with a fresh mug of coffee, Meg sat down in front of her laptop and thought. What was she looking for? She knew very little about what had happened to the Taylor children, and she wasn't about to ask John or Jenn for details—that would be cruel. What did she know? It sounded like they had all been born healthy, and then had sickened and died, usually before the age of five. There was no cure, and all four of their children were affected. Meg typed in "Batten Disease," and when the references came up she started reading.

When she was done with that, she clicked open her genealogy program and started with Violet Cox.

33

Three hours later Meg realized it was past lunchtime and she hadn't even heard from Seth. Was he working? Had he talked to John, and had they come to some sort of an agreement? She hated to think that Seth might fire John just because of what his mother had tried to do.

But she felt a sense of triumph: she had verified that Jenn Taylor, née Morgan, wife of John Taylor, was indeed a direct descendant of Violet Cox, daughter of Unity Warren. Which in some oblique way made Jenn Meg's relative, too. Was everyone in Granford connected?

She hadn't traced John's lineage, but she was pretty sure she didn't need to. Whoever he was descended from, they'd also carried a recessive gene for Batten Disease. It was only when two carriers came together, as John and Jenn had done, that the disease became fatal. Unity Warren's second husband had also come from Granford, and most likely they had both been carriers.

When she reached the kitchen, she saw that Seth's van

was parked in front of his office. Bree was sitting at the kitchen table eating cereal, and Meg realized that she had been so absorbed that she hadn't even heard her housemate come down the stairs. "Good morning," Meg greeted her.

"Uh, it's one thirty. What are you working on?" Bree asked.

"Local connections. I'll fill you in, but I want to see if Seth expects to see John today—I've got some questions for him."

Bree snorted. "If I was John, I'd steer clear."

"Poor John. He didn't do anything. At least, that's what he says—he had no idea what his mother was up to. And Jenn says she didn't know until last night. I wonder what she thought she could accomplish in the barn?"

"I got the feeling Jenn wasn't thinking much at all, just lashing out. Maybe Donna pushed her to do it."

"I know Donna wanted to help her son," Meg said, "but she just ended up making things worse. Poor Jenn."

"If they wanted the property so much, why didn't they just ask if it was for sale?" Bree asked.

"I can't answer that. Maybe the timing was never right. Maybe they did, and Mother's lawyer blew them off without even telling her. I'd bet Mother would've snapped up an offer if she had known about it. Maybe the Taylors were waiting for some divine power to drop the opportunity in their laps."

"Ha! And then they finally got tired of waiting and decided to do something about it, once you looked like you were settling in. Maybe they hoped you'd give up quickly."

"I guess," Meg agreed. "Anyway, I'm going to go say hi to Seth."

She pulled on a coat and hurried toward the building at the other end of the snowy driveway, crisscrossed with frozen tire tracks from all the activity the night before. Seth's office was upstairs, and Meg went up the wooden stairs and rapped on his door.

"Come in," he called out.

Meg opened the door and was greeted with a blast of warm air from the space heater, which explained the closed door. "Hi," she said, shutting the door behind her. Max rose from the floor to greet her.

"Hi yourself. How're you doing this morning?"

"Not bad, all things considered. Relieved. Saddened. A whole muddle. But I've been trying to sort out a few things about the Taylors, and I wondered if you were going to see John today?"

"Yeah, he's coming over later. I had to call him—I know he feels really bad about what happened. Why?"

"I've been looking at Jenn's family history, and at Batten Disease, and I've found some interesting things. Well, interesting to me."

"You want me to bring him over when he gets here? We didn't have any jobs planned for today, and after last night that's probably a good thing. I'm not sure I could hit a barn with a hammer at the moment."

"Want some lunch? I don't know what I've got, but I'll fake it."

Half an hour later they were finishing up canned soup and sandwiches when John's truck pulled into the driveway. Seth went to the back door to wave him in. John came in, hesitating on the doorstep when he saw Meg waiting.

She smiled at him. "Come in, John. I'm not angry at you, or Jenn. Your mother I'm not so sure about. Want some coffee?"

"Uh, okay." He came into the kitchen, leaving his coat on, as Meg made more coffee. "Look, Meg, I'm really sorry. Jenn and I had a long talk last night. She's not a bad person, really. It's just that she's had a really hard time, and when Ma told her what she'd been doing, Jenn just went crazy. She didn't mean to hurt anyone. Heck, I don't know what she was thinking. But that doesn't make what she did right."

"I understand, John." Meg set coffee mugs on the table, and then sat down facing the two men. "You said Jenn's family comes from around here?"

"Yup. They go back a long way in Granford."

"Did you and Jenn have any genetic testing done?"

John looked startled. "Not at first, when Megan died. We had the basic tests done before Sean was born, but he was already on the way by then."

"I'd guess that you found out that you're both carriers for Batten Disease. You don't show any symptoms of the disease, but you passed it on to your children. You were unlucky enough to marry another carrier, but given how limited the population of Granford is, it was likely. It's nobody's fault, and there was no way of knowing ahead of time unless you did some expensive and complicated medical tests."

"You're saying this goes back a long way? Before us?"

"What's your point, Meg?" Seth asked.

"I do have one. It comes back to the sampler. Wait, let me show you." She stood up and went to retrieve the sampler, and the family tree charts she had been working on all morning. When Meg returned, she carefully unrolled the sampler, still in its white towel and turned it so it faced the two men. John looked baffled.

"John, I found this sampler in the house a couple of weeks ago. I was really curious about how it came to be here, so I've been looking for answers ever since."

John shifted in his chair. "What's this got to do with me?"

"This is what's known as a family register sampler, and as you can see, it was made in 1798 by a girl named Violet Cox. I'll keep it short: Violet's mother Unity was a Warren, and sister to the man who lived in this house. Unity and three of her brothers all moved to Vermont. They all married there, and she had one child, Violet, by her first husband. Then her husband died. Unity remarried pretty quickly, and had four more children by her second husband, Jacob Lampson—who, as it turns out, also came from Granford originally. But then the Lampson children started dying."

John made the connection quickly. "You're saying you think it's the same thing? This damn disease?"

Meg nodded. "I think it's possible. Unity's first husband was born in Vermont and had no ties here, and their daughter was fine. But all the younger ones died early." Meg pointed to the lines on the sampler. "I've seen some of the town records from that era, and they say things like 'sickly,' 'poorly,' 'feeble' about the Lampson children. Some of them had fits. Does that sound familiar?"

John nodded, his expression grim. "Sounds like Batten, all right. Our kids have what they call the infantile kind, the one that hits earliest. They don't have good muscle control, and they have seizures and jerk a lot. Eli doesn't only because he's on some pretty heavy-duty meds. They sometimes go blind, too."

Meg reached across and laid her hand on his. "I'm so sorry, John. It must be a terrible thing to watch your child suffer like that." Meg hesitated, unsure whether her next conjectures would give John relief or cause him pain. "But that's not where this story ends. Take a look at the sampler: not long after the youngest child died, Jacob Lampson died, and two days later, so did Unity. Violet had family in Vermont, but she came back here to live with Eli Warren, her uncle. And she married here in Granford, and had children of her own. Her husband's name was Abiel Morgan." She stopped, watching John's face.

"You mean, Jenn's descended from this Violet? And her mother?" he said at last.

Meg nodded. "There's more. I read some early records that hinted at some awful event that made it wise to let Violet grow up somewhere else, away from the scandal, and there's a diary that spells it out. Unity watched her babies die, one after another—like you and Jenn, John. Back in those days, with little medical knowledge, she probably blamed her husband. After all, she'd borne one healthy child, so the problem couldn't be hers. It obsessed her, so much that after her children were gone she killed him. And then herself, a few days later. All those deaths just pushed her over the edge. And that's what may have happened to Jenn. This whole thing with your mother and her crazy scheme was the last straw."

They were all silent for a long minute. Meg found herself thinking of young Violet, all her near family dead, sent away from the only place she'd known in her short life, to end up here, in this house. Had Eli welcomed her, been kind to her? Violet had set about commemorating her lost family in the sampler, and then she—or someone—hid or put it away. It had lain in the house, forgotten, for two hundred years.

Meg began again, "John, Jenn did something foolish, but I can understand why. She's fighting for her son, and for you and whatever happiness you can find. Maybe she's a little out of control, but I can't blame her. Nobody got hurt. I'm not going to press charges, against any of you."

John stood up abruptly. "Thank you, Meg. Maybe it helps a little, to know that this didn't happen just to us, that it goes back a lot further. It's just lousy luck." He turned to Seth. "You want me to come by tomorrow morning?"

"Sure. Eight?"

"See you then." Without looking at them again, John grabbed his coat and went out the back door, leaving Meg and Seth alone at the table.

Seth waited until John had shut the door behind him before saying, "Wow. That's quite a story. Unity Warren Cox Lampson was a murderer and a suicide, and now John and Jenn Taylor are part of the same story, two hundred years later. Donna Taylor was driven to harassing you because she saw getting this house as the only possible bright spot in an otherwise lousy life, and she felt she deserved it. And you're descended from Eli Warren?"

"That's about it," Meg agreed.

"Tell me you're going to explain how Jacob Lampson and his wife died?" Seth joked.

"Maybe. I think Violet left us another clue." She pointed to the sampler. "See the Bible verse? I thought it was just a reference to the deaths of the children, but I think there's more to it."

"What?"

"The verse includes the word 'flower.' What do you see next to the row of tombstones there?"

"Lily of the valley, clearly. So?"

"Most people don't know it, but lily of the valley is poisonous, and it grows throughout the Northeast. My guess—which I know I'll never prove—is that Unity poisoned her husband and waited long enough to make sure that he died, and then took the same thing herself. And I think young Violet knew what had happened. Why else would she have included that particular flower in her sampler? Either her mother told her what she had done, or Violet witnessed it. Poor child! She left this one tiny clue, and then she put the sampler away and went on with her life: she married Abiel Morgan here in Granford, and had children. And Jenn Taylor is her lineal descendant. Sad to say, Violet couldn't have known she was passing on a defective gene; and even then it might not have mattered if Jenn hadn't had the bad luck to marry another carrier here in Granford, where it all started. That's one of the downsides of small-town living."

"I guess so. Do you think you're a carrier? I mean, if it's on the Warren side then you're descended from the same line, if you go back far enough."

"I haven't had time to think that far. Although as far as I know, no other local Warrens have had this problem—not that I've looked. I only figured it out this morning. For that matter, the Chapins could be carriers, too."

"Let's hope not," Seth said, smiling. "And now I really had better get some work done, if John's coming back in the morning."

"Go." She waved him off. "I've got plenty of genealogy to keep me busy."

Epilogue

Saturday morning Meg found Seth pounding at her back door yet again. "It's Saturday. What are you doing here? Are you working today?"

"Nope, but I've got a project. We need to find you a Christmas tree."

"Christmas? Oh, my goodness—it's next week. Where do you want to go?"

"Uh, you'll notice that you have a woodlot back there?" Seth made a sweeping gesture toward the back end of her property.

"You want to cut down a tree?"

"Yes, I do. Don't worry—there are plenty. Nobody's taken a tree out of there for decades, and the woods can use some thinning."

"Okay, if you say so. Sounds good. But I don't have a tree stand."

"I have plenty. You have any more quibbles?"

"I guess not. You have an axe?"

"We're not taking down a huge tree. I've got a saw." Seth waved it at her.

"And how do we get it back to the house?" Meg said dubiously.

Seth recoiled in mock horror. "And here I thought you were a farmer, not a city girl. We carry it. Put your boots on."

Meg complied.

She had to admit it was lovely, walking across the uneven fields that lay behind her house, toward the tree line. The sky was blue, the snow was still clean and fluffy, and they were going to cut down a Christmas tree from her own property. She couldn't have imagined any of this a year earlier.

"I did some more research, after you left yesterday," Meg said.

"Oh?"

"About Batten Disease. Like Jenn said, there are studies going on, and even if they don't promise a cure, they may extend life, or at least improve the quality of life."

"Well, that's good news."

"Maybe. John said his insurance wouldn't cover the experimental drug because it hasn't been approved. But I had an idea."

They'd reached the trees, and Seth was scanning for a likely tree for cutting. "And?"

"I want to give John and Jenn the sampler. It's worth a good deal of money, according to the Sturbridge expert, and it *is* Jenn's family, after all. Maybe it won't save Eli, but it could make his life easier. It's a shame to lose a part of the town's history, but I think it's the right thing to do. The Taylors need it a lot more than I do."

Seth stopped, and Meg stopped, too, looking up at him, their breath fogging the air between them.

"I think it's a wonderful idea. So, any decisions?"

"About what? The next apple season? Us?"

"Both. Either."

"I'm staying, Seth."

Meg's last coherent thought was, *Have I ever been kissed in a snowy wood?*

Acknowledgments

This book was inspired by two unrelated and widely separated events.

Years ago, when I was a professional genealogist, I was approached by J. Michael Flanigan, one of the producers of the *Antiques Roadshow*, to do some research on a sampler that he had acquired through the show. The story was that someone who had bought an old house in Cleveland discovered what he thought was a dirty rag in the back of a closet. It turned out to be a piece of needlework, so the owner decided to bring it to the *Roadshow*, and learned that it was an early nineteenth-century sampler made in Pennsylvania. I remembered the segment, and I was thrilled to be able to investigate the sampler's history. (If you're interested, you can see the segment at www.pbs.org/wgbh/roadshow/archive/199907A26.)

The other event is sadder but no less important to the story. More recently I was asked to give a talk to a chapter of the Daughters of the American Revolution about the Orchard series and the genealogy behind it. Afterward I met a young woman who had brought her two-year-old daughter. She said something that made a profound impact on me: her child had Batten Disease, which is both hereditary and incurable. Yet at that time, the child looked completely healthy. I couldn't begin to imagine the pain of watching a child deteriorate in a few short years, but I could see that it might lead parents to act in desperate ways. Since the disease is passed down through families, and since my fictional Granford has been home to the same families for centuries, it was easy to envision such an unhappy genetic heritage there.

For the sampler I created for this book, I borrowed elements from a wide range of existing pieces (with a few personal additions), but all the elements are appropriate to needlework of the time period and the region. Thanks to Ruth Van Tassel of Van Tassel-Baumann American Antiques in Malvern, Pennsylvania (who restored the *Roadshow* sampler), for her insights and suggestions regarding early needlework. In addition, I was privileged to visit the exhibit of Massachusetts samplers on display at Old Sturbridge Village, which enabled me to examine examples of skilled needlework up close—and the talents of some of the young makers are truly impressive. Betty Ring's well-known book *Girlhood Embroidery* was an invaluable resource.

Finally, as usual I've borrowed a lot of my own family history for this book, because it showed me so well how people in the eighteenth century moved around, and how hard it is to find records that show the reasons why.

Thanks, as always, to my indefatigable agent, Jessica Faust of BookEnds, and my extraordinary editor, Shannon Jamieson Vazquez at Berkley Prime Crime. Thanks also to Sisters in Crime and the ever-helpful Guppies—including Tracy Hayes who suggested the title.

Recipes

Minestrone

There are probably as many minestrone recipes as there are cooks. It's a great dish to keep simmering on your back burner, and the beauty of it is that you can add whatever vegetables (preferably fresh, but canned will do) you happen to have on hand—especially if you're snowed in.

1 cup dried beans (white or whatever you prefer)
2 pounds marrow bones
2½ quarts water
3 slices bacon, diced
1 tablespoon olive oil
1 large onion, minced (about a cup)
1 clove garlic, crushed
1 carrot, chopped
1 cup chopped potatoes
1 cup peas

2 small zucchini, diced
1½ cups chopped tomatoes
1 cup shredded cabbage
salt and pepper to taste
½ teaspoon powdered sage (or fresh)
1 teaspoon dried basil
¼ cup raw rice
2 tablespoons butter
1 tablespoon minced parsley
½ cup grated Parmesan cheese

Wash the beans and put them in a large soup kettle. Cover with cold water, bring to a boil, and remove from heat. Let stand 1 hour.

Drain the beans. Add the water and the beef bones. Bring to a boil and simmer, uncovered, for 1½ hours.

Sauté the bacon until golden. Drain off the fat. Add the oil to the pan, then the onions and garlic, and cook over medium heat for 5 minutes.

Stir in the carrots, potatoes, peas, and zucchini and cook for another 5 minutes, stirring occasionally.

Remove the beef bones from the beans. Add fried vegetables, tomatoes, cabbage, and seasonings. Simmer, uncovered, for 1 hour.

Add the rice and continue cooking for 30 minutes.

Cream together the butter, cheese, and parsley. Add to the hot soup and stir until dissolved.

Hearty Gingerbread

There's something very comforting about warm gingerbread on a cold night.

½ cup (1 stick) butter
½ cup granulated sugar
1 egg
2½ cups all-purpose flour
1½ teaspoons baking soda
1 teaspoon cinnamon
1 teaspoon ground ginger
½ teaspoon ground cloves
½ teaspoon salt
½ cup light molasses
½ cup honey
1 cup hot water

Preheat the oven to 350 degrees F. Grease a 9 x 9 metal pan.

Melt the butter and let it cool. Add the sugar and the egg and beat well.

Sift together the flour, baking soda, salt, and spices.

Combine the molasses, honey, and hot water.

Alternate adding the dry and liquid ingredients to the butter mixture and mix until blended.

Bake about 1 hour, or until the edges of the cake pull away slightly from the pan.

May be eaten plain or with ice cream or whipped cream.

Bree's Jerk Chicken

Bree improvises this dish without a written recipe. Most recipes call for Scotch bonnet or habanero chiles (hot!), so you'll have to decide just how spicy you want this to be.

2 fresh Scotch bonnet or habanero chiles
6 scallions, chopped
3 shallots, chopped
3 cloves garlic, chopped
1-inch piece of fresh ginger, peeled and chopped
3 tablespoons fresh thyme leaves, or 1 tablespoon dried thyme
2 teaspoons ground allspice
1½ teaspoons freshly ground black pepper
1½ teaspoons salt
1 teaspoon ground cinnamon
½ teaspoon freshly grated nutmeg
½ teaspoon ground cloves
1 teaspoon cayenne pepper
½ cup lime juice (if you don't have limes, substitute vinegar)
8 chicken thighs (you may use bone-in breasts if you prefer, but the dark meat stands up better to the spices and cooks more slowly, for better flavor)

Discard the stems, seeds, and ribs from the two chiles and chop coarsely (you may want to use latex gloves for this, if you have them).

In a food processor, blend the chiles with all the remaining ingredients except the chicken until a paste forms. Make slits in the chicken pieces, then rub the paste all over the pieces. Cover and chill at least two hours (overnight if possible).

Heat the oven to 350 degrees F. Place the chicken pieces skin side up on a foil-lined pan or rimmed baking sheet and cook about 45 minutes (until the juices run clear).

THE FIRST IN THE NATIONAL BESTSELLING
CANDY HOLLIDAY MURDER MYSTERIES

TOWN IN A
Blueberry Jam

B. B. HAYWOOD

In the seaside village of Cape Willington, Maine, Candy Holliday has an idyllic life tending to the Blueberry Acres farm she runs with her father. But when an aging playboy and the newly crowned Blueberry Queen are killed, Candy investigates to clear the name of a local handyman. And as she sorts through the town's juicy secrets, things start to get sticky indeed . . .